And Then You Loved Me

And Then You Loved Me

Inglath Cooper

Fence Free Entertainment, LLC

Contents

Copyright

Published by Fence Free Entertainment, LLC

Cooper, Inglath
And Then You Loved Me / Inglath Cooper
ISBN – 978-0-9914997-2-4

Fence Free Entertainment, LLC
Fence.free.entertainment.llc@gmail.com

Publisher's Note

***

People say you can't ever go back. That some of the things that happen to us simply cannot be redone. But the paths of a life journey are rarely straight. They twist and turn and wind back across those once visited and long thought to have faded from existence.

Becca Miller has lived her life trying to do the right thing, even when its cost has been giving up the boy she loved and wanted to marry. The sacrifice she made for her sister isn't one she regrets because there was no other choice for her to make. And for eighteen years, she lives this choice with full commitment and as little looking back as she can manage.

But when Matt Griffith returns to Ballard County for the funeral of his grandmother, the path that had seemed so straight begins to loop back and take her across feelings she thought she had put away for good. As it turns out, those roads we've traveled do not fade at all. They simply wait to be retraveled, leaving us with the decision to follow them exactly as we did before, or make a different choice and find out where it will lead us.

Books by Inglath Cooper

My Italian Lover
Fences – Book Three – Smith Mountain Lake Series
Dragonfly Summer – Book Two – Smith Mountain Lake Series
Blue Wide Sky – Book One – Smith Mountain Lake Series
That Month in Tuscany
And Then You Loved Me
Down a Country Road
Good Guys Love Dogs
Truths and Roses
Nashville – Part Ten – Not Without You
Nashville – Book Nine – You, Me and a Palm Tree
Nashville – Book Eight – R U Serious
Nashville – Book Seven – Commit
Nashville – Book Six – Sweet Tea and Me
Nashville – Book Five – Amazed
Nashville – Book Four – Pleasure in the Rain
Nashville – Book Three – What We Feel
Nashville – Book Two – Hammer and a Song
Nashville – Book One – Ready to Reach
On Angel's Wings
A Gift of Grace
RITA® Award Winner John Riley's Girl
A Woman With Secrets
Unfinished Business
A Woman Like Annie
The Lost Daughter of Pigeon Hollow
A Year and a Day

A Note From the Author

Dear Readers,

This story is set in a fictionalized version of Franklin County, the county where I grew up in southwest Virginia. Some of the early settlers to the county were members of the Old Order German Baptist Brethren, who for generations, have made a life of simplicity a priority.

Brethren homes and farms are scattered throughout the county, but members of the Old Order church are easily distinguished from other citizens by their clothing, a symbol of their faith. Women wear the traditional plain dress with a cape attached at the shoulders. Their long hair is secured in a bun and covered by a white or black bonnet. Men often have long beards. Some live among other members of the community without making use of modern conveniences such as television, radio and computer. Others have moved away from some of these more strict practices.

Like the county that inspired it, my fictional town of Ballard represents an interlocking blend of farms and industry, Super retailers and Main Street renewal. It is a place caught in a visible struggle between past and present.

Maybe this is a universal struggle, one that doesn't limit itself to a place, but applies to the lives of its people as well. The present, after all, cannot exist without its past. The two are inextricably tied, a circle that must eventually find its point of completion. For my characters here, raised in a county of like and different, the ends of the circle are about to connect, the ensuing collision forever altering the journey of those on its path.

Prologue

> *What is deservedly suffered must be borne*
> *with*
> *calmness, but when the pain is unmerited,*
> *the grief is resistless.*
> ***– Ovid***

Then

There's a moon tonight. It hangs in the sky above the barn, fat and full, a summer moon. It lights my path across the backyard, the parched grass beneath my feet making a brittle, crackling sound. Daddy says if we don't get some rain soon, the corn crop won't be worth cutting.

At the thought of him asleep in his bed, worn out from a day spent putting away over a thousand bales of hay, I feel a sharp pang of guilt for sneaking out of the house. I don't like hiding things from Mama and Daddy. But it's not as if they won't know the truth soon enough.

Three weeks from today when I turn sixteen, John and I are getting married. I know we're young, but I'm just glad I found someone who wants the same life I want. Mama says when people are different and don't believe the same things, it's not likely that a life together would ever work. My brother Jacob and my sister Becca are both choosing a different path, and I worry that what Mama said will come true for them.

I've always loved our life. Unlike some of the girls I know from church, I never once wanted to be like the other people we saw in town on Saturday trips to the grocery store. Never wished for things we didn't have. I like the idea of being the same at the end of my life as I was at the beginning.

I tighten the strings of my white bonnet and pick up my pace, nearly running when I reach the big sliding doors at the front of the hay barn. I pull one side back, slip through, leaving it slightly cracked for light.

John is waiting inside for me. He smiles his lopsided smile and reaches for my hand. "Hey, Emmy."

"Hey," I say, and something inside me melts a little at the sound of his voice on my name. I guess at my age it's hard to know what real love is, but I suspect what I feel for him is close enough. He makes me laugh, and seeing him fills me up with the kind of warm feelings I used to get when Grandma Austin would make me hot chocolate on snowy days.

He pushes a bale of hay against the wall for us to sit on, knocking to the floor the old metal pitchfork Daddy uses to dole out flakes of hay to the dairy cows. Once when I was a little girl, Becca left this exact pitchfork lying outside by the water troughs one morning when she was helping Daddy feed. I didn't see it and stepped on it. One of the sharp tines stuck through the ball of my foot, and Mama had to take me to the emergency room to get a tetanus shot. As a punishment, Becca had to do my milking chores for two weeks.

I start now to pick the fork up and prop it back in the corner, but John takes my hand and pulls me down next to him, and I forget about it.

We talk for a bit, sharing little pieces of our day and thoughts we've had about our wedding. He puts his hand on mine and looks at me with a sweet pride. "I'm going to talk to my dad about us living in the little house on our farm," he says.

I lean back and look at him, both surprised and pleased. "You think it'll be okay?"

"Once they get used to the idea, they'll be glad to have us so close."

I feel a wash of relief at this, just knowing that's one thing we won't have to pay for. John and I both realize we'll have a hard time making ends meet at first.

We sit, quiet, his hand still resting on mine. After a while, he leans over and kisses me, and I think how it's nice to feel love in another person's touch. That out of all the things I want from life, this would top the list.

We kiss for a few minutes under the unspoken agreement that until we're married, things won't go any further again. I rub my thumb across the freckles on his cheek and then loop my fingers through his wavy red hair.

"Maaatt! Beccca!"

The voice booms out of nowhere, the names slurred at the edges. John and I both sit up with a start.

"Who is it?" John asks.

"I don't know," I say, straightening my dress and standing.

The door opens, and three shadows fall across the darkened dirt floor of the old hay barn.

"Matt! Becca!" the bigger boy calls out again. "You two in here going at it? Sayin' your good-byes? You know he's gonna forget all about you, Beeecca, once he's at U-V-A with all those hot, smart chicks."

"They're not here," John says, taking my hand and stepping forward into the sliver of moonlight shining through the open door.

"Who the hell are you?" The question contains more slur now than before, and I feel a pang of unease.

"John. John Rutrough."

"John John Root Trough," the boy repeats in a slow, mimicking voice.

Laughter floats out from the other two shadows and seems to hang suspended from the rafters above us.

"Who are you?" I ask.

The boy in front walks over to stand in front of me. I can smell the alcohol on his breath along with the sickeningly sweet scent of something else I don't recognize. "Now what does it matter who I am?"

"Y'all better go on now," I say, shivering even though the night air is muggy and hot.

The boy stares at me as if he's not sure I'm worthy of his attention. "Where are Matt and Becca? His car's parked over at the mailbox."

"I don't know," I say. "Maybe walking in the orchard. They do that sometimes."

He glances back at his friends and snarls a laugh. "Matt's gettin' it in the orchard. I should have known."

"Please. You have to go," I say, afraid my parents will wake up and come down to the barn.

He glances at me, his eyes squinting as if he's having trouble focusing. "What are you two doing out here, anyway? Y'all playin' grown-ups?"

The questions have something ugly at their core, and I feel a new wave of fear. I take a step back, and John reaches for my hand.

"Aww, itn't that sweet?" The boy lurches forward, reaching out to untie the strings of my bonnet. "Maybe we need to give you two a lesson in what real grown-ups do when they're alone. Looks to me, John John Root Trough, like you haven't figured it out yet, seein' as how you haven't even gotten her out of her bonnet. But then what else would we expect from a Dunkard boy? Hard to learn about the world hidin' behind your mama's skirt."

He yanks the bonnet off my head, one of the bobby pins in my hair catching. I yelp, and John lets go of my hand to give the boy a shove. "John, no," I say. "Let it go!"

The boy staggers back and then rights himself like a listing buoy. He stares at John for a moment, as if he can't believe what he just did. His face contorts with anger, a black, drunken thundercloud of it. He pokes John in the chest with one finger and says, "That how you want to play then?"

"Y'all get on out of here," John says, and I hear the fear beneath the words.

"We'll go when we're good and ready," the boy says. "But first I think I'd like to see what's under that dress. It's gotta be somethin' to be hidden so well."

John makes a sound then that sounds like a roar of fury. He charges at the boy. They stumble backwards, and I hear myself scream as if the sound is coming from someone else.

John is no match for him, and they roll around on the dirt floor, kicking and throwing fists. I hear John groan, and I begin to scream for them to stop. The other two boys start trying to break it up, but the first one is much bigger and flings them off like paper dolls. John manages a swing that connects with the boy's jaw and makes an awful cracking sound.

Everything goes completely still then, the boy touching his face and staring at John in disbelief. The moment just hangs there, and I start to pray as hard as I know how that they will leave.

But the boy erupts in a volcano of fury, running at John like a bull aiming to take down a wayward steer. And this is the moment I will relive over and over again. I see it in slow motion, the boy's shoulder connecting with John's chest. John reeling, arms flailing in mid-air. And then a horrible noise I can't identify as he hits the ground. Like the sound of a nail puncturing a tire as the air starts to hiss out.

I run to him, screaming, screaming. His eyes are wide open, an expression of shock frozen in place on his freckled face. And then I lower my gaze to the middle of his chest where the pitchfork tines have pierced straight through.

I put a hand to my mouth and drop to my knees, air refusing to fill my lungs. I think it was this exact moment when for all intent and purpose, I stopped breathing. Trapped in the forever-haunting knowledge that if I had just picked up the pitchfork as I'd known to do, the ending might have been so very different.

1

Fix Sunday

"The happiest moments of my life have been the few which I have passed at home in the bosom of my family."
– Thomas Jefferson

Now

Martha Miller loved Fix Sunday.

Especially one as nice as this warm, early spring afternoon when members of the Booker Hill Brethren Church flowed out the doors of the quaint white building onto the green grass surrounding it. Families extended invitations to follow one another home after the service for a meal and fellowship.

Martha had never felt as adept at pulling it off as many of the women now surrounding her in the front yard of the church. Most of them she had known the majority of her seventy-four years, and she'd often wished that she could be like those who showed not a single sign of apprehension when a dozen cars ended up in their driveway, hungry friends and neighbors pouring out the doors.

Martha's own mother had always managed the day

with grace and hospitality. As a child, Martha remembered Sundays when forty or more men, women and children would fill every table in their home, and even a few makeshift eating arrangements set up under the oak tree in the back yard – sheets of plywood on wooden barrels that were then draped in tablecloths. Martha's mother had taught her well how to handle the preparation of food for an unknown number of guests. How to prepare huge pots of vegetable soup and apple cobblers early in the week that were then frozen and pulled out on Sunday morning where they were left to thaw so they could be quickly reheated after church.

Martha and her oldest daughter Rebecca, Becca as they had always called her, had done just this the previous Monday, using canned jars of vegetables, tomatoes, corn, squash and okra, which they'd put up last summer from Becca's bountiful heirloom garden. There would be no question that they had enough food to go around this afternoon, and for this Martha was thankful.

Exactly one hour past the end of the church service, she stood at the doorway of her own family dining room, holding a pitcher of sweet tea in her hands. There were a dozen guests today plus three of her own family members, Becca, son-in-law Aaron and granddaughter Abby. Multiple threads of conversation could be heard from where Martha stood. She loved the fellowship of these Sunday afternoons, the always-voiced appreciation of a good meal, the comfort to be found in repeated ritual and familiar faces.

She looked down the long harvest table to see who needed a refill, then stepped forward and added more tea to Esau Austin's glass. Aaron had just finished sharing the story of one of their dairy cows who refused to go into her milking lane until Aaron put her favorite alfalfa hay at the front.

Esau thanked Martha for the tea, and then to Aaron, chuckled and said, "Easy enough to see who's running that show."

Warm laughter drifted up, and from her seat across the table, Becca glanced at her husband with affection. "They like to let him think he's in charge."

Once she'd completed a round with the tea, Martha took her own seat next to Abby who had finished her soup and was dipping out another serving from the big white stoneware bowl at the center of the table with the appetite of youth. "This is really good, Grandma," she said.

"Thank you," Martha said, patting Abby's hand. "I'm glad you like it."

Esau put down his glass of tea and ran a hand through his white beard. "I guess you all heard about Millie Griffith's passing," he said, his aging voice suddenly serious.

With the words, something in Martha's heart caught, a spasm of sorts that startled her with its intensity. One hand automatically went to her chest. She lifted her gaze and let herself look at Becca only to find confirmation that Esau's news had hit her with equal effect. Becca's face had lost its color, her eyes brimming with instant tears.

Martha felt the curious gazes of those sitting nearby and forced normalcy into her voice when she said, "I'm so sorry to hear that. She was a kind lady."

Esau nodded. "She was."

"The funeral," Becca said, the words uttered with what Martha heard as deliberate neutrality. "Do you know when it is?"

"Tomorrow morning," Esau said. "At eleven o'clock."

Becca stood and slid back her chair, the legs making a sudden scrape against the wood floor. She grasped the table edge, her fingers white against the grain, steadied herself and then said, "Excuse me, please," before walking quickly from the room.

Martha heard the screen door off the kitchen at the back of the house wheeze open, then shut with a loud clap that made her flinch.

She glanced at her son-in-law and saw that he, too, had made a connection of worry in this news. It was there in the wrinkle of his brow, the firm set to his mouth. Martha could only hope that they were both wrong, and that there was no need for concern. Becca was a mature woman who had long ago put her own desires beneath the needs of her family. It was hardly fair to doubt her now.

But Martha also knew that Mrs. Griffith's passing would bring the woman's grandson back to the county. She knew, too, that there would be no talking Becca out of attending tomorrow's funeral.

A wave of tiredness gripped her, so intense she could barely sit straight beneath its onslaught. Maybe, somewhere along the way, she had become complacent, allowed herself to believe that what was done was done. Even though she had once questioned the path they'd taken, she had deferred to her husband's judgment, certain that their actions had been for the greater good.

Sitting here at this table, a table around which she had raised her three children, Becca, Jacob and Emmy, she could admit she no longer knew. And she could not help but wonder if, in the end, a single choice that had seemed so right at the time, an act of obedience on her part, would be the final definition of so many lives.

2

Departures and Arrivals

"Life can only be understood backwards;
but it must be lived forwards."
– Soren Kierkegaard

Now
The day of Millicent Griffith's funeral dawned as a sparkling April morning, a day when the entire town of Ballard appeared dewy and again renewed under spring's generous return. The back parking lot of the Ballard Methodist Church overflowed with cars and trucks alike, late arrivers for the morning funeral squeezing in along the grass edging. Others left their vehicles in the downtown library's lot and walked north uphill to the church in a somber procession of dark silhouettes.

At two minutes before eleven o'clock, Becca Brubaker lingered at the entrance of the church sanctuary, her hands trembling against the strap of her black purse. With a look of forced determination, she walked down the center aisle and took a seat in one of the back pews. She kept her gaze focused straight ahead, never once letting herself meet eyes with those around her, a representative mix of Ballard County citizens in modern clothing as well as some members of her own Brethren community wearing black shawls and black bonnets with their conservative print dresses.

The organist played a Charles Wesley hymn, the old Methodist song rising up to fill the place with a combined sorrow and celebration. Becca sat with her hands folded in her lap, the words playing through her head, each stanza soothing her with a stoic peace. She'd told herself over and over while she was getting dressed this morning that she had every right to be here, every right to pay her respects to a woman who had meant a great deal to her, her motives void of anything more calculated than a wrenching sense of loss.

Drawing in a steady breath, she let her gaze sweep the front of the church, spotting him instantly at the end of the pew directly in front of the casket. Matt. The sight of him brought with it a start of electricity, a reigniting of something long ago extinguished.

Even from this distance, Becca could feel the waves of his grief, as if the connection between them had never been severed, and she could still feel what he felt.

Guilt clanged inside her like the ring of the church bells that had called everyone into this sanctuary to honor the life of Millicent Griffith. There had never been any question that he would be here today, and maybe that should have been all the reason she needed not to come. Certainly, this was true in the eyes of her mother and her husband. Even after all these years, still swimming upstream when it would have been so much easier to follow the natural path of things and simply stay away. And yet, she needed to say this good-bye.

Becca longed, suddenly, for Matt to turn his head, to drink in the sight of him, imagining that this full on appraisal would quench the thirst inside her the way a glass of cold water cooled her throat after hours of working in her garden. It was wrong, this need that had consumed her in the hours since she'd learned of Mrs. Griffith's death. But a single thought had stuck in her mind, and she could not stop herself from worrying it the way a child worries a loose tooth. This was very likely the last time Matt would have a reason to come back to Ballard County, very likely the last time she would ever see him. She told herself that maybe there was relief to be found in this, as if the end were finally in sight, a final closing up of any lingering what-ifs.

People continued to file into the church, a blend of young, old and somewhere in between. Millie Griffith had been a woman known in the community for her devotion to helping those less fortunate. Programs created through her efforts varied from the collection of Christmas gifts for children with a parent in prison to the creation of a food bank where single mothers could come for groceries every Monday morning.

Despite the gap in generations between them, Mrs. Griffith had been Becca's friend. For more than fifteen years, Becca, along with her mama, and then later on her own, delivered eggs to the Griffith house on Highland Street once a week. By word of mouth alone, Mrs. Griffith single-handedly helped grow the Miller's egg business to the point where Becca could hardly make all the deliveries in one day. And, to Becca, personally, she gave another kindness.

From the very beginning, Millicent Griffith had accepted Becca as if she were any other girl her grandson had chosen to date. As if she believed they had a right to be together.

Becca let her eyes drift to the back of Matt's head again, struck anew with the reality of seeing him. She'd imagined it too many times to count, until their past began to seem like someone else's dream.

During that last summer when they'd been together, Matt had been a seventeen-year old boy. Today, she saw the man he had become, his shoulders wider now beneath his dark suit, his jaw line more defined. He was the kind of man women call good-looking, the kind of man who would never be single. She could not help but wonder, then, why there was no one by his side today.

The reality of that ignited a spark of gladness inside her that seemed beneath her. Had she hoped somewhere deep down that if she could not have him, then no one else would, either?

The thought was a selfish one. After all, she had known from the beginning that the bar had been set too high. That in spite of what they felt for each other, people were different, and no matter how much they wanted to believe otherwise, those differences mattered.

In the end, those differences had separated them.

In the end, they mattered more than either of them could ever have imagined.

3

Collapsed Bridges

Millicent Griffith: County Matriarch's "Influence Will be Missed"
– The Ballard County Times

Now

It was exactly the kind of day Gran would have chosen for her funeral, bright sun and blue skies. "I want smiles at the end, Matt. No tears for me. Where I'm going, there's nothing to be sad about."

Matt Griffith pictured his grandmother as she had been when he was growing up, a spitfire of energy and motivation. Baking biscuits at five in the morning. Ironing his clothes before school. Rehearsing at the piano before choir practice on Wednesday nights. Driving the two of them downtown to Simpson's Grocery in her big black Ford, her hands gripping a steering wheel the size of a tractor trailer tire.

He thought then of the woman she had been during his visits these past ten years, staring at him from the nursing home bed, not a spark of recognition in her blue eyes, a shrunken shell of her former self. Death could be cruel when it consumed a person in stages, each of Gran's strokes stealing a piece of her identity until, in the end, there was little left of the person she had once been.

Sitting on the hard-backed pew, listening to the Reverend Prillaman remind those who had known his grandmother about the life she'd led, Matt wished for her faith, for her conviction that there was a purpose for everything that happened, a reason behind each of the events in a person's life. She had tried to teach him this as a boy, but too young, he had decided that life was made up of little more than coincidence and chaos, that people were merely victims of circumstance, of moments of being in the wrong place at the wrong time.

He squeezed his eyes shut against a sudden deluge of memory, a day over thirty years ago when he'd sat in this same sanctuary as a little boy, two caskets lined up parallel to one another where Gran's now sat alone. He'd been unable to look at the faces of his mother and father that day, burrowing his head into the curve of his grandmother's arm, her soothing hands anchoring him to her.

Throughout his childhood, Gran had been the buffer between him and the memories of the accident that had taken the lives of his parents. They filled his head now, a collage of sounds and images disjointed by time and a concerted effort to forget. The unrelenting wail of an ambulance siren, the cold sting of sleet blowing through a broken back window where he'd sat trapped behind his father's seat. And his own six-year old voice crying out their names, the silence telling him once and for all that they would never again answer.

Matt blinked hard now to erase the images, focusing on the remainder of his grandmother's eulogy even as the words blended with those uttered in memory of his parents so long ago.

Reverend Prillaman closed the service with a prayer,

an uplifting deliverance from this life to the next that Gran would have found satisfying. The pastor stepped down from the pulpit, and a woman with freckles and long wavy, red hair took his place. Matt recognized her as an older version of a young girl who had sung in the choir when he was growing up. She faced the crowd and stood for a moment, eyes closed. There was no music, just the rise of her voice a cappella. Amazing grace. How sweet the sound.

For the first time since he'd received the call that Gran was gone, tears filled his eyes, spilling over and falling onto the sleeve of his suit where they made a dark stain against the gray fabric.

He dropped his head and gave in to the power of the song, its poignant swell rousing in him a well of regret for all the ways in which he knew he had disappointed her. For the knowledge that he was not the man she had tried to teach him to be.

When the song ended, a peaceful quiet settled over the sanctuary, a quiet of acceptance, of closure. No one moved, and Matt felt it was a moment worthy of a woman as fine as his grandmother.

He turned his head to meet the sympathetic glances of those who had come to pay her their respects. Most of the faces looked familiar to him; some the children and grandchildren of people he hadn't seen in almost two decades. He realized then how much he had missed this place, how despite his deliberate efforts to eradicate this town from his life, ties that could not be so easily cut anchored him here.

It was then that he saw her.

The shock of it rolled through him, even as the changes in her appearance registered one by one. She now wore the clothing of the Brethren Church, a traditional black bonnet covering all but the front edges of her blonde hair, a long sleeve light blue dress matched with a cape that buttoned at her neck.

Something painful and raw began to burn low in the pit of his stomach.

Her eyes locked steady on his. *I'm sorry. I know you loved her.*

Staring at her, the years fell away for him, just like that, and he remembered how she once read his thoughts so well, what it felt like to be young and in love.

It had all been so long ago. Eighteen years to be exact. On that last night he'd seen Becca, she had been his. The certainty of this as identifiable upon her features as the symbolic clothing that now singled her out from the others in this church. But this was no longer true, their lives having unfolded along completely different roads. With this realization-though it was hardly a new one—the bridge he'd built to a new life collapsed within him. And it felt like losing her all over again.

4

Links

God can heal a broken heart, but He has to have all the pieces.
– Author Unknown

Now

My name is Emmy Miller. I am thirty-four years old. I live in Ballard County, Virginia.

I recite these facts to myself at least once every day, a habit based on the fear that I might eventually lose even this most basic awareness of who I am or who I used to be.

The center of my world is this room where I've slept since I was a little girl, four solid walls I don't care to venture beyond.

If I had the choice, I would be most content living out the rest of my life right here. But that's not something my sister is willing to let me do. Becca is a fighter. She starts each morning as if it's a new battle, and she has a fresh plan for how to pull me out of this shell, how to get me out into the world again.

She's a worthy general in this war we've all been fighting for more years than I can even remember now. Her determination is like a steel rod in her spine. She will not break. Will not give in. She keeps pulling me along, convinced that one day I'll wake up, and all will be as it used to be.

Maybe I once believed this myself. But now I see the truth of it. The truth is I am the concrete block tied to my sister's ankle. And I fear that one day, I will pull her down altogether, so that neither of us is able to go on.

The thought increases the heaviness in my chest, and I get out of bed and stand by the window of my room. Through a tiny hole in the pull-down shade, I watch Mama hanging laundry on the clothesline. I see the glances she throws this way, the worry she wears full-time the way she used to wear smiles and happiness. All I can think is how lost she looks out there. As if the world she once knew changed in a blink with little of it now recognizable.

I wish I could snap my fingers and make things the way they used to be. Turn this darkness inside me to light, roll back the years to a day when I could direct us all down a different road. If only life gave us that kind of second chance.

When we're young, we think the chances are limitless. That if we make a wrong choice, we'll always have another opportunity to fix it. But I know the truth of this now. The truth is that every decision counts. One leads to another and another and another until the chain is formed, the links forged and unbreakable. And maybe all of it would be bearable if the chain had been my burden alone all these years. If I had been the only one to suffer for my choices.

This is the part that doesn't seem fair. That the people I love should continue to pay for my wrongs. This is the part I would change, if only I could.

5

Butterfly Wings

At night, when the lights are out, when the house is asleep, when I am sure that not a living soul can see in my face that I am thinking of you. That is when I think of you. Remember you. Let myself long for you.
– Entry from Becca's Journal

Now
Becca washed up the remaining supper dishes, relishing a rare moment of solitude. Through the window above the kitchen sink, she looked out across the back yard at the barn and the hundred-year-old oak tree just up the hill from it. It had come back to life once again this year, the same tire she'd swung on as a child still hanging from a sturdy limb. It always amazed her that the tree could have survived so long in the same place, season after season, its leaves no less vibrant now than they had been the year before.

Like that old tree, Becca's roots here ran deep. She loved the farm and the flat lay of the land where it stretched out to the foot of Tinker's Knob, the mountain that ran along the outer edge of their property. As a child, she'd explored every inch of it, except, of course, Tinker's Knob, which as a little girl, had always seemed like Mount Everest to her. She used to try to imagine what might be on the other side. When she was nine years old, she'd actually put together a plan to climb it, complete with a map from the County Extension office that marked her family's piece of the Blue Ridge in yellow highlighter. She'd packed a bag with a flashlight, a pocket-knife, cheese sandwiches and a jar of lemonade, all set to head out when her mother got wind of her expedition and warned her about all the wild animals that lived on the mountain. Bears. Goats. Boars. Live sentries to prevent a girl like her from ever attempting to scale it.

So she'd never actually climbed Tinker's Knob. And she knew now that her mother had been right about that and so many other things as well.

Aaron walked out of the big main door at the barn, and spotting her at the window, raised his hand. Becca waved in return, suds dripping from her forearm.

He wore one of the light blue cotton shirts she'd made for him on her mother's old sewing machine. The shirt was tucked neatly into the denim pants she'd also made, suspenders keeping them in place. His face was clean-shaven. On his head sat the straw hat he refused to replace despite the fact that it had been run over by the tractor twice and never quite regained its original shape. Aaron was a hard worker. His view of life was simple in that he kept his head down, never questioning the existence laid out before him.

But Becca had questioned. Considered the what-ifs. Grieved over them, actually.

She could feel them surfacing again, fluttering against the wall of her chest like butterfly wings. *He came back. He came back.*

She reached into the suds for the heavy wrought iron

skillet her mother had used to fry the ham for supper. She refused to use the Teflon-coated pan Becca gave her a few Christmases ago, preferring the one she'd cooked in all her life, even though it was nearly impossible to clean. Becca both admired and resented this stubbornness in her mother. Martha had never seen the value in trying something new when the old still worked.

Becca opened the cabinet door beneath the sink and pulled out a wire scrub brush, working for a minute or more, using the effort as an escape hatch for the direction of her thoughts.

But it didn't help. She closed her eyes and saw his face for the thousandth time since that afternoon.

Throughout all the years during which she had never once run into him, she'd held onto his image as he was before. Seventeen and confident the world was his for the asking. That boy had disappeared forever today, replaced by a man she did not know, a man whose eyes held shadows of disillusion and something else she wasn't willing to identify.

The back door off the kitchen opened, a smiling Abby flying into the room, all breathless flurry, bursting with a can't-wait-to-tell-you secret. "Mama," she said, her blue eyes sparkling. "Bea just had her calf! Daddy let me help her at the end. It was incredible. The baby just slid out into my arms like she knew I was waiting right there for her!"

Becca set the skillet on the counter, smiling. It was contagious, Abby's joy. People wanted to be near her, some of that joy rubbing off on them, like some special elixir. "Your twenty-four hour vigil paid off then, didn't it?"

"It was so worth it," Abby said, heading for the refrigerator, the long, blonde braid hanging to the center of her back flying out behind her. "I was starting to think she'd never have it, but Daddy kept saying just be patient."

Becca nodded once, picturing Aaron patting Abby's shoulder in quiet instruction, as she had seen him do many times. "I wasn't sure you would be back for supper, but I saved a plate for you."

"Thanks. I'm starving."

She opened the oven door, lifting the plate from the rack and setting it on the table. "Is your daddy coming up?"

"He said he'd be on in a while," Abby said, dropping into a ladder back chair, and then asking, "Where did you go today?"

"To a funeral for a woman I knew," Becca said after a few moments.

"Was she old?" Abby managed around a forkful of mashed potatoes.

"Yes."

"I'm sorry, Mama."

Hearing the genuine empathy in Abby's voice, Becca nodded, turning away to wipe down the sink, a lump of sadness lodging in her throat.

"I could have gone with you," Abby said.

"And leave Bea alone?" Becca said, making her voice light, even as she appreciated her daughter's generous heart. It was Abby's nature to feel things for others, animals, people, on a level that seemed out of character for a seventeen-year old. But Becca had known this about Abby even before she learned to talk. Abby only had to look at a dog or cat that wandered onto the farm without a collar or any apparent owner, and her eyes would turn liquid with sympathy. Just as they were now.

Footsteps echoed on the stairs.

Martha walked into the kitchen, slowed by the arthritis that plagued her knees now on a daily basis, her blue calico dress as crisp as if it had just seen the tip of an iron, her gray hair pulled back into a bun and covered with a white bonnet that fit close to her head. She set a wooden tray stacked with dishes on the counter, then reached for the drying towel.

Becca picked up a plate, scraping the mostly untouched food into the bowl at the edge of the sink, then dipping it in the soapy water. "Emmy didn't eat much tonight," she said.

Martha sighed and shook her head. "Sometimes, I think it all tastes the same to her."

"Maybe Aunt Em just wasn't hungry," Abby offered from the table.

"Maybe not," Becca agreed, even though she'd noticed for some time the way her sister turned her head at the sight of food. The mechanical way in which she chewed, then swallowed, her blue eyes registering no pleasure in the process.

"Were there a lot of people at the funeral today?" Martha asked, as if she wanted to change the subject.

"Yes," Becca said. "Mrs. Griffith had a lot of friends."

"She was a good woman."

A little spurt of anger prodded Becca to ask her mother why she hadn't gone to the funeral then, but she didn't. She knew the answer, after all.

They finished cleaning up the kitchen, Abby intent on completing her homework at the table, the silence in the room blatant. When the last of the glasses had been put away, Martha looked at Becca and said, "Emmy loves your banana pudding. Maybe you could make her one tomorrow. See if that helps her appetite."

For a single moment, a spear of rebellion hurtled up from somewhere deep inside Becca. She felt bruised by everything that had happened today, her mother's words like boulders pressing against her too sensitive skin. An almost impossible to resist desire to simply walk away swept through her, a need to leave this house and the weight of obligation she thought would sometimes completely smother her.

But she glanced at Abby then, seeing the hint of question in her eyes. The rebellion died an instant death, as it always did. "Of course," she said, wiping her hands on her apron. "I'll be happy to."

6

Impending Storms

"The willow which bends to the tempest often escapes better than the oak which resists it."
– Sir Walter Scott

Now
Martha didn't miss the look in her daughter's eyes, the instant flare of resistance, and then its deliberate squelching. She watched as Becca let herself out the back door off the kitchen, nearly called her back, then pressed her lips together and turned to put away the remaining dishes.

She could feel her granddaughter's gaze on her back, all but heard the questions running through the young girl's mind. It wasn't as if Martha hadn't noticed them before. Of course, she had. Abby was an intelligent child, and she often observed the interactions between Martha and Becca with a kind of intensity that made Martha feel as if she were being looked at through some kind of special lense. And falling short on her granddaughter's measuring stick.

Abby had always been so closely bonded with Becca.

As an infant, she would stare up into Becca's face with a look of utter adoration, as if Becca had saved her very life. Which, in so many ways, Martha could not deny that she had.

"I'm going upstairs to do some homework, Grandma," Abby said, sliding back her chair and bringing her remaining dishes to the sink. "I'll do these first though."

Abby's shoulders were stiff with disapproval. Strangely, Martha felt no resentment of this. Abby's conclusions, after all, were based on what she witnessed with her own eyes. And Martha could not deny the strain between Becca and herself, the recently renewed tug of wills that for so long had succumbed to acceptance on Becca's part. It was only in these past few days that Martha had felt the bloom of it in her daughter's bearing. She felt it in the air between them, an undeniable threat to the normal pattern of a day like the humidity that precedes a summer storm.

"That's all right," Martha said. "I'll do them."

"Thank you, Grandma." Subdued, Abby left the kitchen then, her footsteps sounding on the wood staircase. For the next few minutes, Martha busied herself with the mindless task of cleaning up. When the last glass was stored in the cupboard, she braced herself at the sink, both hands grasping its edge while a hollowness echoed up from deep inside her.

She regretted now her earlier abruptness with Becca. Wished, as she had so many other times, that she could take it back, soften the requests she frequently made of her oldest daughter. She realized the unfairness of it, even as she felt the sharpness of her own tongue.

If there were any excuse for her behavior, it was that she depended on Becca, had no idea, in fact, what she would do without her. Not so much, she realized, for the physical help that Becca provided for Emmy, but for the way in which she trudged through each day, pulling Emmy along with firm insistence, when Martha would have long ago given up.

This wasn't something she was proud to admit. But it was true, nonetheless. She loved Emmy with all her heart, but at her very human core, she sometimes wanted to shake her into waking up from the trancelike state she'd succumbed to a little more with every passing year.

Not once had Martha ever seen this frustration in Becca. If she felt it, she never let it show. And as much as anything, it was this Martha feared losing now. She doubted her own ability to give Emmy what she needed. Without Becca, she could not begin to imagine what would happen to any of them.

She turned away from the sink and dried her hands on a cotton towel. She felt the ugliness of her own admission and the single wave of shame flowing up from behind it.

This family needed Becca. And with the return of Matt Griffith to the county, Martha was deeply, desperately afraid that they would lose her.

7

A Secret Room

"A mill cannot grind with water that is past."
–American Proverb

Now

The potting shed at the far left corner of the yard beckoned like a shady maple on an August afternoon. Becca headed across the grass, arms folded across her chest, a knot of something that felt too much like bitterness sitting tight and hard inside her. She quickened her steps, nearly running by the time she reached the front door. Inside, she flipped a switch, and soft light bathed the small room.

She closed the door behind her, the tightness in her chest instantly dissolving. The potting shed always had this effect on her, the only place she ever went that truly felt like hers. A place where she could steep her hands in soil, seeds and plants until she found her own roots again, and the world ceased to tilt around her.

Her daddy had helped her build the shed so she would have a place to put the gardening tools and supplies Granny Miller had left her when she died. Aaron and her mother both had been opposed to the idea of making such a building for something as humble as gardening. But her father had built it anyway, knowing how much Becca had needed this space for herself.

Against the back wall was her work area, a harvest style wood table some nine feet in length and four in width. The table had belonged to her granny. In the right hand corner of the shed sat a refrigerator with a glass front, by far the most expensive thing Becca had ever bought for herself and certainly the most worldly. She'd driven to Raleigh, North Carolina and shopped for it at one of those specialty stores that sold equipment with names like Viking and Northland to high-end restaurants. In it, she kept the seeds passed down from her grandmother along with the ones she'd cultivated since, rows and rows of blue jars with muted silver lids neatly lining the shelves.

She'd bought the fancy refrigerator with its glass door for the simple reason that seeing all those jars somehow grounded her, reminded her that sometimes a thread of the past could weave its way into the present.

Growing up, Becca had loved visiting her Granny Miller's house, especially in the spring when she was busy planting her enormous garden. With each year, the garden had grown to meet the demand of the customers who came back season after season to purchase the produce she raised and displayed in green cardboard containers. Becca loved watching the empty black rectangle of earth transform with row after row of new vegetables, the colors and textures rich and alive.

First the lettuce, tender leaves of Buttercrunch and Mascara. Then the spring onions, fragile green tops peeking through the dark soil. Next, Hubbard squash and Cocozelle zucchini, vine after vine, picked while they were still small and tender. Then the tomatoes, German Johnsons, Marglobes, and Old Brooks, each perfectly staked on its own wooden trellis. And multiple teepees of climbing beans, Scarlet Runners and Yellow Squaws.

Gardening was the same for Becca as it had been for her Granny. There was something wonderfully addictive in the seasonal process, a chance each spring to start fresh, create something from nothing, carrying on the tradition of saving from the best plants the seeds Granny had cherished.

Becca walked over to the long worktable where row after row of starter plants sat waiting for the weather to become consistent enough that they could be transplanted outside. She rubbed a finger across a tomato plant, calmed by the assurance of the work ahead of her. These months, April through August, were the best of the year, the days where she lost herself in the cycle of labor necessary to grow the garden and harvest its bounty.

Now, at the end of April, the lettuces were already planted and would be ready to begin picking any day. The workload would increase steadily from there, and the timing was good. After today, she would need the steady immersion and its distraction.

Becca reached for a plastic jug of water and began dosing each of the plants on the table. The quiet of the shed was peaceful, soothing, and she willed it to settle over the images in her head, suffocate them with reason. But she couldn't blink away the image of Matt's face or the sorrow in his eyes.

She knew the danger of letting herself think about him. But then where Matt was concerned, logic had never applied. Her response to him had always come from her heart, unexpected, unsummoned, and at first, unwelcome.

How, then, did a woman fend off something that came from inside her, as organic as the soil she used to grow her vegetables? She could feel the funnel of it now, rising up from a single pinpoint of energy, the same feeling, really, she'd known the first moment she'd set eyes on him nearly three decades before.

∞

Then

THE FIRST TIME Becca saw the Griffith house, it looked like a castle to her. It had been built in the 1800's, Georgian, Federal or some such style. It was a classic old house, one of the nicest in Ballard. The boxwoods out front formed a defining border all the way around the yard, and they'd already outlived generations of the Griffith family.

Becca had been nine years old the Saturday she rode with her mother into town to deliver the eggs they collected each week for a dozen or so regular customers. Mrs. Griffith was new on their list, and Becca's mother said for her to wait in the car while she took the two cartons to the door.

The day was warm so Becca sat in the front seat with the window rolled down and her door open. A dozen yards away, a boy she'd never seen before tossed a baseball high in the air and caught it with a leather glove. He looked to be about her age. He had dark blonde hair and the kind of face that assured him a future of being chased by girls.

He walked over to the car, not saying anything, just staring. This was hardly a new response for Becca. She'd long ago gotten used to the questions from other children who wondered why her family wore funny clothes and didn't have televisions in their homes.

"Do you always have to wear a dress?" he asked, tossing the ball up again and catching it in his glove.

"Do you always have to cut your hair so short?" she threw back, staring at his head.

He grinned and threw the ball up higher, catching it again with a solid whump. "Only in the summer when it's hot. Why? You don't like it?"

She lifted a shoulder, tipped her head, figuring he already had a big enough ego. "It's okay."

"So, you gonna answer my question?"

"Yeah," she said. "I always wear a dress."

"Why?"

She thought about this for a few moments, startled to discover that she didn't have an immediate answer other than that it was what she was supposed to do. "You have something against dresses?"

A grin automatically lit his face again. "I don't guess so."

She wondered if he would have been shocked to know she was a lot more intrigued by him than he ever could have been by her, even though she was the one who looked different.

He stopped tossing the ball, walked a little closer. "Our house has a secret room."

"Really?" she said.

"Yep. It has a secret door, too."

"What's it for?"

"It was built during the Civil war in case somebody needed to hide from the Union soldiers."

"Really?" she said, impressed.

"Wanna see it?"

She looked down at her hands, laced them together in her lap, her heart thudding hard. She knew her mama would never let her do such a thing, but she nodded anyway. "Not today, though. We've got more deliveries to make."

"Oh," he said, and she was left with the feeling she'd disappointed him. She glanced at the house where her mother still stood at the door talking to Mrs. Griffith.

Maybe it was worth asking. She got out of the car and ran to the porch.

Her mother turned at the sound of her footsteps, the floral-print cape above her dress lifting in the afternoon breeze. "What is it, Becca?"

"That boy said they have a secret room in their house. He said he'd show it to me. Can I go see it, Mama?"

Martha's gaze settled on the boy who had wandered up beside her. "That's a very nice offer," she said. "But we have to be going."

"This is my grandson, Matt," Mrs. Griffith said. "And you must be Becca. Stay and let me fix you some tea, Mrs. Miller. The children can take a look at that room."

"Thank you so much, Mrs. Griffith," Martha said. "But we really do have to be going."

"Well, some other time then," Mrs. Griffith said.

Disappointed but not surprised, Becca lifted a hand and walked back to the big black Impala, opening the heavy door and sliding onto the vinyl seat.

A few moments later, her mother got in and backed out of the driveway. Becca could tell by the press of her lips that she was unhappy with her. They hadn't reached the stop-light on Tanyard before she said in a stern voice, "That was not appropriate, Becca. If you're unable to wait in the car as I've asked you to, you'll have to stay at home next time."

Becca said nothing for a few moments, and then, "What would have been wrong with just looking at it, Mama?"

Her mother drove on for a good bit before answering. "Sometimes, Becca," she said, "we put ourselves in places we would be better off not ever going in the first place."

Becca wanted to disagree. Matt Griffith was just a boy who wanted to show her a room. What could be so wrong with that? She pressed her lips together and turned to the window, aware that arguing would only earn her a stay at home next week. "Yes, Mama," she said in a neutral voice even as her heart knew its first flare of defiance.

8

Frogs and Sunrises

"You don't get to choose, you just fall."
–Author Unknown

Now

The frogs were extra loud tonight. Their voices slid beneath Abby's open window and filled the darkness, familiar and comforting. All her life, she'd loved this sound, nighttime's lullaby. She wondered what it would be like to live in a city where there weren't any frogs, honking horns the only sound to sleep by.

She lay on her back, the covers thrown aside. The night was warm, no air-conditioning in the house. She squeezed her eyes closed, keeping them shut tight, as if that alone would keep him from her thoughts.

But it didn't work. She could think of little else these days. She'd never understood what would motivate a person to take drugs like cocaine or heroine, but thought she might understand the addiction if this was what it felt like when a person's senses were altered to another state.

At nearly midnight, the house was quiet, everyone else long asleep. She flicked on the lamp next to her bed and opened the drawer of her nightstand, removing the white envelope she'd received a week ago. She pulled out the letter from the school principal and read it as she had done a dozen times since finding it in the mailbox. She'd nearly memorized the words by now, and the accolades rang through her head. . .*only perfect SOL score in your class. . .so proud of your accomplishment. . .hope you will consider scholarship opportunities.*

A wave of frustration rolled over her. She put the letter down and got out of bed, crossing the floor to the window and raising it high enough that she could sit on the sill with her feet dangling, her toes barely touching the side roof below.

She was eighteen years old, but sometimes, she felt so much older than that.

Part of her resented feeling this way. Part of her wished she could be like the other kids in her school, getting ready to go to college, thinking about what they wanted to be when they graduated.

Abby longed to be a vet. She was good with animals. She had a sort of connection with them that had been there for as long as she could remember. Mama said God made her special that way. The part of her that questioned this life she'd been born into wondered why she had to feel guilty for wanting to use what He gave her. Would He not understand this desire in her to do something good with her life?

If the answer was no, why had He put it there? Was she to ignore it, hold onto the faith that it would eventually go away? Should she accept without resentment that she should leave school, work as a housekeeper or a nanny until she married?

Beau said that was crazy.

Maybe that had been one of her first mistakes, though. Confiding in Beau Lassiter. They'd started talking one day in Advanced Biology. Beau was smart. Really smart.

He planned to be a doctor. And Abby had no doubt he would do big things with his life. He thought the same could be true for her if she wanted it because she was smart, too.

But then that was one of the weird things about their relationship. Because they went to the same school, had most of their classes together, it was easy to forget how different their lives were when they went home at night. Abby knew what was expected of her. She'd already disappointed her father and her grandmother by not leaving school. Neither of them could see why she wanted her diploma, why acing her SOL test meant something to her. They could only anticipate disappointment in continuing her education, her mama's quiet insistence something else she hadn't figured out and the only reason she was still going.

Though her mother wasn't one to openly disagree with either Abby's father or grandmother, on this subject, she'd taken a stance and refused to yield. Abby didn't understand why her father hadn't put his foot down against it. Normally, if he felt strongly about something, he said so in a voice he saved for the times he really meant it.

She had to believe he knew that school had mattered to her mother, even though she had not gone beyond the tenth grade. Abby remembered a time when she was ten or eleven, and she'd found an old folder up in the attic with each of her mother's report cards from first grade through her last year in school. They were all straight A's, not a single B.

Abby thought her mother was an amazing person. She hadn't gone to Harvard or discovered some miracle cure for a deadly disease, but she'd made a name for herself in the community with the heirloom vegetables she grew and sold to the nicer restaurants and stores on Tinker's Knob Lake and in nearby Roanoke.

In the wintertime, she sold some of her seeds through a mail-order business. Abby knew it hadn't been an easy road. She'd witnessed the resistance her mother endured from Grandma Miller on countless occasions. Once her grandma had questioned her mother about working with restaurants that sold alcohol to its customers. Abby remembered her mama's measured and even voice when she said, "Unless they're using my tomatoes or corn or potatoes to actually make it, I don't see what it has to do with me."

Grandma had walked off without responding. Even now, Abby remembered being proud of her mama for standing up for herself.

From below her window, she heard the rustle of a bush, and then in a familiar whisper, "Abby!"

Beau. Her stomach flipped at the sound of his voice. And she let herself admit she'd been hoping he would come all along. "I'm coming!" she said, keeping her voice soft.

She lowered herself to the tin roof below, set her bare feet against the cool surface. From there, she tiptoed over to the branch of the huge old maple she'd used as a ladder since she was a little girl. She swung across to a wider branch, dropped one lower, then down the trunk on the rungs nailed to its wide base.

Beau waited for her below. They said nothing. They didn't need to. She stepped into his arms, pressing her face to his white Nike t-shirt, inhaling the clean, reassuring scent of him. She lifted her face to his then, because she knew that for a little while, at least, his kiss would make all the stuff she'd been thinking about tonight disappear, like the voices of the frogs with the sunrise.

9

Truths

Farm Tragedy Claims Two Victims:
Miller Girl Still Unable to Recount Events
– The Ballard County Times

Now

I can't sleep.

I want to. I actually long for it, that moment when my eyes close and awareness slips away.

But tonight, it shows me no mercy, and I lie here in bed, staring at the shadows on the ceiling, my thoughts refusing to shut down.

Once when I was twelve, I came across a book in the school library called **The Power of the Mind***. I had to write a paper for my science class on the brain, and I remember flipping through the pages and reading a section on the human ability to block out pain. I ended up writing on Dr. Freud's theory of repression, a theory not all doctors agreed with. He said that people sometimes push painful memories into the unconscious mind where I guess, basically, they don't have to look at them anymore.*

Reading that years ago, I had no way of knowing whether it was true or not. I still don't know what's true for other people. I only know my own truth.

A long time ago, a window closed between me and the world I still live in. I can actually see through the window. And I can hear what's said to me and to others. But the window doesn't let me talk back. I'm locked here in this dark place, just me, separated from the people I love by something so much heavier than anything I can push past.

At first, I was terrified that I might never see light again. But at some point, all my fear turned to gratitude. Because I realized that the scary place wasn't behind the door where I am. I've already seen what's here. It's what's on the outside of the door that I don't know about. That I don't want to know about.

The difference between my reality and Dr. Freud's theory is this: my pain is indeed trapped, but I'm down here with it, reliving it each and every day.

Some people believe in a place called Purgatory, a kind of holding room for those not yet pure enough to go on to Heaven. If there is such a place, maybe this is where I am. But if so, then it is where Becca is as well.

She goes about her life as if it's the one she chose for herself. And to anyone who doesn't know her as I do, she's convincing. Maybe there's something in sisterhood that keeps us tapped into one another, so that we know almost intuitively what the other is feeling.

Whatever the explanation, I feel the sadness she keeps buried so deep in the same way I feel the crushing weight of my own anguish. Regret is the wheel that keeps us both rolling through one day to the next.

Becca has made her life busy enough that there's not a lot of time to think about what might have been. But I know there's a hollow place inside her where something very different once was.

For me, there's actually comfort in the thought that one day I'll be released from all this. And that's the fragile rope I cling to. The knowledge that at some point, it will be all right for me to leave.

The question that keeps me here is where will that leave Becca? How can I go, knowing that she'll still be here, carrying on where I left off?

10

Echoes

Giving up doesn't always mean you are weak; sometimes it means that you are strong enough to let go.
– Author Unknown

Now
The house felt lonely without her, echoed in places Matt had never noticed before. He'd gone to bed earlier, but finally given up on sleep at just after one a.m. The last person to pay condolences had left at seven. Until now, there had been things for Matt to do, decisions to make, people to visit with, places to be.

Gran had always filled up the space around her, added dimension and depth to it by the sheer force of her personality alone, her laugh the kind that made people feel as if the room had been flooded with sunlight. It hit Matt with the harshest kind of finality that he would never hear that laugh again.

Taking the stairs to the living room, he stopped midway down to study the pictures lining the wall. They were mostly of him, a few as a baby, red-cheeked and chubby. And then dozens from age six and on, little

League shots with team after team. He recognized the boys' faces. They'd played both together and against each other. Until now, seeing the old pictures, Matt hadn't recognized how they'd grown from year to year to year, little guys to boys to young men.

There were individual shots of him with Wilks, two teenagers with muscled arms slung around each other's shoulders, lower lips protruding with the Skoal chew they'd first tried at eleven, the nausea instantly turning them both green.

Matt could almost smell the tobacco, the leather of their gloves, a time when baseball had been about hot summer nights, pitching and hitting for no reason other than the love of the game. They'd both lived for it, the simple connect between bat and ball, the solid whack that signaled a great hit.

Somewhere along the way, Matt had lost that. Wilkes, too. Somewhere along the way, it had become more about who made the crowd cheer the loudest. Who got a date with the hottest cheerleader. It had become about the competition between them, the increasing awareness that people compared them, and from those comparisons arose judgment. One of them was better than the other. The question was which one.

Looking back, Matt could see that this awareness had started the change between them, but it hadn't been the deciding factor in where they'd ended up. The deciding factor had been Becca.

Matt took the stairs to the living room where his laptop sat on a desk by the window. He'd brought along plenty of work. Depositions to review. Case notes. Billable hours. Time was what he had to sell and in D. C., he never seemed to have enough of it.

The grandfather clock ticked loudly in the otherwise silent house, reminding him that he hadn't billed an hour in days. The thought left a heavy feeling in his chest, and he felt tired of this constant awareness of time unsold. It was the one thing about being an attorney that he had not expected, the way hours disappeared like water swirling down a drain.

His cell phone rang from the desk where he'd plugged it in earlier to recharge. He considered not answering, but when it stopped ringing and then started up again almost instantly, he gave in and glanced at caller id, biting back a heavy sigh. Phone to his ear, he sat down in the desk chair and leaned back to stare at the ceiling. "Hey," he said.

"I knew you wouldn't be sleeping." Phoebe sounded as if she'd been crying, her voice raspy at the edges. He pictured her face, beautiful by any standard, blotchy with tears.

"Yeah," he said. It was on the tip of his tongue to add that ten years of marriage had at least given them reliable knowledge of the other's habits, but he stopped himself, not wanting to argue.

"Are you all right?" she asked.

"I'm fine."

"I wish you would have let me come."

"It seemed better that you didn't," he said, hearing the razor slice in his response. Ironic that he'd ended up the bad guy in all of this.

Silence stretched between them, until Phoebe finally spoke. "Is there anything I can do for you?" she asked, the question soft in a way he knew was difficult for her. Phoebe's instinct had never been to grovel, but to fight no holds barred for something she considered rightfully hers.

"No. But thanks."

"I can still come down. In the morning. I'd like to, Matt. Let me do this for you."

Pure loneliness tempted him. But the thought of her here tightened the knot in his stomach. For now, he didn't want to think about his life with Phoebe. He ran a hand over his face, said too quickly, "No. I'll be home in a few days."

She started to say something, stopped. He knew she was crying again, and more than anything, he hated the fact that he didn't care. This deadness inside him was the scariest part of what had happened to them. How could they ever find their way back from that?

Matt clicked off the phone then without saying another word. Maybe it was cruel, but anything he had to say would only be more so.

He got up from the desk, wandered into the kitchen, hands in the pockets of his suit trousers, a tension headache now gripping the back of his neck.

Gran had spent a good portion of her days in the kitchen, canning pickles, freezing corn, baking pies or cakes for sick neighbors or friends from church.

The stove and refrigerator were old by today's standards, although they worked as well now as they had when he was a boy. He opened the frig, stared at the shelves weighed down with dishes of food, each labeled with a piece of masking tape describing the contents inside as well as who had brought it. They were people he'd known growing up, people he hadn't seen in years, but whose names he instantly recognized.

Sweet potato pie – Janice Blankenship
Green bean casserole – The Cundiff family
Blueberry oat muffins – Carl and Ida Turner

He closed the door, turned to the kitchen table. Tupperware cake boxes and glass pie plates sealed in Saran wrap covered the surface. He walked over, glancing at the names on the containers. Again, all familiar. But the one at the far corner made his stomach drop.

Carrot cake – Mrs. Aaron Brubaker

Written in neat cursive across the strip of masking tape. *Mrs. Aaron Brubaker*. He'd never let himself think of her this way. In his mind, she had remained Becca Miller. Just Becca.

He edged around the table, lifting the lid and staring at the cake. Three layers, with thick swirls of cream cheese icing. He sat down on a ladder back chair, one elbow on the table, the other hand still holding the lid to the box.

Had she remembered it was his favorite?

Matt got up from the table, opened a drawer and pulled out a knife. He reached for a plate from the cabinet next to the sink--same spot where they'd always been--then lifted the cake out of its box and sliced a piece.

He hadn't been hungry for days. But he cut into one edge now, lifting the fork to his mouth. If memory could be found on the taste buds, then a hundred of them flooded through him now.

And at the very center of each was Becca.

∞

Then

FOR A SEVENTEEN-YEAR OLD, Matt did a better than average job of displaying a healthy respect for authority. Gran had insisted he grow up knowing when and where to use his manners, and as a rule, he did a fine job of backing himself out of difficult situations with a humble apology. A yes, sir, no sir. Yes, ma'am, no, ma'am.

Judge Wilson Anderson, however, had apparently seen it all before. And he wasn't buying Matt's rendition of regret and contrition. On the judge's right stood a stone-faced Deputy Sheriff, a uniformed reminder that the matter at hand was serious business.

Matt stood silent before the courtroom bench, his hands hanging awkward at his sides as if they no longer remembered their purpose. At the judge's request, his attorney remained seated. Gran sat behind him at the front of the room, and he could feel the disappointment in her eyes burning clear through the center of his back.

Judge Anderson peered down at him through round spectacles perched on the end of his long, narrow nose. His steel-colored hair was cut short, military style, and Matt suspected it was good enough validation of his no-nonsense reputation. "So, son," the judge said. "If you were me, what kind of punishment would you consider appropriate for a seventeen-year old boy driving under the influence of alcohol?"

The question caught Matt off guard. He'd expected a slap on the wrist, a couple days of community service cleaning up Mary Elizabeth Park and all would be forgotten. But Judge Anderson looked as if he really wanted his input on the decision. So he aimed a little higher than weed eating around the tennis courts.

"Well, sir," he said, clearing his throat. "I guess some of the roads around town could use a good trash detail."

"That's true enough," the judge said, his face darkening like a July thundercloud. "Dang slobs hurling their beer bottles out the car window as if they're never going to see a trash can again."

Having apparently hit a sore point, Matt thought better of this particular suggestion. "The recreation park," he offered up. "I'd be glad to do some work down there in the afternoons when I'm done at Winn-Dixie."

Judge Anderson raised an eyebrow. "Oh, you would, would you?"

"Yes, sir."

"That where you planning to work this summer?"

"Yes, sir."

The judge rubbed his chin with thumb and forefinger,

studying Matt. "Did you know I knew your granddaddy, son?"

"No, sir."

"He was a fine man, your granddaddy. A mentor of mine, actually. I have to believe if he were here, he'd urge me not to go soft on you, but to do what I could to steer you back to the straight and narrow." He pulled a white handkerchief from beneath the desktop and blew his nose, loudly, thoroughly. When he was finished, he tucked it away and looked at Matt. "So I'm thinking a boy like you could use a job that burns up a sufficient amount of energy every day. The kind of job that makes you tired at night. Too tired to be driving around this town with a blood alcohol level well over the legal limit. When I was your age, I worked on a dairy farm one summer. As I remember, it's the kind of job that should accomplish all of the above nicely enough."

"A dairy farm?" The words popped out before he could think better of his tone. He bit his lip and tempered it with, "But I've never done anything like that before, sir."

Judge Anderson narrowed his eyes, and then said, "You know, son, I realize you've been a fairly big deal in the high school's senior class this year. Baseball hero and such. Kind of thing that can make a young man feel like he's above it all. Not so in this courtroom. In here, you break the law, I'm going to make sure you think twice before you do it again."

He pounded his gavel on the desktop. "Matthew Griffith, I hereby sentence you to eight forty hour workweeks at the dairy farm of my choice. I'll make a few calls and let you know where you'll be going."

For a blank moment, Matt could think of nothing to say. "But, sir, I'm supposed to be at UVa for training camp on August 19."

"Since we're already into the first week of June, I

suggest you make some of those weeks sixty hours instead of forty. I'll be asking for regular updates from your employer. I expect not to be disappointed, son."

Several arguments sat ready to roll off the tip of Matt's tongue, but the look on the judge's face made him think better of it. The summer he had been looking forward to had just turned into three hundred plus hours of wading around in cow manure.

11

Deliveries

> *Don't let yesterday use up too much of today.*
> ***– Cherokee Indian Proverb***

Now

Next to Becca, Aaron slept, the rhythm of his breathing deep and even.

She lay on her back, alternately jacking and twisting her arm beneath her, her head finding no comfort in her too flat pillow. She'd always preferred sleeping on a fat, fluffy pillow, but Aaron liked a thin one. She had conceded, thinking a fat pillow and a skinny pillow wouldn't look right lined up on the bed together.

Unreasonable, she knew, to blame Aaron for her own unwillingness to disagree with him. But then maybe she saw it as one more quarter dropped inside the piggy bank of debt she owed him, a debt she'd been trying to repay for the duration of their marriage. She was only too aware of how inadequate her efforts had been, never having given him the one thing he had really wanted, reciprocal love, pure and true. Granted, from the day she had accepted his marriage proposal, she had committed herself to being a good wife. From the outside looking in, there was little to be faulted. But even though they never discussed it, Becca knew, and Aaron, too, that the inside of their marriage was hollow.

Aaron made a snuffling noise, turned onto his side, away from her. She turned over also, facing the opposite wall and staring into the dark.

They'd been married for so long now that it was hard to remember life without him, what it was like to sleep in this bed alone, the same heirloom four-poster her grandfather had made and she'd slept in as a child.

Growing up, she'd never imagined living here in her parents' house as an adult. Where she would live had never been clear, the picture fuzzy with her own uncertainty about whether she wanted to follow her parents' life. It was hard to love something with all your heart and at the same time want to be something so very different. But throughout her childhood, that was how Becca felt. She'd loved helping her daddy cut hay, picking apples every August in the orchard at one corner of their farm and the daily milking of the Holstein cows she'd grown up knowing by name.

Her family had lived a simple life. They'd shopped at the Winn-Dixie in Ballard on Saturdays and gone to church whenever the doors were open. When Becca was five, they'd driven to Ohio one summer to visit her mother's sister. She didn't remember much about it except being car sick in the back seat most of the way there and back.

At thirteen, she'd swung high in the old tire that hung by a rope in the oak tree in their back yard and wondered about the places she'd never been. Were there mountains in Nevada? What was it like to live in a place that had no winter? Did the people in New York City really walk down the street without meeting eyes with the other people they passed?

She could have found most of the answers to her questions in a book. But even then, she didn't think that was the same as seeing it for herself, living it for herself.

As much as she'd loved those things, she couldn't help wondering what else the world could offer.

She got out of bed now, slipping quietly across the room to the window that looked over the back yard. Beneath the maple tree, she saw their shadows dancing in a single line, Abby and this boy she'd been sneaking out to meet. Something inside Becca broke open with a piercing memory of what it felt like to be young and in love, kissing under the moonlight, dreading an inevitable parting.

She knew that a normal mother would march outside, chastise her daughter for sneaking out and send the boy home with his tail tucked between his legs. But then, she was hardly a normal mother. And wouldn't it be the height of hypocrisy to correct Abby for the very thing she had once done herself?

∞

Then

WHEN BECCA WAS old enough to drive, she began making the egg deliveries alone. The number of customers for the business had increased, and they made two trips into town each week now, Mondays and Thursdays. She'd been coming to the Griffith house for eight years, and although she did at least catch a glimpse of Matt most weeks, she never got to see that secret room.

On this particular Thursday, she pulled into the driveway just behind Mrs. Griffith who got out of her car and waved. "Afternoon, Becca," she said.

Becca opened her door and slid out. "Hi, Mrs. Griffith. You look nice today."

"Probably smell like mothballs," she said, pressing a hand to her plaid skirt and smiling. "I don't have cause to get this out of the closet too often, but I thought Judge Anderson deserved the respect of a good suit. Seems my renegade grandson ran into a little trouble with the law. Hope I haven't kept you waiting."

"Actually, I was a little late getting here myself," she said.

The passenger door to Mrs. Griffith's car opened then, and Matt got out, attitude in the set of his jaw. He took long strides up the walkway, muttering, "Hey," in Becca's direction, then vaulting up the steps and into the house.

Mrs. Griffith shook her head. "Never mind him," she said. "He's having a little trouble adjusting to the taste of some well-deserved medicine."

Curious, Becca didn't ask. She opened the trunk instead and lifted out the two cartons of eggs.

Mrs. Griffith unzipped her purse, flipped through her wallet and pulled out a fifty. "You have change, dear?" she asked.

"No," she said. "But that's all right. You can pay me next week."

"I'd rather do it now so I won't forget. Let me just run in the house and get it. I'll be right back."

She took the eggs from Becca, walked up the steps to the porch in her high heels, the screen door slapping shut behind her. Seconds later, a blast of music cut through the quiet neighborhood, and a classic red Mustang convertible pulled into the driveway behind Becca's car.

Becca recognized the driver as Wilks Perdue, a buddy of Matt's.

Three girls sat in the backseat. Becca knew them, too. Trish McGuire. Andrea Shively. Pattie Watson.

Judging from the empty front seat, she assumed they'd come to pick up Matt.

"Hey, Becca," Pattie called out over the blasting music.

"Hi," she said, raising a hand.

"Matt here?" Wilks asked.

"He's inside, I think."

Wilks hit the horn a couple of times.

Mrs. Griffith appeared on the porch, shaking a finger. "Wilks Perdue! Turn that racket down. Not everyone on this street shares your enthusiasm for such noise."

Wilks leaned over, lowered the volume, then looked back at the girls and rolled his eyes.

Matt jogged out of the house, dressed in jeans, a t-shirt and a baseball hat with the bill in the back, a duffel bag slung over his shoulder.

"Just a minute, young man," Mrs. Griffith said, stern.

Matt stopped and turned to face his grandmother. In his expression, Becca saw something angry, a little wild even. "Yes, ma'am?"

"I trust Judge Anderson made an impression on you this morning?"

"Yes, ma'am."

"Where are you headed?" she asked.

"Out to the lake," Matt said.

Mrs. Griffith threw a glance at Wilks, now drumming the steering wheel with impatient fingers. "You planning on driving your parents' boat, son?"

"Yeah," Wilks said. And then, "Yes, ma'am."

"They know you're going out there?"

Wilks nodded.

Mrs. Griffith shook her head as if she found him completely hopeless. "I better not hear about any more alcohol incidents," she said, looking at Matt.

"Gran. . . ."

"If I do," she interrupted, "you'll be spending your free

time this summer on that front porch with nothing more exciting to do than watch me knit."

Matt's expression held steady, but Becca strongly suspected he was tempted to roll his eyes as Wilks had. "Yes, ma'am," he said, managing to sound humble.

He jogged off then, catapulted over the door of the car into the front seat. Wilks backed up, pulled out with a low roar and cranked the music. But his voice rang out loud and clear when he shouted to Matt, "So why didn't you invite the little Dunkard girl? It'd be a hoot to see her in a bikini."

Becca turned away, but not before catching a glimpse of Matt looking back at her, muted apology in his expression.

And that, somehow, only deepened the insult.

12

Tapestries

Whatever our souls are made of, his and mine are the same.
– Emily Bronte

Now
The worst part of losing Daniel, although there were certainly many, was the loneliness Martha found in her bed each night. It had been six years, and still, the loneliness lingered.

Except for the earliest weeks after his death, the days became manageable enough. Once the initial shock of losing him began to wear off, life's everyday chores eventually served as enough of a distraction to get her through those waking hours. But it was here in this place where they had shared most of the important conversations of their lives that she realized over and over again just how alone she was.

This, she found to be the cruelest piece of her current phase of life. Oh, she had her aches and pains, and certainly those could color a day grey. But less tolerable still was the fact that at seventy-four, she had no one to share her worries and concerns with. It was as if the path of aging thinned out the real confidantes in a person's life. Because in truth, there had only been a few people from whom she kept nothing. Her mother, gone for years now, Clara, her best friend, and Daniel.

She missed this part of her relationship with Daniel in the way she imagined a person who lost an arm or a leg must miss its function. She could not count the number of times throughout the decades of their marriage when she had sought comfort in Daniel's arms, sliding into bed and finding her place against his right side, her head seeking with unerring accuracy a single spot at the center of his wide chest.

"What's wrong, Martha?" he would ask, the question her invitation to pour it all out to him. And she would, talking until she could begin to see reason through his eyes. That was the kind of man he'd been. A man who thought with straight-line logic, able to weigh the positives and negatives of a situation without the smothering cloud of emotion that tended to affect her own judgment.

It was her understanding of this that had allowed her to go along with the decision they made eighteen years ago. If there had ever been a time when she had needed Daniel's ability to weed out all the what-ifs she tended to bring into the picture, this had been such a time.

There had been many moments in the six years since Daniel's death when she considered unraveling the tapestry of deceit they'd woven around the events of that single devastating night, but each time she stopped herself, unable to imagine what good it would do for any of them. Her final conclusion was always the harm that would no doubt be done in recasting the truth.

Now, though, without him, she felt as if she were alone in a boat that had managed to struggle along on calm seas. Finally, now, as if she had been expecting it all along, the wind had begun to pick up, and she could feel her small vessel of security rocking from side to side. All her questions were surfacing again, and she could not manage to anchor herself with the assurances Daniel would have given her.

She lay here on her back in the room's thick darkness, her eyes wide open, sleep nowhere near. In her memory, she searched for his voice, struggled to remember what words he would have used to calm her. She tried for a long time, and when two single tears of defeat rolled down her wrinkled cheeks, they came with the admission that she could no longer hear him. Any resurfacing of the past would be up to her to address alone. It was as if, really, Daniel had never been here at all.

13

Connections

"Do not be afraid; our fate
Cannot be taken from us; it is a gift."
— Dante Alighieri, Inferno

Now

Matt woke with the sun on Tuesday morning. He pulled on shorts and an old Redskins t-shirt, and then went downstairs to brew some coffee in Gran's electric percolator, the kind he remembered as a kid, bursts of hot, brown liquid shooting up through a glass bubble on the lid.

Gran's house was like a living museum of Southern domesticity. Being here made him feel like he'd stepped back in time, everything in the same place it had been in when Gran lived here, even though she hadn't been here in years. Matt had continued to pay Bess Shively, his grandmother's housekeeper, to come in once a week and clean. He didn't know what else to do except keep hoping that eventually she would improve and come back home. When it became clear that she would never return, he didn't have the heart to do anything but leave the house as it was.

Matt grabbed a file from his briefcase, poured himself a cup of coffee, careful to strain the excess coffee grounds with a paper towel. He took a seat at the kitchen table and forced his eyes to follow the words across the document, its meaning hovering at the rim of comprehension.

He realized that he was tired, and not just from the restless night or the weight of Gran's funeral. He was tired in general. Worn down, actually. All those years of school, and no one had told him about the part where the career he'd once used as a place to sink his energy lost its fizz the way the glass bottle Cokes he used to drink as a kid went flat after sitting out with the cap off. Eighteen years. Where had it all gone?

In his senior year of college, Matt had put away his major league baseball aspirations, the decision not the difficult one it had been perceived to be. The papers had written it up as the ultimate curiosity. A star college player with no debilitating injuries, a future bright with possibility, and he had left it all on the table. He'd offered no explanations, other than that he'd decided to follow the family tradition of law school. Time to move on to other things.

The truth was that after that last summer in Ballard County, the game had never been the same for him. As a kid, baseball had been something that just came to him naturally. Something he'd been born with the ability to do and not something he'd ever had to work at. He'd loved everything about it, the challenge of besting his own number of hits, of improving his fastball, the roar of the fans when a ball sailed over the center field wall. "It's outta here, folks!" He could still hear the announcer's exuberant call, still remembered the rush of adrenaline that propelled him from first base to second to third and then home plate.

And now it seemed the same thing had happened with

his law career. He worked for a corporate firm in D.C., fifty attorneys plus, all hustling hours like aging prostitutes.

Lawyers went back several generations in the Griffith line. Before Matt was born, his grandfather had been a small town attorney in Ballard. As a boy, Matt had heard dozens of stories about him. Everybody knew Henry Griffith, attorney to the underdog. Sometimes, he got paid with real cash, others in whatever currency the client could afford, a dozen jars of apple butter, even, once, a white goose that was supposed to be Christmas dinner but ended up living in their backyard as a pet.

Whenever Gran used to speak of his grandfather and what he did for a living, there was a pride in her voice that Matt actually envied now. He'd always thought of his grandfather's profession as an honorable one, thought he would carry on the tradition with the same kind of purpose.

But he'd taken the big-city, big-firm route, and somewhere along the way, he'd sold out to the concept of quantity. More clients equaled more hours equaled more money, and he'd gone along with it all just fine, not questioning where that road would take him. Until now. Until he came home. With that sobering thought, he took one last sip of his coffee, put the file back in his briefcase and headed out the front door without bothering to lock it.

It was just after six, and the sun was coming up full force now, an enormous pink ball ascending the Blue Ridge skyline.

He headed down Marshall Avenue, took a right on Taper and stretched out his stride going down the steep hill. He put himself to the test this morning, the run opening something up inside him the way a yawn popped his ears at the end of a long flight.

Ballard had changed. A Hardee's and a movie theater now sat next to the high school. The school itself wasn't all that different, and he was glad. It looked pretty much the same as it had when he'd gone there, classic brick architecture, tall, white paned windows. The football stadium was in the same place, but bigger.

Down from the high school, he glimpsed many of the same names seen in other small towns, Roses, CVS, McDonald's. He remembered when the only fast food place anywhere near the school was Bert's—where almost everything inside had been painted light blue—now long since gone.

He ran on down Taper, spotting the Kroger and Walmart up on the hill where the Star-Gazer drive-in used to be. He remembered summer nights when he was seven or eight, and Gran would load up her car with him and his friends and take them to a drive-in movie where they would stuff themselves with popcorn and Milk Duds and argue over who got to sit closest to the speaker.

Matt took a left now into Franklin Hills, admiring the steeple on the Baptist church on Martin Drive. He looped through the residential area and hit the backside of town, passing the Comfort Inn and the YMCA, both new additions since he'd moved away.

Another mile and a half, and he was back in the heart of town, passing the old Simpson's Grocery, now an office supply store. He ran by the hospital, turned left and headed up the steep hill toward the courthouse.

A few cars were parked along the street, people going in to work. Just ahead on the right was the old law office where his granddad had practiced. A man stood at the front door, trying to get a key in the lock. A little closer, and he recognized Tom Williams, the attorney handling Gran's estate.

Tom looked up, straightened. "Well, hey, Matt," he said, setting down his briefcase and sticking out his hand.

Matt stopped just short of him, wiped his own hand across the bottom of his t-shirt. They shook.

"I was planning to call you today," he said.

Matt nodded.

"I'm real sorry about your grandmother," he said. "Didn't get to speak to you at the funeral yesterday."

"Thanks, Tom."

"When's a good time for us to meet?" he asked.

"I'll be here for a week or so."

"Would this afternoon work for you?"

"Sure."

"It shouldn't take long," he said. "With just the two of you."

"Two?" Matt asked. When Gran made up her will years ago, he remembered her saying that except for the most distant of relatives, there wasn't anyone other than him to leave anything to.

"You and Becca Brubaker," he said.

The name hit Matt like a mallet at the back of the knees. "Becca?"

"Yeah." Tom faltered, as if unsure what to say. "Apparently, Mrs. Griffith was pretty fond of her."

Matt remained silent, trying to process what he'd just heard. "What makes you say that?"

"Well, it's my understanding that Becca visited her every week over at the nursing home."

He rested a hand against the brick front of the law office, giving himself a moment. "You mean just recently?"

"No," Tom said, shaking his head. "My niece is a nurse there. She mentioned several times over the years how Becca came regularly. Seemed she always brought something with her, a pie or a cake for your grandmother and the other residents. Becca got to be pretty well known around there."

Matt nodded as if this was all old news to him, when the opposite couldn't have been more true.

"Well," Tom said. "I better get to work. Three o'clock okay with you?"

"Fine," he said. "I'll see you then."

Tom unlocked the door and stepped inside.

Matt started up the hill, pushing himself into a jog and then a run. But his legs felt like they'd been infused with concrete now, and he gave it up for a walk, his heart pounding.

All these years, Becca had been making time to see Gran. Bringing her food. Talking with her.

All these years, there had still been a connection between them.

Between Gran and Becca. Between him and Becca. How could he not have known?

∞

Then

FIRST MONDAY OF summer vacation, a high school graduate, and the alarm went off at four a.m.

Matt gave the snooze a good whack and pulled the pillow over his head, refusing to believe that he actually had to get up now. This was worse than punishment. It was torture.

Judge Anderson had called the previous Saturday and told him to report to Daniel Miller's dairy farm Monday morning at four forty-five.

"Four forty-five?" he'd repeated, thinking surely the judge must mean p.m.

"Cows don't much care about people's need for beauty sleep," the judge said in a tone that made it clear he wasn't expecting any protests. "When they need to be milked, they need to be milked."

Matt managed to suppress a groan. "Yes, sir."

"And by the way, Mr. Miller is willing to let you work twelve hour days. They milk at five and again at four in the afternoon. That should allow you to get your sentence completed before training camp starts in August. I assume that's what you'd like to do."

"I guess so."

"Or," Judge Anderson said with a heavy pause that clearly conveyed its meaning through the telephone line, "you could just miss the first couple weeks of practice."

"No, sir. That'll be fine," he said, recognizing when he'd been beaten.

By the time he dragged himself out of the shower and pulled on a pair of jeans and a t-shirt, it was four-twenty. A.M.

Downstairs in the kitchen, Gran had made breakfast. She wrapped a couple of biscuits in aluminum foil, dropped them into a paper bag, then handed it to him with a look of disapproval. "I thought you weren't going to be out late last night."

"I meant to get in earlier," he said, pulling a can of Coke out of the refrigerator and popping the tab.

"Hm," she said, exasperation in her voice, "get going now, or you'll be late."

He aimed a kiss at her cheek and bolted out the door, tossing the bag in the back of his Jeep and climbing in. It took just over fifteen minutes to reach the place, speeding and no traffic. He turned into the driveway and bounced over a couple of potholes, the jolt sending up a fresh pounding in his head that made him wonder why he'd ever taken the first hit off that beer bong out at Wilks's place.

He pulled up at the side of the barn, radio blasting classic AC-DC through the floorboard speakers.

A man with a long white beard stepped outside. Dressed in a straw hat, what looked like homemade denim pants and a plain white shirt buttoned at the throat, he looked directly at Matt. Matt turned off the radio, the sudden silence jarring. The man waved him inside and then disappeared. Matt got out and walked in behind him, newly pissed off at his fate.

The man stood waiting for him just inside the barn door. "You're Matt?"

He nodded. "Yeah."

"I'm Daniel Miller," he said. He held Matt's gaze for a long moment, as if he'd already figured him out and wasn't too sure he liked his conclusion. Matt looked away first, shoving his hands in the pockets of his jeans.

"This way," Mr. Miller said.

Matt followed him down a short aisle and through a set of double doors. "This is the milking parlor," he said.

A row of black and white cows stood side by side on the right and left of the aisle. The floors were concrete, hosed clean enough to eat off.

"Jacob? Becca? Emmy?"

Half-way down the aisle, a guy and two girls popped up like a triple jack-in-the-box from behind the heifers they'd been milking. To have gotten that far already, Matt wondered what time they'd started.

Mr. Miller beckoned them over.

"Matt, this is my son, Jacob."

Jacob dropped him a polite nod, wiping his hands on a pair of pants nearly identical to his father's. Matt nodded back, recognizing him as a year or two older than he was.

"My daughters Becca and Emmy."

"Hello," they said in unison, Becca without looking directly at him, the younger sister sizing him up as if he'd just arrived from another planet. Becca, he knew, of course, from the deliveries she and her Mama had been making to his grandmother for years. She wore a light green cotton dress this morning, her long blonde hair hanging in a braid down her back. Matt had never seen the sister before. She looked to be around fifteen or so, and unlike Becca and Jacob, she wore the Old Order clothing—a white bonnet that fit close to her head and tied under her chin, a mid-calf length dress with a cape over the shoulders that buttoned at her throat.

"Bet your ears are ringing," she said.

He stared at her for a second and then realized she was talking about the music. "Next time, son," Mr. Miller said, "would you be kind enough to turn the music down before you get here?"

"No problem," he said, shrugging and thinking what a pain in the butt this summer was going to be. Could he possibly have ended up at a squarer place than this?

Mr. Miller looked at Jacob. "Why don't you show Matt our morning routine, son?"

"Sure," Jacob said. "Come on, Matt."

Matt stepped past Becca just as she turned to go back to work, and they bumped sides, mumbling simultaneous excuse-me's. As he followed Jacob down the aisle, he heard Becca speak in a soft voice to the cow she'd been milking. When he glanced back over his shoulder, he saw her sit down on a wooden stool and go back to work.

All his life, he had walked past these people in the grocery store. Stared at them in Agee Hardware. On the school bus. And always, they were the ones who were different. Strange, even.

He realized that for the first time in his life, here on this farm, he was the one who was different.

He spent the rest of the first morning helping Jacob hose out the milking room and shoveling manure off the concrete walkway where the cows went in and out of the barn. Halfway through it all, his shoulders ached in a way they never had from baseball practice, and by lunchtime, he'd already eaten everything Gran had packed for him. And still, he was starving.

Jacob invited him to eat with the family at the two-story white farmhouse, but Matt declined, thinking he'd feel like a sideshow in their kitchen. He whiled away the half hour at the back of the barn, wishing he had time to run to the store a few miles away and get something.

Shortly after Jacob came back from lunch, a toothpick in the corner of his mouth, a big Southern States truck rumbled down the driveway, stopping at one end of the barn. The two of them unloaded several dozen fifty pound bags of feed and carried them into the grain room. When they'd finished, they stood outside for a minute, sweating and taking a breather. Jacob turned on a nearby water hose and took a long swig, then passed it to Matt.

As Matt drank his fill, he spotted Becca walking down from the house, carrying what looked like a laundry basket full of folded towels. She slipped into the barn without glancing his way.

Once the Southern States man left, Mr. Miller walked over and said, "We need to pick up a load of sawdust this afternoon. Jacob, take Matt with you and show him where to go in case I need him to handle it by himself sometime."

Becca came out of the barn just then, brushing something from the front of her dress.

"Bec, you want to go with us to get sawdust?" Jacob asked.

Becca looked at her father. "Is it all right, Daddy?"

Mr. Miller glanced at Matt, then Jacob, before saying, "I reckon so. Don't dawdle now. We'll need to get some of it spread before milking time."

"Yes, sir," Jacob said.

The three of them headed for the other side of the barn where a dump truck sat parked under a shed. Jacob got in the driver's side. Matt walked around, Becca behind him. He opened the door, then stepped back and let her climb up first. She slid across to the middle and sat with her hands in her lap, staring straight ahead, as if they'd made a pact not to ever meet eyes with each other. Matt closed the door. When it didn't catch, he opened it and slammed it again.

Jacob started the truck, the old engine groaning as if offended by what was being asked of it. Through his side mirror, Matt could see smoke rolling out of the back. The seat beneath shook under the engine's congested rumble.

"How far's the sawmill?" he asked, skeptical.

"Don't worry," Jacob said, smiling. "Her bark's a lot worse than her bite."

The driveway going out was a fairly steep grade, and it seemed as if it took forever to reach the main road. Once they got there, Jacob pulled out and opened the truck up, fifty-five feeling more like ninety, the trees on the side of the road whipping by in a blur of green. Seriously hungry now, Matt thought he might pass out if he didn't get something to eat soon.

They drove for a few minutes without saying anything, Matt conscious all the while of Becca sitting straight as a light pole a few inches away, her elbows tucked in at her sides in an obvious effort to prevent any chance of brushing up against him.

Jacob reached under the seat, pulled out a pack of cigarettes, lit one with the lighter from the truck. He took a deep pull, exhaling out of the left corner of his mouth.

Becca glanced at him, shook her head, then looked back at the road. "If you're going to smoke that thing," she said, "at least roll down the window."

Matt raised his eyebrows. Now this was interesting. Jacob Miller smoking.

In Ballard County, the people of the Old Order Brethren Church stood out from everyone else because of the plain clothes they wore, the plain cars they drove, radios removed, and their rejection of worldly things. Matt was pretty sure smoking cigarettes fell somewhere under worldly things.

"So what are you in for, Matt?" Jacob asked, releasing a stream of smoke through the left side of his mouth and blowing it out the window.

He hesitated, not sure how to answer, his stomach rumbling so loud now that it was getting embarrassing.

"Oh, come on," Jacob said, grinning. "We know you're not here on a charity tour."

"DUI," he tossed out, telling himself he didn't care what either of them thought. He would have bet they didn't even know what it was.

"What were you drinking?" Jacob asked, one hand on the steering wheel, his smile wide enough to indicate he was enjoying himself. "Ballard County moonshine?"

"Budweiser," he said, looking straight ahead, aware of Becca looking at him.

"And Judge Angle's hoping we can reform you?" Jacob slapped the dashboard with his right hand and laughed. "What do you think about that, Becca? Think we can turn Matt around?"

"I don't think that job was put to you," Becca said, chastising. "And it's a good thing."

Jacob took another drag off his cigarette, flicked the ash out his window. "Yep. I expect you're right about that."

Matt's stomach protested again, loudly enough to be heard over the truck's roaring engine.

They were headed through town now, and he was

about ready to put aside his pride and ask if they had time to grab something to eat when Becca leaned toward Jacob and said, "Why don't we stop and get some gas? The needle's just about on empty."

Jacob shrugged. "You know that thing's never right."

"Yeah," she said, "and that explains all the times you've run out on the side of the road."

He flipped the turn signal and side wheeled the big truck into the Franklin Minute Market, pulling up at a pump. He opened the door to get out, reaching for his wallet on the dashboard.

"Need some help?" Matt asked.

"Nah. I got it," he said.

Becca slid over a bit, widening the distance between them.

"I think I'll grab a snack," Matt said. "Want anything?"

"No. Thanks. I'm fine."

He nodded once, popped the handle and slid out. They looked at each other, straight on for the first time that day, and he knew as well as he knew his own name that Becca Miller had guessed how miserable he was. And for whatever reason, chose not to draw attention to it. Maybe she didn't want him to look like a wimp in front of her brother.

Once Jacob finished filling up the truck, they headed out of Ballard and down Route 40 to the sawmill. Matt whistled between his teeth, while he worked on his second bag of peanuts, a bag of Fritos and a pint of chocolate ice cream still lined up on his lap.

From the corner of his eye, he saw the smile on Becca's face. He looked at her and said, "What?"

She shook her head, and then, "Where do you put all that?"

"Growing boy," he said, tossing back another handful of nuts.

"Hm," she said, still smiling.

They drove through Gainer Hill, past the Quickette and the Elementary school. At the road marked 842, Jacob hit the blinker to turn left.

"Jacob," Becca said, surprise in her voice. "Daddy said we need to get back."

"I won't stay but a minute," he said.

"I know how long your minute will be," she complained.

"Okay, maybe two," he said, grinning.

At this point, Matt was more than curious about this unexpected side to Jacob. They drove on another mile or two, then turned right onto a gravel road, dark red cows grazing in the pasture beside a ranch style brick house. A girl in jean shorts and a halter top ran to meet them, braids of dark hair flying out from either side of her head. Matt recognized her from school and thought she might have graduated the year before.

Jacob turned off the truck, then hopped out, swooping her up against him and twirling her around, her giggles echoing across the yard, his straw hat falling to the ground. She glanced over his shoulder, waved at them, then took his hand and pulled him around to the side of the house.

Matt stared at Becca. "She's. . . ."

"Black?"

"Yeah."

"I'm sure she's noticed," Becca said, surprising him with the pluck in her voice.

Matt dropped his empty ice cream container into a paper bag. "I thought you people didn't mix with the rest of us."

She looked at him then. "You people?"

Realizing none of this was coming out right, Matt said,

"What I meant is I thought members of the Brethren Church only dated other members."

"We're not like the Amish," she said, her voice suddenly stiff. "The Church doesn't shun those who marry outside the faith."

"So your family has no problem with the two of them dating?"

She was quiet for several moments, and then, "I didn't say that."

"Do you have a problem with it?"

She glanced at him, then back at the house where a Border Collie lay snoozing on the front porch. "Jacob's life has been very different from hers."

"Maybe that just makes the combining of the two more interesting."

She lifted both shoulders, neither conceding nor disagreeing. "It also makes it very difficult."

"How long have they been seeing each other?" he asked.

"About a year," she said.

"Your folks know about it?"

She shook her head.

"Just you, huh?"

"Just me."

"That's a pretty heavy secret."

"It's Jacob's life. He's got to figure out what to do with it."

"But you think he's doing the wrong thing."

"It's not for me to decide."

"Uh-huh," he said, then leaned forward for another glance at Jacob and Linda.

"You've never seen two people kiss before?" she asked, disapproving.

"Once or twice," he said, amused. A few seconds passed before he added, "Have you?"

She gave him a look. Rolled her eyes.

"That's hardly an answer," he said.

"Of course I have," she answered quickly.

"Ever been kissed yourself?"

At this, her face lit up bright red. "I don't think that's any of your business."

"No, huh?" he said, openly flirting now.

"I see your reputation is mostly accurate."

"And what exactly is my reputation?"

"It's yours. You should at least be aware of it."

Matt laughed, unable to stop himself. "Well, you're sure not what I expected."

She looked him in the eyes. "And what exactly was that? The little Dunkard girl who might look good in a bikini but lives such a sheltered life that she'll never get the chance to find out?"

Matt leaned back, stared at her for a few moments. "So you did hear that?"

"I heard it."

"Sorry."

"For what? It's not as if I lost any sleep over it."

"Wilks can be—"

"Don't, okay?" she said, folding her arms across her chest.

"Okay. So what do you go swimming in?" he teased.

She jerked her head up, eyes flashing.

He grinned. "No impertinence intended. Just a cultural curiosity question."

She tucked her hair behind her ears and lifted her chin. "Do I look like an encyclopedia?"

A short snort of laughter escaped him. "As a matter of fact, no. You don't look anything at all like one," he said, letting his gaze fall from her face down the front of her dress and then lower still to her bare legs.

She sat up straighter and tugged at the hem. "Could we change the subject, please?"

"I make you uncomfortable, don't I?" he said, somehow pleased by the thought.

She leaned over and stuck her head out the driver's window. "Jacob!"

"Oh, is that how it works? Big brother saves you from guys like me?"

Becca sat back, looking at him again. "There are no guys like you."

"I know that wasn't a compliment, but there's something to be said for being the first."

"Is this what you do when you're bored?"

"I'm not bored," he said, all the teasing now gone from his voice, surprising even to him.

They looked at each other then, eyes locked, an awareness he'd never felt for anyone in his life taking up all the air between them.

Becca started to say something, but Jacob was suddenly back, leaping into the cab as if he'd been renewed with some kind of wonder drug.

"Did somebody say we needed sawdust?" he asked with a big grin, cranking the truck and backing up, then jamming the gear into first and tearing up the driveway.

Becca looked relieved at her brother's timing and made a point of not looking at Matt again. But he wasn't ready to let her off the hook. As soon as he had the opportunity, he planned to ask her about that kiss again.

14

Wishes

A kindness may be repaid
In the most unexpected of ways.
– ***Author Unknown***

Now

Becca was on her way out of the kitchen with Emmy's breakfast tray when the phone rang. Aaron had long since left for the barn and Abby for school. Martha had gone out to the hen house to collect the eggs.

Becca turned around and set the tray on the counter, picking up the wall phone with a quick hello.

"May I speak to Becca Brubaker, please?"

"This is she."

"Mrs. Brubaker. This is Tom Williams, the attorney for Mrs. Millicent Griffith's estate. I wondered if you would have time to come by my office this afternoon around three o'clock."

She was silent for a moment, her heart kicking a beat. "May I ask in regard to what?"

"I'll be happy to discuss all of it with you here at my office, Mrs. Brubaker. Can you make it today?"

"I don't know," she said.

"This won't take long," he assured her.

"I'll have to get back with you a little later."

"Certainly," he said and gave her his number.

Becca hung up, her hand shaking on the receiver. She had no idea what to make of the call. Or why Mrs. Griffith's attorney could possibly need to see her. She did know, though, that to go would only create more tension between her and Aaron and her mother as well. In the interest of peace, she would call back and say she couldn't come.

She picked up the tray from the counter and climbed the stairs to her sister's room. The door stood ajar, and she slipped inside. Emmy lay with her back to Becca. She seemed to be sleeping more and more, and this worried Becca. For the past two weeks, she hadn't opened one of the books Becca had brought her from the library. Normally, she would have finished them all by now. "Emmy?"

Without responding to the greeting, Emmy turned over to face her, her eyes devoid of light.

"I made pancakes this morning," Becca said, putting the tray down on the table next to her bed and busying herself with adding the butter and syrup.

Emmy eyed the plate with skepticism and sat up. Becca cut up the pancakes with the fork and knife she'd brought with the hope that Emmy would use them. She offered Emmy the fork with a bite-size pancake portion.

"There's juice here, too," Becca said. "Orange. You go ahead and eat while I get your clothes out."

Emmy took the fork and another bite of the pancakes, chewing slowly, dutifully. Becca walked to the closet and pulled out a white dress with tiny green flowers that did nice things for Emmy's coloring. She reached for Emmy's shoes on the floor below, and after placing the clothes at the foot of the bed, began to tidy up the room.

A few minutes later, she checked her sister's plate only to find she'd eaten little. "Aren't you hungry, Emmy?"

Emmy pushed the plate away, the gesture resonating with Becca as so much more than lack of hunger. She stacked the dishes back on the tray, trying not to notice her sister's thin arms beneath her white nightgown.

Emmy put her legs over the side of the bed, and Becca unwound her hair from its bun and brushed it one hundred strokes. Gray had woven its way into the dark strands. Emmy was two years younger than Becca, and yet they'd switched places, the lines in her face depicting a much older woman.

She rewound Emmy's hair into a bun, put her white bonnet on and tied the strings under her chin. She helped her put on her dress, then slipped her sister's feet into her shoes and tied the laces. She glanced up at Emmy's face, something small and tight catching in her throat. She tried not to let herself wonder whether Emmy felt the restriction of her days or how far past the immediate her thoughts went. To do so, draped Becca in a curtain of guilt so heavy it felt as though she might smother beneath it.

"It's a beautiful day," Becca said. "I'll take you outside and come back for the tray."

They took the stairs with care, Emmy's steps slow and measured as if her body had little energy for the trek. Becca made hers equal to her sister's. Outside, Martha pulled weeds from the base of an old rose bush. She smiled at the sight of her youngest daughter, wincing a little as she got up to give her a hug.

"You're looking mighty pretty this morning, Emmy," Martha said.

Emmy looked off into the distance, the compliment not visibly registering.

"She didn't eat very much, and I think she's losing

weight," Becca said, trying to keep the worry from her voice. "Maybe we should make an appointment with the doctor."

"She doesn't need a doctor," Martha said, straightening Emmy's cape, then glancing down at her shoes. She knelt and retied one of the laces. "Be sure you knot these good and tight. She could fall coming down those stairs."

"I'll finish the dishes," Becca said, her voice deliberately neutral as she turned for the house.

At the back door, she stopped and looked out at Tinker's Knob where it rose up from the back of the farm. She thought about Mr. Williams' phone call then and the knot of indecision that had sat in her stomach ever since.

She had checked the lettuce in her garden early this morning, deciding she would pick several bags today and deliver them to Asher's, a restaurant on Tinker's Knob Lake that had started calling two weeks ago to get on her list. Maybe she would go by the attorney's office afterward just to hear what the man had to say. What harm could there be in it?

15

Mending and Judging

Rutrough Death Declared "Tragic Accident"
Ballard County Times
The Ballard County Sheriff's Department has declared fifteen year old John Rutrough's death a "tragic accident."
Sheriff Oatey Hamilton stated in an interview Monday afternoon that "Extensive invesitagtion into the boy's death led to the conclusion that it was accidental."
"It is believed," the Sheriff stated, "that the boy fell from a hayloft where he and another minor girl had met to talk. It is just an unbelievable tragedy. A waste," Sheriff Hamilton added. "Our hearts go out to the families involved."
When asked if he could identify the minor girl, Sheriff Hamilton declined to comment any further due to her age.

Now
Martha ate lunch outside under the oak tree with Emmy,

tomato sandwiches on homemade whole wheat bread with a light spread of mayonnaise. As a child, it had been one of Emmy's favorite meals, and one of the few foods she seemed to still show some occasional pleasure in eating.

Today, though, Emmy's expression was distant, and she showed little to no response to Martha's comments about the weather and plans for the upcoming summer.

Becca had left the house shortly after noon on an errand. Martha did not ask where she was going, and Becca didn't volunteer the information. But Martha could not shake the feeling that Becca was hiding something, and each time her thoughts settled on this suspicion, she shooed them on to something else simply because she was afraid she did not want to know the answer.

Martha cleaned up the lunch plates and took them into the house, coming back outside just as a dark blue minivan pulled into the driveway. She lifted a hand and waved at her next door neighbor, Clara Bowman, who got out of the vehicle and crossed the yard with a small basket of clothes on top of which lay a sewing kit. Clara was short and round, nearly white hair visible at the front edges of her white bonnet. Her cheeks were always bright with color, and she made her way through life with the kind of joyful, trusting spirit that Martha seemed to find herself in ever-short supply of.

"I was hoping you could use a little company while I finish some mending," Clara said. "It was too pretty a day to sit in the house."

Martha smiled and waved her over to the chairs where Emmy sat with her hands in her lap.

"We would love some company, wouldn't we, Emmy?" Martha said.

"Hello, Emmy," Clara said. "How are you today?"

Martha and Clara had known each other since they were small girls, and Clara was one of the few people outside Martha's own family who spoke to Emmy as if she might answer in a normal way. Martha cherished this in her friend. It had long ago become difficult to witness the questioning looks on the faces of visitors who were less sensitive.

"Let me get my basket, and I'll be right back," Martha said.

Clara sat down next to Emmy, and Martha could hear her speaking softly to her as she went into the house.

An hour later, Martha and Clara had worked their way through half of their baskets, mending holes in socks, stitching loose dress hems, replacing missing buttons from pants and shirts. Emmy had dozed off in her chair, her head resting against the wooden back. Like this, she reminded Martha so much of the little girl she'd once been.

"I've been meaning to get over here in the last few days," Clara said, regretful. "I heard that Millie Griffith died last week."

Martha nodded, pausing to lift her needle from the hemline of a dress. "Yes."

"I suspect Becca went to the funeral."

"Yes, she did."

Clara was quiet for a few moments, and then said, "You shouldn't worry, Martha. Becca made her choices."

"I know," Martha said, nodding.

"But you are worried."

Martha glanced at Emmy and then back at Clara, exhaling a long sigh. "I wish I could say I wasn't."

Aside from Daniel, Martha had never talked about any of this with another person. Eighteen years ago, Martha needed the wisdom and advice of her friend who understood the choices that Daniel and Martha made that awful August. Clara respected Martha's commitment to following through with what Daniel believed best for their family and everyone involved. As children, they had both been raised to respect a husband's decision-making, to submit in times of disagreement. And this was what Martha had done.

She turned her hand over and squeezed Clara's in return. "Thank you. You somehow manage to arrive just when I most need one of our chats."

"Friends should be good for something, shouldn't they?"

Martha pressed her lips together and then said, "You have no idea, Clara, what it means to me that you've never judged me. Sometimes, I don't think I've done the same for my own children."

"I think I do understand. But let me say this as someone who loves you. In the end, none of us will be the one doing the judging. We'll have to do our own individual accounting."

Long after Clara left, her words still rang in Martha's head, impossible to deny. Because, in truth, she feared she wouldn't even know where to begin.

16

Maybes

What happens to the wide-eyed observer
when the window between reality
and unreality breaks
and the glass begins to fly?
– Author Unknown

Now

They think I didn't hear them talking. Mama and Mrs. Bowman.

But I wasn't asleep. And I heard the awful worry in Mama's voice when she'd talked about Mrs. Griffith's passing.

That explains then the differences I've sensed in Becca. The way she stares off out the window when she's in my room, the longing in her eyes.

Matt came back.

I wonder now how I could have thought Becca had forgotten him.

When Becca and I were girls, I saw her as the strong one. The one who could do things I never imagined myself doing. When I was four years old, I had Scarlet Fever. It didn't respond to the antibiotics at first, and it took a really long time for me to get better. I guess it's true that I was never as strong afterwards. I was always the one to get anything that came along, and Mama said things just hit me harder than everybody else.

Maybe that's how I began to see myself as the weak one, convinced throughout the years of my childhood that I didn't have what it took to beat the really hard stuff.

Somewhere along the way, it became clear to me that Becca did, that if I stood back and let her, she would shoulder the difficult things, and I wouldn't have to. Like the time we broke Mama's mantle clock, and Becca took the blame even though I was the one who said we should open it up and see how it worked. She had to do extra chores for a week, and neither of us ever told Mama about my part in what had happened.

I told myself I hadn't really meant to do anything wrong. I just wanted to know what the inside of the clock looked like.

Does anyone ever really mean to do wrong?

The first time I considered this question, my answer was yes, of course. People think, plot, and figure out the best ways to carry off their wrongdoings every day. People go to great lengths not to get caught. Each of these facts makes a good argument for intent.

But I don't think it's that simple.

I've looked at the possible answers from a dozen different angles. And what I've come up with is this: most people justify their actions with excuses they believe cancel out their own accountability. Most people believe they had no choice to do anything other than what they did.

I think this theory mostly holds water. That if it didn't, the world would be full of people like me, people forever changed by a single choice.

As for me, I believe that what I did was wrong. I knew better. I did have a choice. If John and I hadn't met in the barn that night to figure out how we were going to provide for ourselves as newlywed teenagers, maybe he would still be alive today. Maybe I would still be living in this world rather than existing somewhere in between.

Maybe. . .so many maybes.

None of which matter now.

Perhaps then, what does matter isn't intent. Perhaps in the end, what matters is remorse.

I do have this.

I can only hope that when all is said and done, it's what will count.

17

Hope and Boxes

"Nothing is certain but the unforeseen."
– Proverb

Now

Matt pulled into the small parking lot at the side of Tom Williams' office and cut the engine on the Land Rover.

He leaned his head back against the seat, closing his eyes and telling himself this was no big deal. It would be a short meeting. He and Becca would sit across from Tom's desk for a few minutes, hear what he had to say, and then go their separate ways again. That was it. One small intersection in eighteen years. And probably the last of their lives.

He opened his eyes against the blackness of the thought, looking out at the cars stopped at the light on Main Street. Not for the first time since running into Tom that morning, he wondered what Gran had been thinking when she put Becca in her will. Why she had never told him they'd kept in touch. Had Becca asked her not to?

The thought brought with it an actual stab of pain to the center of his chest. He got out of the Land Rover, shutting the door a little too hard, as if he could reseal all those memories, leave them out here where they would have no chance of getting in between Becca and him today.

Inside the office, he stepped up to the receptionist's desk. An older woman with white hair and wire glasses that sat perched on the tip of her nose glanced up and said, "May I help you?"

"Matt Griffith," he said. "I have an appointment with Tom."

"Of course. He's expecting you," she said, picking up the phone and then directing him down the hall to the last door on the left. He stopped just outside, his feet refusing to move. Through the partially open door, he saw Becca seated in front of Tom's big desk, her back to him.

Tom looked up, waving him forward. "Come in, Matt. Have a seat, please."

Becca turned her head and looked directly at him. "Hello, Matt," she said, her voice polite and even.

"Becca." He cleared his throat, adding, "How are you?"

"Fine, thank you. I'm so sorry about your grandmother."

"Thanks," he said, managing to cross the floor and take the chair next to hers, all the while feeling as though he were walking the deck of a listing ship.

"Well," Tom said, "before we get started, can I get either of you anything? Some coffee? Bottled water?"

Becca shook her head. "Not for me, thank you."

"I'm fine," Matt said.

"All right then, we can get started." Tom opened the file in front of him. "As you know, the two of you are named as the sole beneficiaries of Mrs. Griffith's will. At her request, I'll read the following out loud."

Matt sat back in his chair, his heart suddenly beating

so hard he was sure Becca could hear it from her seat. He leaned forward and anchored sweaty palms to his knees.

Tom slipped on a pair of glasses, then picked the paper up off the desk, cleared his throat and began to read.

Dearest Matt and Becca,

I'm sure you must have many questions about this meeting involving you both. In some peoples' eyes, what I have done will seem a curious thing. To me, though, it is nothing short of logical, and I hope you will each see it that way.

Matt, you are my beloved grandson, more like a son to me, as you know. When your father and mother died, I could not imagine how the pain of that would ever recede enough for me to go on living. Losing a child is the closest thing to having your heart cut from your body that I can imagine. You, dear boy, were my saving grace. I love you more than I could possibly ever tell you with words. I leave to you the remains of any and all bank accounts bearing my name as well as the Highland Street house and all of its contents.

And dear Becca. I have so much admired your honor and integrity. I hope you will take what I am leaving you in the spirit in which it is given. A token of appreciation from an old woman who believes you are a special person. I leave to you my house on Tinker's Knob Lake and its surrounding thirty acres of land.

Matt and Becca, I never voiced aloud my hopes for what might have been for you two. Life is full of blind curves, and who am I to question the rightness of the direction you chose? But I do know this to be true. Sometimes, it is nearly impossible to look beyond the parameters of the boxes we put ourselves in. And maybe that is the one thing we should somehow find a way to do.

With deepest love,
Gran

Tom placed the paper back on the desk, coughed once, removed his glasses, his voice wavering a bit when he said, "Well. Either of you have any questions?"

Matt stared at the attorney, as if to set his eyes anywhere else would mean acknowledging what had just been said. "No," he finally managed, breaking the silence.

Becca got to her feet abruptly, her chair teetering backwards and then crashing to the floor. Matt quickly stood and picked it up. She looked at Tom, shaking her head. "I can't possibly accept this."

"I think it's very clear that she wanted you to have it, Mrs. Brubaker."

Becca looked at Matt, her hands clasped tightly around the strap of her black purse. "I had no idea," she said.

"It never occurred to me that you did," he said quietly.

"I'm sorry," she said. "I really have to go."

"Becca, wait," he said, but she was already out the door and running down the hall.

Matt stood there for a moment, not sure what to do, even less sure that he had a right to do anything. *Sometimes, it is nearly impossible to look beyond the parameters of the boxes we put ourselves in.* Gran's words echoed in his head, forcing his feet to move. "Thanks, Tom," he said and left the office.

18

Beans and Boys

A person often meets his destiny on the road he took to avoid it.
–Jean de La Fontaine

Now

Becca forced herself to walk up the street to the parking space where she'd left her car. One foot in front of the other. Walk. Walk. Walk. When she wanted to run. But even that wouldn't do. What she really wanted was to turn the clock back to that morning when Tom Williams had called, to tell him there couldn't possibly be any reason for her to attend a reading of Millie Griffith's will. In the back of her mind, she'd thought maybe the kind old lady had left her a few of her books. They used to talk about them, their favorite stories. Mrs. Griffith had loved Willa Cather and William Faulkner, writers Becca had discovered the last year she'd attended school. They would drink tea and talk about the characters in the books they read as if they were people they'd met on the streets of their own lives, full-blown, real.

That first year after Becca had married Aaron, it was hard for her to continue going to Mrs. Griffith's house.

Becca had known the older woman was lonely for Matt, just as she was. The stark difference in their grief being that Mrs. Griffith's loss was temporary while hers was permanent. Maybe at first it was this mutual mourning that fueled their conversations. But it eventually became more, and Becca grew to look forward to their visits as a high point in her week.

Mrs. Griffith understood things about her that no one else did. That it was not an easy thing to turn away from something you knew was real and good. That sometimes there was no other choice.

After her first stroke, Mrs. Griffith stayed at home for a while with a nurse who came in every day. When she could no longer take care of herself, Becca heard from others how Matt tried to get her to move up to D.C. He'd wanted her to stay with him, but she had chosen not to leave the county. She'd been born there, she'd said many times, and it was her intention to die there.

Eventually, she moved to the nursing home that sat on a hill at the lower end of Main Street. It was a hard place to visit, an even harder place to be. Most of the nursing assistants there tried with the patients, smiles, kind voices, but there was always the sense that people in a place like that were just waiting for the next phase.

As time passed, Mrs. Griffith became less and less the person she had once been. Becca continued reading to her, hoping some piece of the stories would reach her, give her a small nugget of the joy it had once given her.

Becca stopped beside her car now, fumbling through her purse for the keys. She heard again the last of Mrs. Griffith's letter. . .*my hopes for what might have been for you two.*

"Becca, wait!"

She couldn't look at him now. Not with her own emotions so unrestrained. She opened the door, slid onto the seat and tried to stick the key in the ignition. But her hands refused the simple task, and she dropped the key onto the floor, reaching down for it with a cry of frustration.

"Becca."

He stood by her window, rapping gently against the glass with his knuckles. She found the key, sat for a moment, then finally opened the door.

"Are you okay?" he asked.

"Yes," she said, still without looking at him. "I'm fine. Really."

"The coffee shop up the street," he said. "Could we go get a cup?"

"I can't," she said quickly. "I have to get home."

"Ten minutes, Becca. That's all."

She finally looked at him then. His eyes were guarded, uncertain. She wondered if he was anything like the Matt she'd once known. Or if he had become someone completely different.

The desire to know won out. She got out of the car, and they walked the half block to the shop in silence, a good wedge of space between them. She felt as if none of this could be real, that it must be one of the countless dreams she'd had over the years where she woke up with a crater of emptiness inside her.

But this time it was real.

He held the door open, waving her inside first.

The Second Cup had been in town for a couple of years, but this was the first time she'd been inside. The walls were painted the color of toast, and the artwork of local middle school and high school students filled up one entire side. The place smelled of fresh-brewed coffee. A couple of teenagers sat at a table by the window, sipping some kind of concoction covered with whipped cream, laptop computers blinking in front of them.

At the counter, a young girl with an earring in the left side of her nose greeted them. "What can I get you?" she asked.

"Becca?" Matt said.

"Just a regular coffee," she said, opening her purse and pulling out her wallet.

He motioned for her to put it away. She wanted to insist on paying for herself, but it was awkward, so she didn't. "Two coffees," Matt said.

"I'll bring them over," the girl said, smiling.

They picked a table in a corner opposite the students. Becca felt their eyes on them. She thought how odd they must look. She in her cape and bonnet. He in jeans and a white oxford shirt. This part felt too familiar, exactly the same as it had so many years before when they'd gone out together.

They sat, and the waitress arrived with their coffee. Becca busied herself with sugar and cream. When she'd taken as much time with that as she could, she was left with no other choice but to look at him.

His dark blonde hair was still thick and unruly. His eyes an unsettling blue, fine lines now at the sides. His nose was still straight and almost too perfect. His jaw line had not softened, and she could see that he'd taken care of his athletic body over the years.

"It's been a long time, Becca," he said, as if he, too, couldn't quite believe they were sitting there together.

"Yes." She tried to smile, but the effort failed, and she ended up pressing her lips together and wrapping her hands tight around the white coffee mug.

"Your family. How are they?" he asked.

"My father passed away three years ago."

"I'm sorry," Matt said, sitting back. "Your father was a good man."

"Thank you. And yes, he was."

He glanced away, then raised his eyes to hers again. "I've thought of you, Becca," he said, hesitating, and then revising, "I wanted to call you so many times."

She swallowed hard, searching for something to say that wouldn't lay her heart out as the raw and vulnerable thing it was just then. "It's better that you didn't," she said.

"Is it?"

She took a sip of her coffee, buying time. "Yes."

"I didn't know you and Gran kept in touch."

She nodded. "It must seem kind of unusual, but we enjoyed each other's company."

"No," he said. "I'm glad."

"About the will," she said. "I can't accept that."

He was quiet for a moment, before saying, "She left it to you, Becca. It's yours."

She shook her head. "I could never feel right about it."

"And since it was her wish, I could never feel right about it being any other way."

"What would I do with something like that?" she asked. "It would be wasted on me."

"Maybe it could be a place to go when you need something of your own."

She wanted to say how remarkable that sounded, how wonderful, and yet there was no way she could ever choose that house as a place to get away from anything. It could never be a place of her own. It had been *their* place, and for her, it held too many memories, too many shadows of their past.

She pushed her cup away and stood. "Thank you for the coffee, but I really have to go."

"Becca," he said. "Stay. Please."

"I shouldn't have come. I'm sorry." She crossed the wood floor of the coffee shop, feeling the stares of the teenagers by the window. She stepped quickly outside into the late afternoon sun and made her way to her car, and then home, all the while feeling Matt's searching gaze on her skin, as if he had in fact, touched her.

∞

Then

EVERYTHING CHANGED AFTER Matt Griffith came to work on the farm. Overnight, Becca became too aware of the way she walked, not trusting her own feet, worried she would trip in front of him or that her voice would squeak when she talked. When she was near him, her hands refused to function the way they normally did, clumsy and inept.

During the two weeks he'd been on the farm, she'd tried hard to avoid him. But it seemed as if everywhere she turned, he was somewhere within her line of vision.

Becca couldn't quite remember what it was like before he came. She only knew she hadn't walked around with a bubble in her stomach, half hoping they'd run into each other every time she stepped out of the house, half dreading that they would.

For the past couple of hours, she'd been sitting at the picnic table in the back yard, stringing green beans. Matt and Jacob were down at the barn, changing the oil in the tractor. The temperature had hit around ninety today, and Matt's shirt stuck to his back and shoulders, making it hard not to notice the lines of muscle beneath.

Emmy walked up from the garden with another wash pan full of beans. She sat down at the table next to Becca and started breaking off ends, dropping them in the white plastic bucket between them.

"You're awfully quiet. Something wrong?" Becca asked.

Emmy glanced down at the barn, then back at Becca. "You look at him all the time."

Becca stopped snapping for a moment, then went on again, faster. "At who?" she said, keeping her voice indifferent.

"The new boy," she said. "Matt."

"I do not."

"Becca. I'm fifteen, but I'm not blind." Emmy hesitated, as if choosing her words. "He's cute. But he's not like us."

"Does everyone have to be like us, Emmy?" Becca asked the question quickly, hearing the irritation in her own voice.

"You know what I mean," she said.

At the barn, Jacob banged a wrench against the tractor. It made a loud, clattering sound. Matt looked over his shoulder, directly at Becca, and for a moment, she could not bring herself to look away. Since the day they'd gone to pick up sawdust, they'd caught each other's gazes time and again, the connection between them making her insides drop like the grain released from the hopper bottom bin at the barn.

"See," Emmy said.

Becca looked away from Matt and went back to stringing beans, focusing on the pan in front of her.

"You're not going to be like Jacob, are you?" Emmy asked after a few moments, her voice low and concerned.

Becca looked up. "What do you mean?"

"Jacob wants out," she said. "To live another way."

"Did he tell you that?"

"I know about Linda," she said.

Becca snapped a few more beans. "Jacob has to make his own choices, Emmy."

"But it'll be sad if he goes."

"Being with Linda doesn't mean he can't ever see us again," Becca said.

"You know Mama and Daddy could never accept the two of them together. What kind of life would they have?"

"If it's one started on love, shouldn't that be enough?" Becca paused and then added, "And why shouldn't they accept her?"

Emmy shook her head, looking much older than her age. "Isn't it just as easy to love someone who's the same as you as it is to love someone who's different?"

"I don't know," Becca said. "But what about you and John? When you were thirteen, you said you wanted to marry him one day. Wouldn't you still love him if he weren't like us?"

Emmy remained silent for a few moments, and then said, "I don't think I would have let myself."

The answer surprised Becca. Even when they'd been little girls, Becca knew Emmy had no desire to look outside their life. Maybe it was easier that way. But she could not bring herself to view the world with blinders.

A dark blue Chevrolet truck turned in off the main road, scattering gravel and dust as it pulled up to the barn. Aaron Brubaker, a friend of Jacob's, got out and walked over to the tractor where Jacob and Matt were still working.

"I bet he came to see you," Emmy said, the words light and teasing.

"He did not," Becca said, her face flushing.

But a couple of minutes later, Aaron left the barn and headed up through the yard to where they sat.

"Hey, Becca. Emmy," he said, stopping just short of the table.

"Hey, Aaron," Becca said, noticing that he wasn't wearing the work clothes he normally had on during the day when he stopped to see Jacob. His light blue shirt was fresh-pressed, his dark pants spotless. He had blonde hair, blue eyes and skin that always had color in it, as if he'd gotten a little too much sun. Some of the girls she hung around with from church thought he was cute and would giggle when he walked by. Standing here in front of her with his appealing smile, she could see why they thought this.

"Hi, Aaron," Emmy said, getting to her feet. She picked up the bowl of beans they'd finished snapping and added, "I'll take these inside. Be right back."

Aaron folded his arms, then unfolded them, anchoring a palm at each hip. "Looks like you've been busy today."

"The beans have done well this year," she said, wiping her palms on the apron tied at her waist.

"Our garden's overflowing. Not like last year when it was so dry," he said.

"Would you like something to drink?" Becca said.

"Thanks, but no. I can't stay. Actually, I was wondering. . . ." He cleared his throat, and then went on. "Some of us are getting together over at Eli's tomorrow. Would you like to come with me?"

Despite what she'd said to Emmy, Becca wasn't really surprised by the invitation. Aaron had been seeking her out at the end of church lately, talking past casual interest. And it seemed like he'd been dropping by to see Jacob more often. Behind Aaron, she could see Matt Griffith looking up at them. She leaned to the left a bit, Aaron now blocking him completely from view. Maybe the timing of this was right. Maybe going out with Aaron would give her some place else to put her thoughts. "That sounds like fun," she said. "What time?"

"Pick you up at five-thirty?"

"Five-thirty," she agreed.

"Okay, then," he said with a quick nod, smiling. "See you Saturday."

He headed across the yard, and she watched him go. He stopped to speak to Jacob who looked back at her and clapped Aaron once on the shoulder.

Matt, however, went inside the barn without looking her way at all.

19

Questions

There is no pain so great as the memory of joy in present grief.
– Aeschylus

Now

Stepping out the back door of the two-story white farmhouse in which she'd lived her whole life, Martha Miller carried the heavy wicker laundry basket to the clothesline, wondering if she'd finally let her worries get the better of her. She should have gone with her daughter to the funeral today. Maybe if she'd been by Becca's side, she would avoid talking to that boy. Though he was hardly a boy now. Matthew Griffith.

Just his name set up a quiet roar of anxiousness deep inside her.

She yanked a bleached white sheet from the pile in the basket and pinned an edge to the wire clothesline. She slid the other side down the line until the sheet hung straight, securing it with another wooden pin. A breeze lifted the bottom and snapped it forward, then back again, before it settled into place.

Martha had always retreated to work as a way to

redirect her thoughts when she was upset about something. Putting the mind to a task diluted the power of worry, which she'd long ago learned was one of the devil's handiest tools.

Not for the first time, she searched her memory for the moment where she'd gone wrong with her oldest daughter. She concluded just as quickly that there had never been a single instant. Instead, a growing awareness from the time Becca was a little girl that she would not, as Martha had, walk the path of their family with complete acceptance.

From the beginning, her questions overwhelmed Martha, marked as they were by a clear resistance to take anything at face value. *Mama, why do we dress different from the people we see in town? Why does Daddy have a long beard? Why doesn't our car have a radio? Why can't I finish high school?*

Martha's answers had never seemed to satisfy her, no matter how many times she tried to explain that their choices were based on their desire to live a plain and humble life without getting caught up in the ways of the world.

As a child, Martha had never once questioned anything about her life. She had accepted her parents' choices as her own. This had made it more than difficult to relate to a daughter who accepted nothing without question. In truth, a daughter who questioned her mother and what she had chosen to be.

Martha had been raised to believe that a mother had an obligation to teach her child right from wrong. And there had never been any doubt in her mind that their way of life was the right way for them.

It all went by so fast anyhow, the years that strung together a person's time here on earth. Lately, she'd felt a need to settle things. She couldn't explain it, but the need hung tight in her chest.

She glanced up at the window to Emmy's room. Her youngest child. The curtains were drawn, and Martha pictured her in the chair by the bed, staring at a wall, her mind settled in a place none of them could reach, no matter how hard they tried.

A wave of tiredness gripped her, so intense that she could barely stop herself from sinking to her knees. Standing there in the back yard of this house where she had grown up, where she had raised three children of her own, a son and two daughters, she'd never felt more lost. Jacob, gone for so long now that she sometimes had to pull out photos of him as a boy to keep his face from fading in her memory. Emmy, here in this very house, but so unreachable. And Becca.

She thought of happier times, when the children were small, when her husband Daniel had been alive, of early morning breakfasts around the table after the first milking at the barn was done. Of fall afternoons when they'd fill up bushel baskets with apples from their orchard to make apple butter the next day in the big copper pot handed down through Daniel's family. And of the much loved Fix Sundays.

How long ago it all seemed, those days when she had somehow thought they would always be happy.

There was so little of any of it left. Somehow, she had to hold on to what remained.

20

This Kiss

Do not tell secrets to those whose faith and silence you have not already tested.
– Elizabeth I

Now

Becca didn't tell Aaron about her meeting with Tom Williams or the incredible gift Mrs. Griffith had left her. Nor did she tell him that she'd had coffee with Matt. Guilt for each of these things ate a little hole inside her, but she made a pact with herself that she would just get back to her regular life. There was no point in letting something that in the big picture was insignificant upset an existence that worked as it was.

Today, she headed for her garden, and a goal of setting out a row of tomato plants despite the advice of the Farmer's Almanac, which still predicted a few more cool nights. In the past two days, she'd plucked every visible weed from the rich, dark earth and prepared another row for some extra squash plants.

Mostly, the work had succeeded in distracting her. But

it was the nighttime that did her in. She dreaded the nights.

Standing before her bathroom mirror, she smoothed moisturizing cream on her face and tried not to acknowledge the discontent in her own eyes. A knock sounded at the door. She opened it to find Aaron standing there, his expression set, serious. "Is something wrong?" she said, feeling the sudden rap of her heart.

He handed her a piece of paper, Tom Williams' number scribbled across the top. "He called this afternoon," he said, his voice perfectly even. "Asked me to tell you that he'd really like to tie up the loose ends of Mrs. Griffith's estate. Apparently, she left you something?"

Even as she heard the confusion in his last words, a response eluded her. She ran the brush through her hair one last time, and then secured it in a ponytail, before looking at Aaron. "Yes," she said, attempting indifference. "Her house at the lake."

Aaron's eyes widened. He didn't speak for a few moments, as if he couldn't quite absorb what she'd said. "Why would she leave you such a thing?" he asked finally.

"You know I delivered her eggs for years," she said, glancing away. "We used to talk sometimes."

"And she put you in her will based on that?" Skepticism underscored the words, the set of his jaw suddenly hard.

"I kept in touch with her," she added. "I visited her at her house and then at the nursing home after she moved there."

Aaron stared at her, his eyes glazed with sudden hurt, as if she had just revealed an affair about which he knew nothing. "Why would you do that, Becca?" he asked in a careful voice.

"She was always kind to me," she said. And this much was true.

"Your family was not enough for you?"

"Aaron. She was a friend. Am I not allowed to have friends?"

"A friend you never managed to mention that you were visiting over the course of how many years?

She flicked off the bathroom light and walked into the bedroom, her back to him. "I thought you might not understand."

"You were right about that part," he said, his voice thick with an anger she had rarely, if ever, heard in him. "I do not understand why you would maintain a friendship with her and never tell me about it. Surely, that must mean something."

Becca didn't want to do this with him. No good could come of analyzing her motives. She turned to him then, her voice pleading. "Aaron, it means nothing. We had some things in common. She loved to read. We talked about books. That's all."

He leaned against the frame of the bathroom door, arms folded across his chest. Several moments passed before he said, "You will not accept such a ridiculous thing, of course."

The words burned her skin like the spatter of grease from a hot stove. She removed the pillows from their bed, pulling back the bedspread, fussing with the sheets, willing herself to answer in agreement. But there was something in his absolute certainty that she would agree which clogged her resolution, forcing words from her mouth that came as a complete surprise. "I'd like to think about it," she said, propping her pillow against the bed's headboard.

"Becca," he said, her name a harsh rasp. "What is this about?"

She let herself look at him then, saw that her defiance had shocked him. Maybe it shocked her a little as well. "Simply that I would like to think about it."

He remained quiet for several long moments. “I forbid you.”

Aaron had never before used such words with her. It wasn’t as if they’d never disagreed on anything before. There had been a few major things, the most memorable of which had been Aaron’s desire to move to Ohio after his family sold their farm and moved there several years ago. Aaron had thought it would be good for them, give them a fresh start of sorts. He’d brought it up one night after they’d gone to bed, and she’d thought him already asleep, his voice in the dark startling her.

“There’s a farm for sale adjoining my folks’ place in Ohio. I think we should buy it, Becca.”

For long moments, she couldn’t summon a response. “Do you mean just you and me?” she finally asked.

“And Abby, of course,” he said.

“What about Emmy?” She spoke carefully, as if suddenly alert to uncertain ground.

Aaron’s silence took on weight. “Becca. You have your own life to live. Emmy’s not your-”

“Burden?” she finished for him, the question rising up before she could stop it.

He reached for her hand, entwining it with his. “That’s not what I was going to say.”

“Isn’t it?”

“Do you think she would expect you to give up your whole life to care for her, Becca?”

“My life is here, Aaron. And she’s my sister.”

“You’ve been here for her for so long. And your mother is here.”

“Mama couldn’t do everything herself.”

“She could get help. We could pay for that.”

“Aaron.” Becca pulled her hand from his and sat up in bed. “What’s brought all this on?”

“This place has never felt like mine, Becca.”

"It wouldn't be what it is if it weren't for you. After Daddy died—"

"I know," he said, "but it's not the same."

She heard his quiet appeal and understood suddenly how much he wanted this. "I'm sorry," she said softly. "But I can't leave. I can't."

Aaron didn't say anything more. He got up after a bit, went into the bathroom and dressed, then let himself out the door, the lock making a dull click as he pulled it closed.

They never spoke of the conversation again, but Becca often thought that what held Aaron and her together, what served as the foundation of their marriage, was a mutual sense of sacrifice.

And now with this latest conflict between them, a house left to her, she could see in his face awareness of his own sacrifices, his willingness to accept something less than he'd wanted in their marriage. In his voice, she heard a note of ownership that made her skin feel as if it were being rubbed with sandpaper. Her heart began to race, and she pressed her lips together to keep herself from saying something she would later regret. "I'm tired, Aaron," she said, without looking at him. "I'm going to bed."

He stayed where he was while she slipped under the covers, her back to him. He went into the bathroom and closed the door. She let out a deep breath, only now realizing that she had been holding it. She had never intended for any of this to end up here. Deciding today while standing at the edge of her weed-free garden that she would call Mr. Williams in the morning and tell him she could not take what Mrs. Griffith had left her. Why then had she just defied her husband over something she had already decided she could not do?

Rebellion sat like a rock inside her, hard to breathe

around. With the exception of moving to Ohio, Becca had always yielded to Aaron during the times they disagreed, submission a character trait that had never come easily to her, but again, one that she felt she owed him. She had gone along for what she believed to be the greater good. Only now, it all felt muddled inside her head, and she was no longer sure what exactly that was.

Maybe she was simply being selfish. Refusing to consider the damage her actions might incur. But it felt like something else. It felt as if she'd been swimming underwater for half her life, holding her breath the entire time, and now she was about to surface. As if in being a woman who yielded to her husband's opinions, she'd closed off all her own needs and desires for so long that she thought they'd actually gone away.

But sitting across the table from Matt Griffith yesterday, she'd discovered this wasn't true. And ever since, she'd felt a steady throb of pressure against the wall of her chest, as if there were someone else inside her who finally wanted out.

It would be so much easier to give in. Let it go. But wasn't that what she'd always done? Accepted the warnings laid out for her as absolute truth. Like the wild bears and boars on the mountain she'd once wanted to climb. Danger lurked everywhere in this world. And for most of her life, she'd obeyed the signs. Steered clear as advised.

Now, as in the past, she felt sure it would be the safe thing to do. Call Mr. Williams and tell him she could not accept the house. Restore the peace in her home.

Outside the open bedroom window, moonlight illuminated the ridge of Tinker's Knob. She stared at its dark outline against the night sky. And she wondered then how many amazing views she'd missed from the safety of her spot here at the bottom.

∞

Then

IT WAS A RARE thing for Becca to have the house to herself. Emmy and her mother had gone into town. Jacob and her father were cutting hay in one of the back fields. Becca had worked in the garden for most of the morning, and then decided to use some of the baby carrots she'd pulled to make a cake.

The warm smell of baking now filled the kitchen. Becca had set the three round layers on the counter thirty minutes before to cool. She put a hand to the center of one now and decided it was ready for the cream cheese icing. She pulled the bowl from the refrigerator and a rubber spatula from a nearby drawer.

She began coating the first layer, glancing at the window where she could see Matt Griffith outside the barn working on a piece of haymaking equipment. She ran a finger across the tip of the spatula and tasted the sweet icing, wondering if he could feel her watching him, if he felt the same pull she felt, or whether it was all her imagination.

She started to turn away, but he straightened then and wiped a hand across his forehead. The day was typical hot June, the temperature expected to reach the low nineties by mid-afternoon. She'd thought about taking him some ice water earlier, going as far as filling a pitcher and glass with ice and then dumping it all down the sink when she'd lost her courage.

Matt looked around once as if to make sure no one was watching, then pulled his t-shirt over his head and tossed it on the ground. Becca stepped back, the spatula dripping icing onto the kitchen floor, guilt catching in her throat as if she'd summoned this action with her thoughts.

The clock on the nearby hutch ticked loudly in the otherwise quiet room while Becca stood, motionless, telling herself it was wrong to stare when he didn't even know she was there. She closed her eyes, searched for resolve, the pull of him impossible to resist like the undertow at the center of the creek where she and Emmy swam on hot days like this.

She finished the cake with quick, sure strokes, standing back to study it with a critical eye. The center had fallen a little, but hopefully the taste would make up for it. She pulled a knife from the drawer and cut a thick wedge, placing it on a white saucer and then pouring a tall glass of milk from the pitcher in the fridge.

She walked out of the house and across the yard to the barn, her confidence thinning with each step. By the time Matt turned to look at her, she'd decided this was a really bad idea.

"Hey," he said.

"Hi," she said, trying not to look at his bare chest.

"That for me?"

She nodded. "I thought you might be hungry."

"Thanks," he said, reaching down to pick up his shirt and then shrugging it on.

Becca looked away and then back again, her eyes following the line of muscles in his arms while something in her stomach dropped.

"Sorry about the shirt," he said, running a hand through his dark-blonde hair.

"I've seen boys without their shirts before," she said quickly.

"Kind of like the kissing thing, huh?"

She ignored that and said, "Do you normally offer apologies to girls for taking off your shirt?"

Matt grinned. "They don't usually ask for one."

"I'll bet."

He leaned back and looked at her. "And that's supposed to mean-"

"I'm sure you've taken your shirt off for lots of girls."

He laughed and shook his head.

She held the plate and glass out. "Here. I have to get back to the house."

He took the cake and milk, tipped his head toward the shade of the nearby oak. "Stay while I take a break."

Becca folded her arms and looked at the ground. "I should go."

"Stay anyway."

She looked up at him then, and there it was again, the undertow. She felt it swirl around her, a gentle yank of concession. "Just for a minute," she said.

They sat down at the base of the tree, inches apart. Matt leaned his back against the trunk and tucked into the cake. He ate half of it before he spoke again. "Wow. That is good."

Becca's face went warm with the compliment. She looked down at her hands. "Thanks."

"You like to cook?"

"Sometimes."

"You're good at it."

"I like to use things from the garden."

"Did you grow these carrots?"

She nodded.

"Really?"

"Yeah."

He considered this for a moment, and then, "Cool."

She looked at him, trying not to smile. "You and your buddies like to garden on Friday nights?"

He laughed. "Not exactly. But it is cool. Being good at something."

"Like you and baseball?"

"Yeah," he said, shrugging, surprisingly modest.

"It's really not the same. I haven't noticed any cheering fans outside the kitchen when I'm cooking."

"I'd cheer for this," he said, finishing off the last bite of cake and then taking a swallow of milk, a rim of white lining his upper lip.

Becca smiled and reached out to wipe it away, stopping herself just short of touching him. "You have milk there," she said, making an arc in the air near his mouth.

He wiped it away with the back of his hand. Becca's gaze hooked with his, and she could not bring herself to look away.

"Thanks for the cake," he said, his voice threaded with something that told her she should get up at that very moment and head back inside.

"You're welcome," she said, her own voice barely audible.

"About that kiss," he said.

"What kiss?" Again, the words a whisper.

He leaned in then, stopping a few inches from her face. "This kiss."

A sound that might have originated as protest slipped past Becca's lips only to yield to something altogether different. Matt's hand slipped to the back of her neck, his mouth warm and insistent against hers. He tasted of the cake she'd made, and he smelled of an appealing combination of citrus and hard work.

It wasn't as if she'd never been kissed before. She had. Once. In a clumsy, unimpressive encounter that really hadn't left her in a hurry for a repeat experience despite her big talk with Matt on the sawdust run.

But this was different. Very, very different.

He pulled back, both hands now on each side of her face. They studied each other for several long moments before he said, "Okay if I do that again?"

Becca didn't answer but kissed him this time. He leaned

back against the tree and hooked an arm around her waist, bringing her with him, her chest pressing into his, heat rising up from their skin to meld with the humid June afternoon.

She understood then in a way she never had before what it meant to find the one against whom all others would forever be judged. The one for whom there would be no comparison.

The thought simultaneously lifted her up and left her hanging beneath the realization. She sat back then, one hand to her still tingling mouth. "We shouldn't have done that."

"Why?" Matt said, his voice warm, amused.

She looked down at her lap. "So what are you going to tell Wilks? Do Dunkard girls kiss like other girls?"

"Becca."

The surprise in his voice made her look up; she wished she could take the words back. They sounded petty and mean. He hadn't done anything to deserve them. But just then, a car pulled into the driveway. Her mother and Emmy were back.

Becca got to her feet and reached for the plate and glass Matt had left on the grass next to them. "I have to go," she said.

"Becca, wait," he said, standing.

She didn't stop, but walked back to the house where her mother stood waiting. She pulled a bag of groceries from the trunk of the car and carried them inside, unable to meet the knowing look in her eyes.

21

A Boy's Life

Study the past if you would divine the future.
*– **Confucius***

Now

The past was something best left alone.

Martha had never been able to see the wisdom in revisiting things that could not be redone. This had been Daniel's philosophy as well. Once a decision was made, he'd believed in moving forward and not ever looking back.

But it seemed now that Martha could do little else. She had only to look at Becca's face to see her daughter's discontent. It was, she imagined, the way a house must look after an earthquake has rippled beneath its foundation, the top permanently askew from the bottom.

Worry cut at Martha with the sharpness of a paring knife, and she found herself questioning the reasoning behind the decisions they had made, decisions that were thought to be in the best interest of everyone involved.

It had been some time since she had driven out to see the Rutroughs. Almost two years, in fact, since her last visit. Her only explanation for doing so now the guilt that continued to funnel up from its buried place, the volume she'd managed to squelch for significant streaks of time renewed to a dull roar.

Over the years, she'd visited the Rutroughs maybe a dozen times. It had never been easy for her, and something she did out of a sense of obligation to maintain the connection, to check in on them, even after all this time.

She drove the dozen or so miles from her house to the Rutrough's place at a pace slow enough to have four or five cars lined up behind her by the time she turned in at the end of their gravel road. A red Trans-Am blew the horn and roared off with a squealing of tires.

Martha pulled into the driveway and turned off the car. Lydia Rutrough stood outside watering a large Crepe Myrtle bush. She looked up, and in that second just before she caught herself, Martha saw the flare of upset on the other woman's face, and then the deliberate effort to school her features into pleasantness. It wasn't that Martha didn't understand Lydia's discomfort. She was only too aware that in her eyes, Martha would always be associated with the delivery of unimaginable news.

Lydia put down her watering can and walked over to the car, wiping her hands on the apron tied at her waist. "Hello, Martha. How are you?"

"Fine, Lydia," Martha said, a waver in her voice. "And you?"

The two stopped short of a hug, clasping their hands and squeezing once. "Good," she said, and then after an awkward moment, "Come in. I just took a pound cake out of the oven. Let's have a slice."

"That sounds wonderful," Martha said, following her into the house. They entered through the front door, the foyer much like Martha's own, the furniture plain and unimposing with its straight lines. The floors were made of wide pine planks, the dull honey-colored finish spotlessly clean.

Lydia led the way, and Martha followed, her gaze snagging on a collection of pictures hanging in the hallway just short of the kitchen. Unable to stop herself, she stood and stared at this progression of a son's life, infant to toddler, young boy to young man. The pictures ended there, of course, and Martha wondered if Lydia's suffering renewed itself all over again every time she walked past these photos.

She forced herself to walk into the kitchen where Lydia removed the lid from a cake box.

"Mark had to go into town, or else I'd call him to join us," Lydia said, giving no indication that she had noticed Martha staring at the pictures.

"That's all right," Martha said. "And please don't go to any trouble."

"No trouble," Lydia said, cutting the cake and placing it on plain white saucers, before pouring them both a glass of iced tea and bringing it all to the kitchen table.

They sat, awkward now as they both took a bite of the moist cake. "Um," Martha said. "Delicious."

"Thank you."

Through the open window at one end of the kitchen came the sound of a tractor starting up, its engine sputtering once and then finding a steady rhythm. A light breeze brought with it the scent of grass, freshly mown.

Lydia looked up then and let her eyes meet Martha's. "Is everything all right, Martha?"

There were any number of ways Martha could have answered, but somehow she didn't have it in her today to say anything other than what she felt to be true. "Do you ever wish we'd acted differently, Lydia?"

Surprise flitted across Lydia's face. Since the day of

John's funeral, they'd never once spoken of the decisions that had been made. It was as if by some silent pact, they'd agreed it was better left alone. Martha felt instantly guilty, as if she had violated some unspoken trust.

"I don't let myself question it," Lydia said.

"But do you regret it?"

Lydia rubbed a thumb across the rim of her saucer, considering her answer. "Do I wish I knew the absolute truth? Yes. Do I think it would make what we've had to accept any easier? No."

Martha thought about those pictures in the front hall of this house. The chronicle of a boy's life. She thought of her own son and all the time that had been lost, years and years during which he lived a life of which she was not a part. This had been deliberate on her behalf, an unwillingness to accept Jacob's choices. She wondered what Lydia would give to be in her shoes.

Martha felt a sudden wave of shame, for the fact that she had come here today to somehow salve her own conscience and in the process, pulled the permanently flimsy covering from Lydia's wounds.

"I'm sorry," she said. "I don't mean to cause you any further grief, Lydia."

"What is it that you want to know, Martha?" Lydia asked, sounding suddenly weary.

For a few moments, Martha was silent, unable to answer. When she finally did, she barely recognized her own voice. "If you could do it over again," she said, "would you choose differently?"

Lydia lifted her gaze to Martha's, her eyes suddenly liquid with regret, as if a curtain had been pulled to reveal something previously well hidden. "Yes," she said. "Yes, I would. Would you?"

The conviction in the answer took Martha by surprise. She realized then that this was not what she'd expected to hear. And that maybe she had needed to reaffirm in her own mind the soundness of the logic behind all that had been done. Looking at Lydia's face now, seeing her temporarily unveiled despair, she thought of the individual events that had been set into play by their actions. And how questioning something that was already said and done could do nothing but remove the covers from the deepest wells of pain.

It was this which gave her pause. And this that made her question whether all those years ago, she had acted for the good of those she loved or for reasons that could be deemed far less selfless.

22

Destinations

It behooves a father to be blameless if he expects his child to be.
– Homer

Now

As a child, it's hard to understand our parents. I remember thinking when I was a little girl that my mama spent most of her day fussing at Becca, Jacob, and me about one thing or another. Then, I couldn't understand why everything we did seemed to bother her. I even wondered at times why she ever wanted children if we were such a nuisance. If everything about us needed to be changed to a different standard.

When we were little, Becca was the one who challenged Mama and Daddy's rules, refusing to take anything at face value. Jacob, too, but with more subtlety. If he stepped over the line, he usually got his foot back inside before anybody noticed. At least until he met Linda.

For the most part, I went along with what was expected. I was the good girl. Which makes it hard to understand how I could have done something I knew would shame my mama and daddy in the eyes of our community and church.

In all the years I've had to think about it, I've taken the question apart a thousand different ways. And the only thing I've come up with is this: I wanted my own life. I didn't want to live under my parents' rules any longer. I wanted to be married to John. And I knew Mama and Daddy wouldn't have let me until I was eighteen.

I don't know if I believe that God deliberately punishes us here on earth when we disobey and do wrong. I guess I'd understand if He did. But I wonder if it's more that He lets the consequences of our actions play out their natural course. We tip the domino, and the track is set, each piece falling in upon itself until the end result is the only one it could have been.

Maybe it's inherent in human nature that we are drawn to those things we should turn away from. And I guess, really, that's what Mama's daily fussing was all about when we were little. Trying to teach us the things that would help us get through this life without pain. I didn't see it that way then. But I do now. I just don't think it's something that can be taught. In one way or another, pain is something we will all know. Even when the danger signs are held up in front of us, we have to travel the road ourselves, hoping all the while that it will have a different destination for us than the one our parents warned us about. Only to figure out after it is all but too late that they were right all along.

23

The Other Parts

We must not say every mistake is a foolish one.
– Cicero

Now

It was an overwhelming task, the act of closing down another person's life.

Matt started in the attic, the fourth floor of his grandmother's house. He quickly realized that the things accumulated over decades of living could not simply be piled up and hauled off, but required careful scrutiny. He discovered boxes of dresses his grandmother had worn as a girl, an old trunk filled with Life magazines from the forties and fifties. He felt an enormous responsibility in being the one to declare their worth or lack thereof. What if he threw away something that had been especially meaningful to his grandmother, a family memory that once discarded by him would no longer exist?

The attic had no air conditioning or windows, and the May afternoons grew warm enough that he could only tolerate working there in the mornings. On the third day of sorting and boxing, he headed back downstairs at just after noon, wiping sweat from his forehead with the back of his arm. Just as he reached the foyer, his cell phone jangled in his pocket. He glanced at the caller i.d. screen. Phoebe. He considered not answering, but they hadn't spoken in days, and under the weight of a pricked conscience, he flipped it open.

"Matt, let me come down and help you," she said by way of greeting, a plea in her voice. "I know it's an enormous job, going through your grandmother's things. I remember how hard it was when my dad died."

"I'm fine, Phoebe."

"But it's so much. And what about work? Won't they expect you back soon?"

"Actually, I've taken a short leave of absence."

"Oh," she said. "For how long?"

"I'm not sure." And he wasn't. It wasn't something he'd intended to do, but late yesterday afternoon, he'd found himself calling the senior partner of his firm to say he needed some time off. Life suddenly felt too complicated. Phoebe. Gran's death. Becca.

He blinked at her name, as if he could brush her image from his thoughts. But there it was, etched against the back of his lids. Becca, sitting across that coffee shop table from him a few days ago. Becca, leaving, as if she couldn't get away fast enough.

"Matt?"

"Yeah?"

"I want to come. Can't you give me a chance to make this right?"

"What makes you think that's possible, Phoebe?" he asked, anger edging his voice now.

"Maybe it's not. But I want to try," she said, humble with a contrition he had never before heard in her. A prosecuting attorney for the District of Columbia,

Phoebe had been referred to as a ball-buster more than once by opposing counsel.

"You threw our marriage down the toilet, and I'm supposed to fish it back out again?"

She said nothing for a few moments, and then, "I messed up, Matt."

He forced himself to consider that she was trying, reaching for a softness he didn't feel. "Phoebe, what exactly do you expect of me?"

"Just a chance. You don't know how much I wish I could change what I did. I'd give anything to go back and make a different choice. But I can't do that."

"No. You can't," he said. They were both silent then, and it felt as if there was nothing else to be said. "I'll call you," he added and then hung up.

He dropped the cell phone on the foyer table, going outside to sink onto the front porch swing. It creaked beneath his weight, and he moved to the center to keep it from tipping too far to one side. It was the same sensation he'd felt getting out of bed on the mornings leading up to Gran's funeral. As if his life had lost its fulcrum, and he'd been left swinging crazy out of control.

The truth had spilled out like something on a less than original soap opera. He'd found the number on her cell phone one afternoon when he'd borrowed it without asking her. Mentioned it to her more from curiosity than suspicion. With the single question, she'd confessed the whole story, as if she'd been waiting for him to catch her. As if she needed him to. He'd wanted to stop her in mid-admission, push the pause button, rewind to the part where he saw the number, decided the attorney must have been looking for him and let it go.

If confession was good for the soul, Phoebe should have been completely recovered by the time she finished laying out how the whole thing had started, how many times she and Larry had met, etc. Larry. Lawrence. Metcalf, Esquire. Matt had stood mute and immobile, as if he owed it to her to listen. As if he had done something to cause it, and this was the price for his screw up.

Wasn't there something inherently selfish about confessions, anyway? The guilty party's chance to purge their guilt. Never mind that another person got flattened in the process. Ignorance *was* bliss. No pain in not knowing. He wished she'd kept it that way. Even if every other attorney in his firm knew his wife was spending her extended lunch hours at the Four Seasons. At least he could have gone on about his business, head buried in the sand. The view from there really wasn't that bad.

But now he'd been handed the hat of forgiveness, expected to wear it with a-gosh-Phoebe-that's-okay-graciousness he didn't feel.

He got up from the swing, walked around to the back of the house and pulled a pair of pruners from the old shed where Gran's lawn tools were still stored. He headed to the front and started shaping the enormous boxwoods that lined the walkway. They hadn't been touched in years and long ago lost their roundness, unruly sprigs jutting out here and there. He aimed at restoring their shape without making them look like someone took a mower to them.

Matt worked for a couple of hours, breaking a good sweat. The constant clip, clip, clip of the pruners distracting him from his previous desire to put his fist through one of the columns on the front porch.

Finished, he stood back and surveyed his handiwork. Not bad. He suddenly felt energized, challenged, by the work at hand and it felt good. Really good.

On a roll now, he decided to take the weed trimmer around the house and fence. He pulled it out of the shed only to discover there was no gas in the red tank marked

MIX. He threw it and a couple others in the back of the Land Rover and headed to the Exxon downtown. When he turned into the station, a car sat at the unleaded pump, so he pulled in behind it to wait. An older man with a cane walked out of the station. It took a moment, but Matt recognized him as Mr. Blankenship, the old man's face transporting him back. He remembered the man decades younger when he and his wife Ruth sat in the front row at church every Sunday. Spotting him, Mr. Blankenship waved and stopped to speak.

"Real sorry about your grandmother, Matt," he said.

"Thank you," he said through his lowered window.

"She was a good woman," he added. "Don't come much better."

"Yes, sir."

"Been a long time since I've seen you around here. Where you living these days?"

"Washington, D.C."

"Fast lane, huh?" he said, the grooves in his cheeks deepening into a smile.

Matt smiled back and opened his door to get out.

"Those were some good years of baseball you had at UVA," he said. "We were rooting for you to go on to the pros around here."

"Shoulda taken better care of this shoulder, huh?" Matt said.

"You're not blamin' your defection on that, are you?" The comment came from behind them. He turned around to find Wilks Perdue wiping grease-stained hands on a blue shop towel.

"Gotta blame it on something," Matt said.

Mr. Blankenship opened the door of his car and got in. "I'll let you boys debate that one. Y'all take care now," he said and pulled out of the station.

Matt had heard Wilks was still living in the county.

They hadn't run into one another since before he'd left for college, the punches they'd ended up throwing at one another that last night, a final guillotine to their friendship.

Wilks looked like an older version of himself now, his hair a little thinner at the front, lines etched at the sides of his eyes. The smile was the same though, let's-get-past-it-today's-a-new-day.

"This your place?" Matt asked, noticing for the first time the Perdue's Exxon sign above the garage door.

"It was either this or neurosurgery."

"You never could stand the sight of blood."

Wilks grinned. "You're the one who threw up on the side of the road the night we hit that deer."

"That how you remember it?"

"That's how I remember it."

Matt opened the back of the Land Rover, pulling out the gas cans. Wilks lifted the nozzle off the unleaded tank and handed it to him. "Thanks," he said.

"I was sorry to hear about Mrs. Griffith."

"Yeah." Awkwardness took over, and Matt concentrated on the sound of the gas streaming into the can.

"Seen any of the old gang?" Wilks finally asked.

"Nope. Who's still around?"

"Joey Mathers."

"He still keeping the town in pot?"

Wilks shook his head. "He's a pastor for a Holiness Church in Ferrum."

"No way."

"Way."

Matt shook his head. Apparently, the road to reform could be taken up by most anyone.

"I heard Angie's back. Divorced and living in her

parents' old house. She's a teacher over at the high school."

"Really?" This was the first Matt had heard about his old girlfriend in years. He'd dated Angie before he met Becca, and after he and Becca had broken up, Angie came up to UVA a couple times during his freshman year. They'd made a few false starts and then finally let go for good.

"How about Becca? Run into her since you've been home?"

Matt looked up, found Wilks waiting for his answer with an expectant expression. "Yeah. As a matter of fact."

Wilks paused, as if weighing what to say. "I guess that was a shock, seeing her in that Little House on the Prairie get up?"

Something in his tone hit Matt wrong. He didn't want to talk to Wilks about Becca.

"Hey," Wilks said when Matt failed to respond. "I didn't mean that as a slam."

Matt wanted to ask him how he did mean it, but that was a place they didn't need to go again.

"Besides," Wilks said, "she's done all right for herself from the sound of it. All those fancy restaurants around the lake think she's some kind of magician in the garden. They buy her vegetables like it'll get them a mention in *Southern Living* or something."

Matt remembered then Becca's interest in growing things, how she'd taken him through her garden the summer they'd dated, proudly showing him the prize vegetables she'd grown from seeds handed down through the generations of her family. He could see her continuing the work her grandmother had taught her, knew she would find satisfaction in it.

"So I guess you never got over her, huh?" Wilks went on, railroading past Matt's silence. "I figured if she'd mattered to you, you wouldn't have wiped this place off your map."

"It wasn't like that," Matt said.

"Really?"

"Really."

Wilks lifted a shoulder, clearly disagreeing. "You married?"

He hesitated, then said, "Separated."

"Bummer." Wilks pulled a tin of snuff from his pocket, took out a pinch and put it between his lower lip and gum. "Hey, the Red Robin's still open up on 40. Come on out tonight, and I'll buy you a beer."

"Thanks," Matt said. "But I'm working on getting Gran's house ready to sell."

"You can't stay at it 24-7."

"Lot to do," he said, noncommittal, handing him a twenty for the gas.

Wilks gave him his change, staring hard for a moment, before saying, "Man, we were good friends once."

"We were," he agreed.

"Think we're old enough to put all that crap behind us?"

The question held an earnestness that didn't sound like the Wilks Matt had known. To rebuff his effort would make Matt the smaller of the two of them. Besides, it was Becca who had cut him out of her life. Becca who had walked away and chosen someone else. Holding a grudge wasn't going to change the truth.

∞

Then

MATT HADN'T BEEN out in over two weeks. He'd been so tired after getting off work at the Millers that all he'd done every night was eat and go to bed. Wilks had left dozens of messages with Gran for Matt to call him back. Which he'd yet to do.

He took a shower, standing under the cold spray long enough to perk himself up. He didn't really want to go anywhere, but decided he needed to do something more progressive than stare at the backside of a cow. And, too, he needed a diversion from thinking about Becca.

He didn't know what to make of what had happened between them. Kissing her wasn't something he'd planned. Or expected. But he hadn't been able to think of anything else since.

And she had clearly been avoiding him. The few times he'd seen her today, she'd acted as if it had never happened, as if she would erase all of it if she could. He alternated between wanting to know why and being thoroughly pissed off.

He pulled on jeans and a t-shirt and went downstairs to dial Wilks's number. He was cool at first, asking where Matt had been. Wilks was working the deep fryer at Burger Queen for the summer, no great challenge to mind or body, so Matt didn't bother to enlighten him about the fact that he'd been getting up at four every morning.

Gran had gone to a special choir practice at church, so he went out on the porch to wait. Wilks rolled up in ten minutes, grudge forgotten as he talked about how he and some of the other guys from the baseball team had driven out to the lake yesterday and jumped off the cliffs, a tall face of rock where locals went to dive.

"Man, we got so wasted," Wilks said, peeling out of the driveway. "I think Morris topped your high jump."

"Yeah?"

"Don't worry. You can rechallenge." He grabbed a beer from the floorboard and handed it to Matt.

Matt popped the top, took a swallow, grimacing a little and setting it in the cup holder beside him.

Wilks gave him a look. "What? A job with the Dunkards, and you can't drink a beer?"

Matt ran a hand around the back of his neck, beginning to seriously wish he'd stayed home. "Hey, man, why don't you ease up?"

"Let me guess. You've got a crush on–what's her name?"

Matt looked out the window and ignored the question.

"Becca. Right?" He snorted a laugh. "I guess if you've been looking at cows all day, she might start to look pretty hot, huh?"

"Shut up, man."

Wilks laughed, stopping for the red light across from the Methodist church. "What you need is some fun. You been out in the boonies too long. We need to get that corn cob out of your butt."

"You're a jerk, you know?" Matt said. He and Wilks had been friends since second grade when Wilks's family had moved to Ballard. They'd played t-ball together, then graduated to baseball. Wilks was going to Ferrum College for his freshman year, and if he got his grades up, transferring to JMU the next year.

He'd given Matt a load of grief about the scholarship to UVa, telling everybody Matt would turn into a preppie, leaving a pair of kelly-green pants hanging on the outside of his locker one day at school. There had been a point when this difference seemed like it was going to get between them, but Wilks had finally cooled it with the ridicule.

"Where are we going?" Matt asked.

"The Minute Market. Joey said he'd be there."

"Aw, man," he said, definitely not in the mood for Joey Mathers.

"What? He's cool."

Joey Mathers was usually so stoned you could tip him over with your index finger. Wilks and some of the other baseball players kept him around as their only connection to scoring dope.

"Right," he said, picking up his beer and taking another swig. This time, it tasted a little better.

It was nearing dark when they pulled into the Minute Market beside Blake Harmon's Chevelle. A group of kids stood around the back of the car, Joey holding court.

"By the way," Wilks said, smiling. "Forgot to tell you Angie was supposed to be here."

"I'll bet you did," he said.

Wilks threw a punch to Matt's shoulder. "Can I help it if she's still got it bad for you?"

Matt rolled his eyes, getting out of the car and leaving the beer inside. Most of the crowd they hung out with was there, ball players, a few cheerleaders. Wilks walked over, put his arm around Mimi Parker, one of Angie's best friends. "Hey, Joey," he said, "you bring any of the good stuff with you?"

Matt stayed where he was, somehow wanting to be on the sidelines tonight.

Dale Brooks wandered over, leaning up against Wilks's Mustang and hooking his thumbs through the pockets of a pair of faded overalls. Dale was a good guy, valedictorian of their class, headed for MIT in the fall.

"You're at the Miller place this summer, right?"

"Yeah," Matt said.

"What's it like out on the farm?"

"Not too bad."

Dale ran a hand across the top of his blonde buzz cut. "Becca's family, right?"

Matt nodded.

"I had some classes with Becca before she left school. That's one smart girl."

For whatever reason, Matt had never had a class with Becca, and he was intrigued by this piece of information. "Really?"

"Yeah, not just book smart though. She had the common sense kind, too. This intuition for when something was right or wrong. If she'd stayed in school, I probably wouldn't have been first in the class."

Dale was prone to modesty, but Matt could hear the sincerity in his voice, and something else, too.

"You have a thing for her?" he asked, keeping his voice casual, as if it didn't matter one way or the other whether Dale answered.

He tipped his head, conceding. "Maybe a little," he said.

Matt folded his arms across his chest. "So why don't you ask her out?"

Dale lifted his shoulders in a shrug. "Figured it would be a waste of time, you know?"

"What do you mean?"

"Just that I'm not one of them and that kind of thing probably wouldn't work."

He thought about Jacob and Linda and what Becca had said about them. "Yeah, I guess not," he said.

Angie edged up beside Dale then, giving him a playful bump with her shoulder. "My turn," she said.

"Oh, pardon me," Dale said, grinning. "I didn't realize there was a Griffith line." He gave Matt a thumbs up behind her back, then headed over to Wilks and Joey who were retelling their diving stories from the day before.

Matt leaned back against the Mustang, palms planted on the trunk. "Hey, Angie," he said.

"Hey." She smiled, her green eyes nearly level with his, her straight, dark hair pulled back in a ponytail. Voted Most Popular in their class, Angie Taylor was one of those girls born knowing what she wanted. And she'd never been shy about going after it.

When they'd broken up last spring, Wilks summed up Matt's stupidity with his usual elegance. "What the hell are you thinking? Every guy in this county would give a nut to date her."

Angie put her back to the car now, close enough that their arms touched. "Haven't seen you out this week," she said. "Where you been?"

"Working," he said.

"I heard."

"Seems everybody has."

She smiled. "Not exactly where I would have pictured you this summer."

"Me, either. What are you doing?"

"Helping my dad. Answering the phone and stuff."

A general practitioner, Angie's father had been Matt's doctor since Gran stopped taking him to the pediatrician in Roanoke. "That's probably interesting," he said.

"A lot more interesting at five o'clock when I get to leave," she said, laughing.

They talked for a while, and it was like it always was with Angie. She was warm and flirted like somebody who'd had a lot of practice. Which she had.

They hit on the subject of college, what it would be like not to see all the kids they were used to seeing every day.

She turned around, planted her elbows on the trunk of the car, looking up at him. "Sweet Briar's not that far from Charlottesville, you know," she said. "Maybe we can plan a weekend road trip."

"Yeah," he said, not sure where they were going with this, even less sure where he wanted it to go. "That'd be nice."

She smiled, glanced away.

"What?" he asked.

She traced a finger through the dirt on Wilks's car, making a question mark. "That thing you do. Go along just to change the subject."

"I don't," he said.

"Yeah, you do," she said, still smiling. "But that's okay. I'm on to you now."

They studied each other for a moment, and he decided to let it go.

"I've got my car here," she said. "Wanna take a ride?"

Matt thought about Becca and the way she'd refused to talk to him throughout the day. Every time he'd tried to approach her, she'd found some reason to go the other way. "Yeah, sure," he said.

He walked over and told Wilks he was getting a ride with Angie. A couple of the guys let out a wolf whistle. Wilks just shook his head, giving him a two-finger salute.

Angie pulled up in the white convertible she'd gotten for graduation. Matt got in, and she made a right out of the Minute Market, heading down Route 40 and then left on 122, the opposite direction from his house. He knew where she was going, considered telling her not tonight, but instead, sat back in his seat and closed his eyes.

A couple minutes later, she turned onto a gravel road. A quarter mile down was the asphalt paving company her uncle owned, a secluded spot they'd made use of more than a few times. She pulled around to the back, cut the engine.

There weren't any lights on that side of the building, dark except for the few stars overhead. They sat for a minute or two, not talking.

"I think about us a lot, Matt," she said, the first to speak.

"We had some good times," he said, one shoulder against the door.

"So why did we break up anyway?"

"Seems like we were doing a lot of arguing."

"Um," she said, turning in her seat so that her knee pressed against his thigh. "I can't even remember what about."

She leaned over, kissed the side of his face, pausing a second before nipping the lobe of his ear with her teeth.

"Look, Angie—" he began.

"Hey, I know we got this part right," she said.

He turned his face to hers, and she kissed him, nothing soft and introductory, just picking up where they'd left off, two people who knew each other's bodies. He closed his eyes, but it was Becca's face he saw on the back of his lids. Intent on erasing it, he kissed Angie back, and she leaned against the driver's door. Matt followed, half lying across her.

She pulled his shirt over his head, and he unbuttoned her blouse, popping the snap on her bra, willing himself not to think. Just like that, and they were back to the way it had been when they were together.

He pulled away after a few minutes, drawing in a few deep breaths. "Angie," he said. "This is nice. Real nice. But like you said, this was the part we got right the first time. If we're going to start up again, maybe we ought to work on the other parts first."

"I don't have a problem with that." She leaned over, kissed him again. "How about a date then? Saturday night?"

He'd started this thread. Not so easy to let it go now. "Saturday sounds good," he said.

She hooked her bra and buttoned her blouse, then started the car. They drove back to town, music from the radio taking up the silence between them. And the whole way he wasn't thinking about the girl beside him, but about the fact that everything he'd done tonight had been nothing more than an unsuccessful effort to get Becca Miller out of his head.

24

One Simple Truth

Each day provides its own gifts.
– American Proverb

Now
On Saturday morning, Becca asked Abby if she'd like to take a drive. She didn't tell her where they were going, wanting it to be a surprise. They climbed into the old white farm truck, driving the few miles into town where Becca stopped by Tom Williams' office to get the keys to Mrs. Griffith's house. She'd called earlier to let him know she was coming, and he'd left them for her at the front desk. Cowardly, maybe, but she was glad she didn't have to face him, pretend she didn't see the questions in his eyes. Walking back to the truck, she held the keys tight, the metal cold against the palm of her hand. They headed out of town and down 122 toward the lake.

"Okay, so what's the big mystery?" Abby asked, her window lowered to let in the spring breeze.

"It's a house," Becca answered, keeping her eyes on the road, mostly to avoid the questions in Abby's.

"What kind of house?"

"At the lake."

"Really? Whose?"

"Actually, it's mine."

"Yours?" Abby turned in the seat, her back to the door, eyes wide.

Becca nodded, realizing she was starting to like the sound of it. Hers. She'd lived her whole life in the house where she grew up, a house that officially belonged to her mother. Aside from her potting shed, she'd never yearned to own anything that was strictly her own, but something here had struck a chord deep down. "Mrs. Griffith, the woman whose funeral I went to last week, left it to me."

"Wow," Abby said, amazement underlining the words. "Have you seen it?"

"A long time ago."

"Are you going to keep it?"

"I'm not sure," she said.

The drive from Ballard to Tinker's Knob Lake took some twenty-five minutes. Becca made the right hand turn off 122 onto the gravel road that led to the house, surprised she remembered it so well and then at the same time realizing that part of her felt as if it had just been yesterday that she'd last come here with Matt. The bushes along the edge had grown out far enough that the old truck had to elbow its way down the half-mile stretch until they reached the clearing where the house sat a couple hundred feet back from the edge of the lake. The yard was in a similar state of disrepair, the grass knee-high, blackberry vines growing up against the side of the house.

"What a great place," Abby said.

"It is," Becca agreed. They got out of the truck, wading through the grass to the back door. She inserted the key, swinging it open and inside to find the kitchen basically the same as it had been eighteen years ago.

Only now cobwebs abounded, and mouse droppings

dotted the linoleum floor. Becca's fingers itched suddenly to make the place look as it once had when Mrs. Griffith had taken pride in it.

They walked outside, standing on the front porch and looking out at the lake, sunlight glistening off its blue surface. Across the cove, a deer peered out of the woods at the edge of the water. Overhead, a hawk soared, announcing itself. There were no other houses within sight, and the place had a peacefulness to it that made her imagine for a moment a lovely stretch of garden between the house and the lake.

"It's beautiful," Abby said.

"Yes," Becca said, remembering the times she had come here with Matt, how in this place, it had seemed as if they might have been the only two people in the world. She put a hand on Abby's shoulder. "Feel like doing some cleaning?"

"So that's why you brought me along," she teased.

Becca smiled and gave Abby's ponytail a gentle tug. "Would ice cream on the way home help persuade you?"

"Cookie dough Blizzard at the Dairy Queen?" she negotiated.

"Deal."

They headed back to the truck where Abby climbed over the tailgate and retrieved the mop, bucket and cleaning supplies. They started in the kitchen, scrubbing grime from the sink and counters, making the faucet and stove shine again.

They hit the baseboards next, rubbing away the caked-on dust until the white paint once again gleamed. The old wood table in the center of the room perked up beneath a good dusting and a coat of polish. Abby found a ladder in a closet and used it to reach the ceiling light fixture.

They worked until mid-afternoon without a break. It

was nearly three o'clock when Abby said, "Okay, I'm starving. When do we get to eat?"

"Some mother you have. I forgot to feed you lunch."

Abby smiled. "If you brought peanut butter and jelly, I won't report you this one time."

"I'll try to do better."

They got the cooler out of the truck. She'd brought along an old quilt as well, and they spread it close to the water. Over the years, waves from ski boats and Sea-Doos had eroded the shoreline so that it ran not so much in a straight line as a zigzagged edge like the hems Granny Miller used to sew in Becca's dresses when she was a little girl.

The water was smooth today, its color a deep green. Across the cove, black Angus cows grazed the grass that ran to the water's edge. Much of the lake had been built up, enormous houses occupying quarter acre lots with golf course quality yards. But this cove looked much the same as it had eighteen years ago. Mrs. Griffith had leased the grass pastures of her land to a farmer who lived nearby. Once, on a hot July day when Becca had been here with Matt, they'd floated across the cove on a tube to pet a cow who'd decided to wade out and cool off.

Becca blinked away the memory, handing Abby a thermos of lemonade. They ate in comfortable silence. When Abby finished her sandwich, she stretched out on her belly, chin propped on her hands, facing the lake.

"So it seems like there has to be more to this," she said.

Becca took a sip of lemonade. "What do you mean?"

"Well, obviously, Daddy and Grandma are bent out of shape about something. They're not speaking to you, and I'm guessing it has to do with this place. Why would they mind a nice old woman leaving you something?"

Sometimes, Becca wondered if Abby would grow up to be an investigator of some sort. Or maybe a psychiatrist.

She'd always looked for clues in people, mulled over their words and actions, rearranged the pieces of the puzzle, until she became satisfied with the fit.

"My English teacher was talking to Ms. Taylor, one of the other teachers, about Mrs. Griffith yesterday. I heard her say something about a grandson who was here taking care of her will and stuff. She told Ms. Taylor that he was hunkier than ever and that she should never have let him get away."

"Really?" Becca said, studying the crust of her mostly uneaten sandwich.

"Did Ms. Taylor date him?"

"Yes," she said.

"Did you know him?"

"Yes." With this, she shifted her gaze to the fishing boat now idling into the cove.

A man in a baseball cap lifted his hand in greeting, then cut the engine and cast his line. Becca wondered how much to tell Abby, sick inside at the thought of adding another single lie to the pyre she'd built in the past eighteen years.

"Were you friends with him?"

Becca felt the angle of Abby's questions, and she wanted with sudden conviction to bring something of the truth out into the light where it had at least a hope of being seen for what it was. "We were," she said. "Actually, we were more than that for a while."

Abby looked at her, blinking in shock, as if she had cast her fishing line into the ocean under the assumption she would never catch anything, and now there was a whale on the end. "Oh. What, exactly?"

Becca stuck her sandwich back in its Zip-loc bag, buying herself a few moments. "We dated."

"But he's not—"

"No. He's not."

Abby processed this, her gaze on the boat sitting silent in the cove. "Did you love him?"

"I guess I thought I did," she said.

"What happened?"

"Our lives were very different."

"And you married Daddy?"

She nodded, looking up at the hawk making another pass over the cove, its shrill cry resonating inside her. "Yes."

They were quiet for a good bit before Abby said, "Do you love him?"

"Who?"

"Daddy."

She glanced down. "Your father is a good man, Abby."

Abby considered this, and then, "But you don't love him the way you loved Matt."

Honesty compelled Becca to say, "I don't compare the two."

Another span of silence took up the space between them, before Abby finally said, "I'm in love with someone, Mama."

"I know, honey."

Abby's eyes widened. "How?"

"I've seen you outside the house at night."

"And you haven't said anything?" She shook her head as if it were again the last thing she would have expected.

"Abby, I trust your heart. It will tell you what to do."

Abby pulled a blade of grass from the edge of the quilt, rubbing it between her palms. "But he's not like us, either."

"I know."

"Daddy will have a cow."

"He just might."

Again, they were silent, letting these new revelations

between them find balanced footing. "Was it like this for you? With Matt?"

"That was a very long time ago," Becca said, feeling as if she'd said enough, that more would make her a traitor to Aaron. She got up from the quilt, brushing the crumbs from her dress, then leaning down and taking off her shoes. "Let's see if the water's warm."

Abby followed her to the edge of the shore. She stepped down into the water, holding her dress above her knees, the soft red clay squishing up between her toes. Abby slipped off her shoes, stepping in beside her, giggling when a tiny fish nipped at her calf. The sun lay warm across their shoulders. Abby reached for her mother's hand, entwining their fingers. "I love you, Mama. I'm glad we can talk like this. That we can be honest with each other."

Becca swallowed hard, tried to answer, but the words stuck in her throat. How did she explain, after all, that one simple truth could not possibly obliterate such a tangle of lies?

25

Smudged Lines

If you would be a real seeker after truth, it is necessary that at least once in your life you doubt, as far as possible, all things.
– Rene Descartes

Now
On the drive home, Abby struggled to gain a clear focus on what had happened today. It almost felt as if she had found out something she'd always suspected, that her parents' marriage wasn't altogether what it appeared to be. She'd never heard them argue, never heard her mother say a critical word against her father, but the playfulness, the joy she'd seen in the parents of some of her friends wasn't there between them. From the outside, their marriage looked as if it had been touched up with one of those computerized airbrushes, made to look perfect when the original had plenty of flaws.

Her grandmother had Aunt Emmy's supper tray waiting when they walked through the back door of the house and into the kitchen at just after five-thirty. "Becca, please take this up to your sister," Martha said, her voice cool and disapproving. Once her mother had left the room, a little ribbon of resentment unfolded inside Abby. Sometimes, she hated the way Grandma talked to her mama.

She opened the refrigerator, pulling out the milk bottle and pouring herself a glass before taking a big sip.

"Supper will be ready soon, child," Martha said. "Don't spoil your appetite."

"Yes, Grandma," she said, opening the door to the hutch where the dishes were kept and picking up four plates. She set the table as she did every night, adding the silverware and napkins.

Martha placed a bowl of steaming green beans in the center, adjusting a wayward fork and speaking without looking at Abby. "I hope you won't encourage your mother about this house."

"Why?" she asked, for some reason unwilling to make this easy for her grandmother.

Martha met her gaze then, direct. "A wife should not go against her husband's wishes," she said in an even voice. "To do so puts the whole family in jeopardy."

Abby knew how her grandmother saw the world. Anything that pulled her from the path of the familiar was simply unacceptable. Not that Abby had ever disapproved of this. She thought it was okay for her grandmother to choose her way. But shouldn't it also work in the reverse? Shouldn't it also be okay for others to choose theirs? "It's just a house, Grandma," she said.

Martha refolded a napkin, fitting it close to the edge of the plate. "Ah, but that's where life gets complicated, Abby. Sometimes, things look harmless from the surface. When that's not really the case at all."

She untied her apron then, leaving it on the counter and walking outside, the screen door wheezing shut behind her. Abby watched her go with a funny feeling in her stomach, wondering why she'd sounded so sad.

In some ways, Abby thought being a child a far preferable thing to being a grown up. She'd once seen the world in clear squares of black and white, right and wrong, nice and mean. Lately, though, she'd begun to see that the lines were sometimes smudged, and it wasn't always easy to know what fell on which side. For a child, why never entered the picture in sizing a person up. They either were or weren't. So much simpler.

Today had brought two questions into a picture Abby had never wanted to examine too closely, questions she'd managed to push away whenever they popped to the surface. But this time, she couldn't make them disappear. They blared through her head as if they'd been posed through a megaphone, refusing to be ignored.

26

First Cry

To give birth is a fearsome thing; there is no hating the child one has borne even when injured by it.
– Sophocles

Now

I remember the day she was born, the details of her birth forever forged in my mind.

It was the coldest kind of March day, the wind beating at the windows of the Ohio hospital where Becca had driven me at four in the morning, as if it had every intention of getting inside. I remember, too, the antiseptic smell that hung in the air and the cheerful voices of the nurses on the maternity floor, how they'd grown sober at the sight of me, figuring out I guess from the look on my face that I was not typical of the women who normally arrived lit up with happy anticipation.

Abby's entrance into the world was no easy thing, the labor a stretch of hours that seemed to have no end. My body felt as if it were being wrenched in half, and maybe in more ways than just the physical, it was.

Nothing prepared me for the sound of her first cry, a weak little mewling at first, and then a full-fledged wail of protest.

At the sound of it, I started to cry, too, an entire well of sorrow pouring up and out of me.

I couldn't look at her face, the terror of seeing John in her tiny features more than I could summon the courage to do. I looked at Becca, instead, her eyes liquid pools of compassion, and I turned away, refusing to hold my baby, even as my breasts ached in response to her hungry cries.

Throughout my childhood, I had seen cows reject their babies many times, my heart throbbing for the helpless calf bleating in fear. I never understood how the mama could go through everything she went through to bring a life into the world and then simply turn away with no interest whatsoever in sustaining that life.

Many times, Daddy would bring another cow into an enclosed area and place the wobbly calf next to her, all of us holding our breath that she would accept it. Relieved beyond words when she did.

I guess this is what I felt that day watching Becca leave the delivery room with my newborn baby in her arms. Utter relief for the fact that she would take over from here. That my child would know love, rationalizing that it didn't matter where that love came from as long as she had it.

What I didn't let myself consider that day was the cost of this act of love on my sister's part. Only much, much later would I understand the full reach of it.

27

Paw Paw Trees and Whippings

Helping one another,
is part of the religion of sisterhood.
*~ **Louisa May Alcott***

Now

Becca read until Emmy's eyes grew heavy, and her head relaxed against the pillow. She closed the book, but remained in the chair next to the bed, wishing they could talk as they had as girls, when they had been closer than close, confidantes.

Emmy's breathing grew even and steady, and Becca started talking about things she thought Emmy would like to know. "Abby's in love, Emmy. I know she's young, and part of me wants to tell her all the reasons why getting serious now will complicate her life. But another part of me knows that my disapproval will probably only push her away."

She reached for Emmy's hand, lacing her fingers with hers. "She's such an amazing young woman. Smart and kind. She reminds me so much of you."

A single tear slid from Emmy's closed eyes. Becca felt as if her heart were caught in a vice, and she pressed her lips together to keep the sob rising in her throat from escaping.

Emmy squeezed Becca's hand, and for a moment, Becca thought her sister might speak. But the moment passed. The silence stretched out between them, and Becca regretted her own neediness. "Everything is fine, Emmy. Abby is fine. It's all going to be okay. I promise."

Emmy closed her eyes again, but kept her hand clasped with Becca's. Becca sat in the hard-back chair until her sister's breathing altered and the steady rhythm of sleep took hold. Only then did Becca get up and quietly leave the room.

∞

Then

BECCA WAS TEN years old and Emmy eight the summer they went for a swim in the creek that ran through the middle of their farm. Their mama had gone into town for groceries, their daddy helping Dr. Thompson, the local vet, castrate calves since early that morning.

The day was typical July in Virginia, hot and muggy, the air so thick it was hard to breathe. It hadn't rained in two weeks, and even the trees looked thirsty, their normally green leaves tinted with brown.

It had been Becca's idea to slip off for a quick dunk in the cool water. That was usually the way it had gone with the two of them, Becca the instigator of anything questionable they might do. Emmy went along because she trusted her the way younger sisters trusted older sisters, as if they had the secrets to the universe already figured out.

Under the heat of a July day, the creek was an inviting

oasis, and there on the bank Becca immediately began shucking off her dress.

"What are you doing?" Emmy asked, unbuckling her shoe.

"I'm tired of swimming in my clothes," she said.

"But we're not supposed to swim without them," she said.

"Who's going to know?" Becca pulled off her camisole and underwear.

Emmy stared at her, gasping. "Well, we will. That's who."

"Don't be silly. I don't want to wear a wet dress back to the house. I won't tell if you won't."

Naked, she scrambled up the bank to the rope their daddy had hung for them from the sturdy limb of an old paw paw tree.

"Becca Miller, have you lost your mind?"

Not once in her life had Becca ever done anything like this. What initiated it, she didn't know, but it felt alarmingly good to be on the other side of the rules for once. She climbed the tree and grabbed for the rope, leaping out and holding on. The rope swung over the creek and then back. She yelped once in sheer happiness, ignoring Emmy's shrieks from below. Midway over the creek, she let go, plunging into the cool water. She came up laughing.

Emmy stood glaring at her with her arms folded across her chest.

"Come on," Becca said. "You're not going to believe how good it feels!"

"Mama will kill us if she finds out."

"How's she going to find out? It's so hot our hair will be dry before she gets back home." Becca headed up the bank again, waving for Emmy to come on. "Chicken!"

Grinning now, Emmy began unbuttoning her dress,

watching while Becca swung out over the creek again and took another plunge. This time, she followed her naked up the bank, and Becca let her go first, cheering when she released the rope and dropped into the water.

Emmy popped back to the surface with a look of amazement on her face. For the next hour, they hooted and hollered like two wild children, racing each other back to the shore to see who could get up the tree first.

When their daddy appeared on the other side of the creek, a look of crushing disappointment on his face, Emmy immediately began to cry.

"Put your clothes on right this minute," he said in a voice Becca had never heard him use before.

They both slunk toward the pile of clothes on the bank, like Adam and Eve being banished from the garden. They tugged their dresses on as quickly as their wet skin would allow and then followed him back to the house, Emmy in front, Becca behind her. She stared at Emmy's back, her little sister's head hung in shame. She walked with her own chin in the air, still holding the position that they hadn't done anything wrong.

The two of them followed their daddy to the barn where he pulled out the belt he had threatened to use before, but never had. Becca supposed that this time, he didn't feel he had any choice.

"Daddy, can I take Emmy's whipping?" she said, stepping forward. "It was my idea. She wanted to swim in her clothes."

Her father looked at her, then shook his head. "Maybe you'll think about that the next time you pull your sister into your decision to do wrong."

Emmy went first, and as Becca stood there watching the red welts rise on her little sister's legs, she felt sick with regret. The whipping she received afterwards was almost a relief. Years down the road, she would wish that the other mistakes she'd made could be so easily paid for.

28

Legends Get Dumped, Too

> *"Study the past if you would define the future."*
> — ***Confucius***

Now

There is truth to the old adage that some things never change, no matter how much time passes.

The Red Robin was one of them.

From the front entrance, Matt spotted Wilks Perdue across the room at one of the pool tables. Wilks held up a stick and waved him back. Matt weaved his way through the crowd, smoke hanging over the tables like low grey clouds.

"Hey, man," Wilks said, clapping him on the back, a cigarette dangling from the corner of his mouth. He'd cleaned up well. Gone were the grease-stained overalls, in their place a white button-down and Levi's. His dark hair had been combed back with some kind of gel that made him look somewhere between hip and behind the times.

"Hey," Matt said, nodding at a couple of younger guys standing nearby, curiosity clear on their faces.

Wilks introduced them, then dropped an arm around

a passing waitress, ordering a fresh round of beer and a glass for Matt. He started to decline, then decided why not.

"You still play?" Wilks asked, crushing his cigarette in a nearby ashtray and passing him a stick.

"Probably not since the last time you and I were here," he said.

The waitress came back with the beer and filled their glasses. Wilks handed her a twenty, telling her to keep the change. She smiled, thanked him, and headed back to the bar. He reached down as she passed and gave her backside a squeeze. She threw him a look over her shoulder. Wilks gave Matt a what's-a-guy-to-do shrug and a wink that brought him back to those days in high school when he and Wilks both thought they'd been put on earth for the sole purpose of indulging their sexual needs. He'd felt every bit as deserving as Wilks in those days. He'd been so high on his own local fame that if a girl didn't fall at his feet, he just raised the heat of his efforts until she did.

He took a swallow of his beer, watching while Wilks racked the balls and nodded for him to break. Matt aimed the cue ball at the center, sending the red and green zipping into parallel side pockets.

"Damn," Wilks said, chalking the end of his cue. "You sure you haven't been playing?"

"I'm sure," he said.

They went at it a while, one shot better than the next. A crowd began to gather around. Someone ordered another pitcher of beer. Wilks took the first game. Matt conceded with a nod. They finished off their glasses and racked the balls again. He felt the old competitiveness between them take hold, telling himself he should stop this and go home, that if not, they would very likely end up in a pissing contest. But he didn't want to go, unable to shake the feeling that something between them never got played out, that he needed to tie up loose ends.

The second game was Matt's, the third belonged to Wilks. They were two-thirds of the way through the fourth when he said, "So what happened between you and Becca, anyway?"

"She dumped me," he said, aiming at the solid purple and smacking it into a side pocket.

"That had to suck."

"Actually, it did."

"So legends get dumped, too?"

Matt looked around, spotting one of Wilks's groupies smiling at him. He wondered if she were even old enough to be in the bar. She was blonde, lean and leggy, a combination of fresh-from-the-farm and been-there-done-that. "Dumb girl," she said.

There had been a time in his life when he would have taken the opinion, unsolicited though it was, as confirmation of his own conclusion. Becca was the one who missed out. The one who took another road, got left behind. He'd gone on to bigger and better, and she'd stayed here with Aaron.

Now, he wasn't anywhere close to sure who got left behind.

"See, man," Wilks said, offering him a high five. "Even chicks who were in elementary school when you were the big star around here know who you are."

Matt took his next shot. "Then I guess it was all worth it, huh?"

Wilks laughed, shrugging off his sarcasm. "Hell, yeah, it was worth it. Don't tell me you wouldn't go back if you could. Cheerleaders hanging all over you like you were box office gold."

"The glory days," Matt said, while the ladies who had

gathered around for the show erupted in a chorus of giggles.

"You got that right," Wilks said, angling an arm around the waist of the blonde as if to prove he still had it. She raised her face to his, and Wilks claimed her with a kiss.

By ten-thirty, Matt had grown weary of the whole scene. They played a couple more rounds, ending up with an equal number of games on their scorecards. He put the pool stick back on its wall rack just short of midnight. "I'm done," he said. The groupies had gone to the bathroom to freshen up, so he and Wilks were the only two at the table.

"You want some company tonight?" he said. "Sandy gave Mimi the cue. She's yours if you want her."

Matt heard the words, and yet it took a moment for them to register. Had he ever been such a jerk? But then he knew the answer, felt himself blanch beneath its truth. It occurred to him that maybe Becca had been a lot smarter than he'd given her credit for.

The women returned, freshly powdered and poofed. "All yours, Wilks," he said, raising a hand and heading for the door.

"Hey, man," he called out over the music, "you start getting tired of this, then you're old. Just old."

Matt pulled out of the parking lot a few minutes later, Wilks's proposition still fresh. From Ferrum, he headed back down Route 40. On impulse, he took a shortcut he remembered taking with Jacob on sawdust runs to a mill in the Miller's old dump truck. The road wound and turned for seven or eight miles. He stood on the brakes when a possum darted out in front of him, disappearing in the grass on the opposite side of the road. Matt didn't let himself admit where he was going until he turned into the driveway at the top of the hill.

The house sat a quarter mile or so away, a two-story

white farmhouse, L-shaped after an addition in the forties. He remembered this as if it were part of his own history, pieces of information about the place coming back to him now, Becca's voice attached to each of them.

Her mother had grown up here, as had her mother before her. The two-hundred acre farm had once been over five hundred acres, but the family had been forced to sell off part of it during the Depression-era years.

A single light shone from the front porch now. The rest of the house was shadowed in darkness. He wondered which room belonged to Becca and Aaron.

Matt felt like an intruder, sitting there in the dark and staring at this place where Becca still lived. But he couldn't help himself. He imagined her garden, pictured her working in it during the morning hours before the heat bore down with too much intensity. He wondered if the farm looked the same in the light of day. He remembered Aaron as a good man, a hard worker and a friend to Jacob. Could Aaron's influence be seen in the fields around the barn?

Matt cut the engine and the lights and rolled down his window. The farmhouse was no longer visible, but enveloped in the pitch darkness of night, he knew one thing now with sudden glaring certainty. Since the day Becca cut him out of her life, he'd been searching for what the two of them had.

And he never found it.

Not even close.

∞

Then

MATT PICKED ANGIE up at six, and the two of them drove to Roanoke for a seven o'clock movie. They were mostly quiet during the thirty minute ride, making a few false starts at conversations that petered out within a couple of minutes.

Something about the night felt different to Matt, forced, as if they were trying to fix something they had already agreed was unfixable.

Matt had never been good at that, going back on a decision once he'd made it. He wasn't sure why he was doing so now, why he kept looking at her and wishing he felt something, anything that might justify the two of them being together.

But after spending a portion of the past two days listening to Jacob talk about Aaron Brubaker's crush on Becca, Matt had decided a date with Angie was exactly what he needed. That maybe being with her would force him to quit thinking about Becca.

Besides, he could probably count the number of words they'd actually said to one another since that kiss under the oak tree. And yet, he was aware of her in a way he'd never been aware of anyone in his life. It was like he had a sixth sense for when she was going to walk out of the house, or suddenly appear at the barn. His palms started sweating, and his heart felt like it was going to trip out of his chest. A girl had never had this effect on him before. His ability to stay cool was something he'd always taken pride in, bragged about in the locker room with the other jocks who viewed dating as a necessary detour on the road to getting laid. All of a sudden, he was thinking about asking Becca out on a real date, found himself creating scenarios that might impress her.

As for Becca, he was beginning to think she'd erased that kiss under the oak tree from her mind as something altogether insignificant. She found other things to look at when she was around him. Like he was the most uninteresting person she'd ever met. But then he would find himself wondering if maybe she was aware of him, too.

Matt and Angie both found the movie less than stellar, the popcorn pretty much its only selling point. Afterwards, they stopped for pizza, even though Matt wasn't hungry.

It was almost ten-thirty by the time they pulled into the Dairy Queen parking lot in Ballard, the mutually agreed upon meeting place where everyone ended up on Saturday nights. Within shouting distance of the Minute Market, it maintained a steady stream of cars circling in and out. As soon as Matt cut the engine to the Jeep, Angie hopped out and headed for a group of friends who waved her over with smiles that demanded she tell all. Matt wondered if she would be honest and say that so far their date had sucked or if she would dress it up as something other than what it had been.

He walked over to Wilks's Mustang, shooting the breeze with a few guys sitting on the hood of his car. Wilks came out of the Minute Market, a pack of cigarettes and a lighter in his hand. He clapped Matt on the shoulder, shaking his head. "I didn't figure you two would be wasting any time hanging out here tonight," he said, shooting a glance at Angie a few car lengths away. She laughed at something Mimi Parker had just said, her head thrown back a little so that her dark hair swung in a curtain against her bare shoulders. "If I could have a night alone with that work of art," he added, "there's no way I'd be wasting time with this bunch of jerks."

Matt leaned up against the door of the car. "Maybe you should've asked her out then," he said, his tone not quite as lighthearted as he had intended.

Wilks lit a cigarette, taking a long pull and then blowing it out through the center of his lips. "Maybe you hadn't noticed, but she's not aiming it at anybody but you."

He heard the envy in his friend's voice and realized it should bother him.

A dark blue Chevrolet pickup idled by, a plain black sedan right behind it. Matt glanced at the truck and recognized the driver as Aaron Brubaker. Sitting next to him in the middle of the seat was Becca, a younger boy on her right.

His mouth went completely dry, and he barely listened as Wilks told him he should invite Angie out to the lake tomorrow. He stared at the truck where it sat parked in front of the Dairy Queen, headlights flashing off. The driver's door opened. Aaron slid out, holding up a hand for Becca, who put her palm in his and slipped down, releasing his hand to smooth the skirt of her dress. The younger boy riding with them walked around the truck, and they joined the two guys and girls getting out of the sedan. One of the girls Matt recognized as Becca's sister, Emmy.

The group stood out in the parking lot full of teenagers wearing cut off jeans and t-shirts. Aaron and the other guys wore dark pants and long-sleeve shirts, straw hats on their heads. Emmy and the other girl wore the dresses and capes of the Old Order, white bonnets covering their hair. Becca's dress was light green and simple, her long hair caught in a ponytail that nearly reached her waist.

Aaron said something, removed the straw hat from his head and made a mock bow. They all laughed. It was the sound of Becca's laughter that his ears automatically singled out, and jealousy ignited inside him. Unfounded as it was, it hovered over him like smoke from a wood stove, filling his lungs to choking point.

"Hey, it's the Little House on the Prairie girl," Wilks

said, his voice booming under the effect of a six-pack of Bud.

Becca looked back, first at Wilks, then Matt. She missed a step, tripping a little. Aaron took her arm, leaned in close, said something, and then smiled.

They followed the rest of the group inside the Dairy Queen, and he gave Wilks a look.

He tossed his cigarette on the pavement and ground it out with the toe of his boot. "So that's how it is. Angie's out and Dunkard babe is in."

Matt's fist itched with the sudden need to wipe the smirk from Wilks's face. "Shut up, man."

Wilks laughed, hooked an arm around Joey Mathers' shoulders and pulled him over. "Hey, Joey, tell Matt Becca Miller's never going to let him under her skirt."

Joey shifted a slow gaze in Matt's direction, his voice flattened with the effects of a recently inhaled joint. "What skirt?"

Wilks gave him a half-playful shove backwards. "Get out of here. You're too stoned to have a valid opinion, anyway."

"Ease up, Wilks," Matt said, taking a step closer.

Wilks held up both hands and grinned. "She brings it out in you, doesn't she? So how you planning to compete with straw-hat boy?" he asked, tossing a glance at the Dairy Queen where Becca and her friends stood at the front counter.

"What is your problem?"

"Hey, I'm not the one trying to figure out which piece of ass is the right one for me," he said, looking at Angie who was now staring in their direction.

Matt turned and started to walk away. Wilks grabbed his arm, laughing now. "Man, can't you take a joke?"

Matt pulled his arm free. "Get off me."

He headed for the Dairy Queen door then, not sure

why he was doing this, aware with every step that he should turn around.

They were all at the cash register, ordering. Matt fell into line behind them. Becca stood in front of him, Aaron beside her, studying the menu. She glanced over her shoulder, her eyes widening at the sight of him.

"Hey," he said.

"Hey." Her voice was cool, and he could see she hadn't missed Wilks's remark.

Aaron turned around, smiling and sticking out his hand.

Matt shook it. "How's it goin'?"

"Matt's helping out at the farm this summer," Becca said, her voice stiff.

Aaron nodded. "Yeah. We met." He put a hand on Becca's shoulder, and Matt didn't think it was his imagination that there was a statement behind it. "We better get something to eat. This girl plays a mean game of softball."

"I'm sure," Matt said. Becca looked up at him then, the same awareness he'd been feeling all week clear in her eyes. The glance between them couldn't have lasted more than a couple of seconds, but it was enough to make him feel as if he'd been given a shot of adrenaline.

"Matt?"

Angie's voice brought him back to the present. Becca glanced over his shoulder, and he felt Angie's hand on his arm. "Wondered where you got off to," she said, stepping in front of him and leaning back against his chest. "Hey, Becca," she said, lacing her fingers through his. "Gosh, I haven't seen you in forever. You quit school, didn't you?"

Becca took a breath. "Yes, I did."

"We used to have English together. Tenth grade, right?"

"Right," Becca said.

"I thought I'd never get through that class," Angie said.

"All those poems. Chaucer and Beowulf. Who actually reads that stuff, anyway?"

Becca smiled a smile that Matt already knew was not her real one, this one stiff and failing to reach her eyes. "Chaucer takes a little time to get used to," she said.

"Yeah, if I remember right, you and Mr. Simmons were the only two in class who got it."

Aaron turned back from the guy he had been talking to. "Our turn to order, Becca," he said.

Becca faced the register and ordered a banana split.

"I could go for one of those," Angie said, tilting her head back to look up at Matt. "Wanna share?"

"You go ahead," he said.

Becca and Aaron took their ticket and walked over to the table where the other kids in their group were sitting. Angie ordered her banana split, and they waited at the front counter. She put her arms around his neck, pulling his head down so that her mouth was close to his ear. "Wilks said I better get in here and protect what was mine. Why don't we take our ice cream out to my uncle's place?"

Matt looked over her shoulder to find Becca watching them. He put his hands on Angie's arms, removing them from his neck and making some comment about an early day tomorrow. He glanced back at Becca then, but it was too late. She had already looked away.

29

A Single Seed

> *If you judge people you have no time to love them.*
> – ***Mother Teresa***

Now

As a young person, I'm not sure I ever thought about prejudice. We studied it in school, of course. History classes about our country's time period of slavery, and then later on, segregation between blacks and whites. And, too, its reach to other parts of the world where men like Adolph Hitler killed millions of Jewish people because they were thought to be inferior.

I remember wondering in those history classes how hatred could get so big and out of control. How it could lead to such acts of horror. That there must have been some enormous instigating factor to justify turning a person's life into a nightmare. It seemed unbelievable to me, almost like someone must have exaggerated the eventual outcome, that people couldn't have been as evil as history recorded them to be.

And if they had been, how did they get that way?

The answer is still hard for me to accept. But I know it's true. I've seen with my own eyes the tragedy that can result from a single seed of hate. That's all it takes, really, just one.

It's easy to miss at first, a seemingly benign judgmental word, resentment, jealousy. In the same way that the wind blows spores of a dandelion across a green yard, and they begin to pop up everywhere, the same is true of hatred, the seeds multiplying one by one until the landscape it has fallen upon is forever changed.

30

Unexpected Encounter

You don't choose your family. They are God's gift to you, as you are to them.
*– **Desmond Tutu***

Now

It was just after one-thirty a.m. when Martha pulled into the Wal-mart parking lot, seven or eight cars scattered about in nearby spaces. She saved her shopping for the night hours when real sleep was nothing more than a distant memory.

The first couple of hours after she went to bed, she usually managed to doze off from sheer fatigue. But the rest of the night she would lie on her back, staring at the ceiling, one thought after another flitting through her mind until they were so tangled, she would wrest herself from bed just to escape their hold.

Tonight had been no exception.

She got out of her car and hurried into the store, nodding a greeting to an employee in a blue vest who was sweeping the walkway at the main entrance.

Inside, the whir of a vacuum cleaner competed with the music playing from ceiling speakers. Martha reached for a cart and pulled a shopping list from her purse. She headed with purpose then for the aisles containing cleaning supplies. To her basket, she added Comet, Windex, and Johnson's furniture polish. From there, she made her way to the back of the store, picking out some white hand towels to replace those of her own that had grown thin with use.

She passed two other customers, the only other people in sight a young woman with frizzy red hair counting items on a shelf and making notes on a clipboard. She found the towels, counted out a half-dozen and made her way toward the grocery section. She turned a corner and bumped the edge of someone else's cart.

"I'm sorry," she began to apologize, glancing up with a smile and then feeling it freeze on her face.

The woman staring back at her wore the same expression, both of them standing there for several long moments, the silence hovering between them awkward and choking.

Martha supposed that this had been inevitable. Amazing, really, that it hadn't happened before now. Ballard wasn't that big a town, after all.

"Mrs. Miller," the younger woman said.

"Linda." Martha nodded, trying to say something more but feeling as if her vocal chords had suddenly been cut. She could not make a single sound come out. It was then that she noticed the young boy standing next to her daughter-in-law.

"Mrs. Miller," Linda said, her voice respectful, "I'd like to introduce you to your grandson."

Martha stared at him, one hand going to her chest as if she could still her heart's sudden flutter. She could see her son in the boy, the features so clear and familiar that it was as if Jacob were right here in front of her, ten years old again. The only difference that the boy's skin was darker, the color of caramel candy. Everything else about him had the clear stamp of her son.

"Hello, ma'am," the boy said, his voice shy.

"Hello," she managed. "Are you here alone?"

"Jacob's at home with one of the goats. She's in labor," Linda said, putting a hand on the boy's shoulder. "Michael's had a cold. Our humidifier broke, and since neither of us was sleeping, we came out to get another."

"I'm sorry you're not feeling well," Martha said, gripping the handle of her cart.

"Thanks," he said. "My daddy's told me about you. Why don't we ever come to see you?"

The question hung there between the three of them, issued with nothing more than a child's honest curiosity. Martha had no idea how to answer. Over the years, she'd built up a fortress of reasons, and yet not one of them came to her now.

"Michael," Linda said, touching his shoulder, and then saying, "we'd better go."

"Of course," Martha said, unable to look at the boy.

Linda took his hand and pushed her cart on. A few feet away, she stopped and said, "Mrs. Miller?"

Feeling as if there were a knife stuck in her back, Martha said, "Yes?"

"Jacob would love to see you. You're welcome at our home anytime."

They walked on without looking back again. Martha stood there in the same spot after they disappeared from sight. Never in her life had she felt more alone.

A sob welled up in her throat. She pressed her hand to her mouth, and left the cart where it sat. She began walking then, her steps faster and faster until she was almost running from the store.

31

Cherry Picking

> *"Nothing ever becomes real 'til it is experienced."*
> — ***John Keats***

Now

Becca got up with the sun and picked another round of lettuce from her garden, tucking the tender leaves of burgundy and green inside large plastic Ziploc bags and labeling them with the name of the restaurant to which they had been promised. She then set out another row of tomato plants along with a row of Crookneck squash.

She woke Abby around seven-thirty and asked if she'd like to go back to the lake house today. Abby mumbled something that sounded like yes and then groped her way to the shower through half-open eyes. Becca went back downstairs and started a pot of vegetable soup to have for supper later. She carried Emmy's breakfast up, helped her dress and then took her down to sit under the oak in the back yard where their mother could see her from the kitchen window.

Emmy clung to Becca a little this morning, as if she knew she was going somewhere different and didn't want her to go. Becca sat with her a few minutes, looking out at the fields behind the house, at the blue-tinged crest of Tinker's Knob farther beyond. If Emmy was happy anywhere, it was here under this old tree. The two of them had spent so much of their childhood playing beneath it, entertaining their rag dolls with picnics of acorns and pokeberries. It seemed so long ago, and she wanted to ask Emmy if she remembered, but stopped herself, knowing she wouldn't answer.

"Mama will be out in a few minutes to check on you," Becca said. "Abby and I will be back this afternoon."

At this, Emmy looked to the mountain and folded her hands in her lap, as if resigned to Becca's going.

A few minutes later, Becca found Abby waiting at the front of the house. They slid in the truck and drove the twenty-some miles out to the lake with only a few words of conversation between them. It was a good quiet though. It had always been like this with them. As if they communicated through silence as easily as with words.

They'd almost arrived at the turnoff when Abby looked at her and said, "This house will be good for you, Mama. I'm glad you have it."

"Thank you, honey," Becca said, hearing the catch in her own voice.

"Can I be honest with you about something?"

Becca flipped the blinker, tapping the brakes and steering the old truck onto the gravel road. She glanced across at the child she loved more than she could even find the words to express. "Of course you can."

Abby pulled her braid over her left shoulder, worrying the end with her fingers. "You're always there for everybody in our family. Daddy, Grandma, Aunt Emmy and me. I don't see what could be so wrong with you having something for yourself."

Tears clouded Becca's vision then, and she couldn't

speak for the knot of gratitude lodged in her throat. She did not deserve this child or her unflagging loyalty. "I don't begrudge my life, Abby."

"I know. But sometimes, I just wonder why we have to choose between the way we live and wanting to do something else with our lives. Did you ever question it?"

Becca didn't answer for a moment or two. It seemed impossible to find the words. Finally, she said, "At one time, I wasn't sure which life I would choose. I remember how bad it felt to even consider giving one up for the other. Is that what you're thinking about?"

"I guess," she said, rubbing a thumb over the back of one hand. "I love our life. But I want to go to college. I want to be a veterinarian. One of my teachers told me about the Griffith scholarship. I'm going to apply for it."

A little stunned, Becca slowed the truck to a stop at the back of the house and cut the engine. Abby had never said anything like this before.

She turned in the seat, putting one hand on her shoulder and giving it a squeeze. "Abby, you're the only one who can decide what's right for you. One of the hardest things about being a grown-up is the choices we have to make. I wish I could say you can have everything you want. But it doesn't work that way. The one thing I can say for sure is that no matter what you choose, I will always love you. That, you never have to doubt."

Abby scooted across the seat, putting her arms around Becca's neck and hugging her hard. They sat this way for a bit, and Becca wondered if it would always be like this between them. If the truth ever found its way out, would Abby still love her with this kind of fierceness?

Abby pulled away first, wiping her face with the back of her hand. "Do you mind if I apply for the scholarship?"

Becca glanced down at her hands and then into Abby's

earnest eyes. "If it's what you want, Abby. Just be sure, okay?"

Abby hugged her again then. "Thank you, Mama."

Becca pressed one hand to the back of her head, feeling somehow as if they'd reached a divide in the road, and that, soon, Abby would veer off in a different direction, finding her way out into the world and possibly never coming back. The thought flooded her with a wash of panic, and she wondered, suddenly, if this was what her own mother had felt at the thought of losing her.

They spent the next few hours in the house, working in the living room downstairs and then the bedrooms upstairs. It was almost three o'clock when Abby declared it time for a break. They went outside, taking the jug of lemonade she had brought along down to the water. Abby took off her shoes and danced in, holding her yellow cotton dress up above her knees.

Becca sat in the grass and watched, enjoying the summer sun on her face.

They'd been sitting for a few minutes when a car pulled up to the house.

"Mama, someone's here," Abby said.

Becca turned around and spotted Matt walking through the overgrown yard toward them. Her heart thumped once and then started beating way too fast. She set her own cup of lemonade down and got to her feet, pressed shaking hands to the skirt of her dress.

"Hello," he said from a few yards away, his voice low as if he were unsure of his welcome.

"Hi," she managed to answer.

"I'm sorry for barging in. I just drove out to take a last look at the place."

"Oh," she said, awkward. "Of course. We were just doing some cleaning."

He nodded. "I stuck my head in the back door when I saw the truck. You've been busy."

Suddenly remembering that Abby stood behind her, Becca turned with reluctance and beckoned her forward. "Abby, this is an old friend of mine, Matt Griffith. Matt, this is my daughter Abby."

Abby walked up, taking Becca's elbow as if she somehow knew she needed the support. "Hello," she said. "It's nice to meet you."

Matt stared at Abby, a flicker of question in his eyes. "Nice to meet you, too," he said. He took a step back then, raising a hand. "I didn't mean to interrupt your day. I'll come back another time."

Becca told herself to let him go. There was no doubt it would be the wisest choice. She hadn't expected to see him, but now that he was here, she didn't want him to leave. "You should look around," she said.

He stopped, glancing from her to Abby.

"I mean, you drove all the way out here," she added. "Please. Stay as long as you want."

"Yeah, Mr. Griffith," Abby said. "But watch out. Mama might just put you to work. She pays well though. DQ Blizzards."

He raised an eyebrow, a smile touching his mouth. "Persuasive."

Abby smiled back at him, picking up her shoes and saying, "I'm going to finish working. You two probably have some catching up to do."

"Abby, you don't have to—" Becca began, even as she jogged toward the house.

"She's a beautiful girl," Matt said.

"Yes." Becca folded her arms and looked at the lake. "Inside, too."

"I see that."

"I don't take any credit for it. She was born that way,"

she said and then wondered what he must think of such a comment.

"She reminds me of you," he said. "Her manner. The way she smiles."

Whether he meant to or not, there was no greater compliment he could have paid her. "Thank you," she said.

It was hard to look at him. Harder still to believe they were here together in this place where they'd once spent some of the most memorable hours of her life. Her face heated at the memories. She wondered if he remembered the same things.

"This is the first time I've been back to the lake since I left for college," he said, shoving his hands in the pockets of his jeans, his gaze somewhere left of her.

"Why?" she asked before she could stop herself. Over the years, she'd pictured him coming here for visits with his wife, the two of them swimming off the dock, lazing on the grass in the summer sun.

He looked at her then, direct, as if she should know the answer. "It didn't seem right," he said.

She knew she should ignore the unspoken implication beneath his words, but she couldn't find the will. "Why?"

A string of moments slid by before he said, "Because you weren't here."

There. She'd wanted to know if he remembered. If she were the only one of them who felt a genuine ache for the happiness they had known here. "Matt—" she began.

"Would you rather I lie?" he asked. "Would that make it easier?"

Bitterness edged the questions. Maybe this surprised her most. Somehow, she had imagined him reading her letter all those years ago and tossing it in the trashcan on his way out to some college frat party at UVA.

In his face, she saw that she had been wrong to make

such an assumption. "No," she said, glancing away before letting him see something she shouldn't.

"Becca," he said. "Look at me."

For several moments, she refused. She felt completely transparent, as if he could see every feeling pulsing through her heart the way an x-ray brought into clear view the individual bones of the body. She was vulnerable in a way she did not want to be. She finally looked at him and said, "I should go."

"Mama! Mr. Griffith!"

She turned to see Abby running toward them, a white bucket swinging from one hand. All smiles.

"What is it, honey?" Becca asked, forcing a normal note into her voice.

"There's a cherry tree in the field on the other side of the house. It's loaded with ripe cherries. Is it all right if we pick them?"

Becca glanced at Matt, but he said, "Becca? They're your cherries."

"I—sure, honey."

"I could use some help," Abby said. "There must be a million back there."

Matt looked at Becca and said, "Guess we'd better pitch in then."

An hour later, the three of them had filled Abby's original bucket to the top and were half-way through another one. Abby took charge as the leader, climbing from limb to limb, pointing Matt and Becca toward the largest clusters. Their fingertips turned red, their tongues, too, from the vast quantity they ate while working. Matt's ease with Abby was something Becca had not expected. He told them how his grandmother used to make cherry pies every summer with the cherries they picked here. And how he could still remember eating until he couldn't hold another bite.

"Mama makes a wonderful cherry pie," Abby declared, popping another into her mouth. "Maybe she'll make you one."

Becca looked at Matt, her face warm from the sun, warmer still from the way he studied her. For whatever reason, Abby had taken a liking to Matt. Assumed they would be seeing him again. "I'm sure Matt's wife is a very good cook," she said.

"Then you should take some cherries back with you," Abby said.

He remained quiet for a moment, and then, "She's never cared too much about cooking. Actually, we're not together anymore."

At this, Becca's bucket slipped from her fingers to the ground. Cherries rolled out from it like a red velvet carpet. She dropped to her knees and started picking them up. Matt squatted down beside her, helping without saying anything. "I'm sorry," she finally managed. "I didn't realize you were–"

"Yeah," he said.

She wanted to ask more, but Abby made no attempt to hide her interest. Becca pressed her lips together and kept quiet.

They took their full buckets back to the house, and at Abby's insistence, rinsed them beneath the spigot out back. Once they were finished, Becca stood and said, "It's getting late, Abby. We'd better get home."

"Okay," she said, drying her hands on the skirt of her dress. "I'll go inside and get our things."

Becca and Matt watched her dart across the grass, the screen door at the back of the house clapping shut behind her.

Matt looked at Becca then, his eyes searching her face. "Will you be back tomorrow?" he asked.

She looked down, not sure how to answer. She wanted

to say yes and knew with unequivocal certainty that she should not. "I can't," she said.

"Why?"

She looked at him then, unable to ignore the quiet plea in his voice. "Matt, you know this isn't something we should do."

"I just want to talk, Becca. Isn't what we had worthy of a conversation?"

She tried to answer, but couldn't seem to make any words come out.

The door opened, and Abby headed toward them, a bundle of cleaning towels under one arm.

"I'll be here at noon," Matt said, his voice low. "Come back, Becca. Please."

She didn't answer him. Couldn't. She picked up the buckets of cherries and headed for the truck, certain Abby would see the guilt on her face.

Abby followed her across the yard, getting in on the other side. Becca started the truck and backed out of the driveway, waving in Matt's direction without looking at him.

They were a mile or two down the road when Abby said, "We sure did leave fast."

Becca stared straight ahead. "I have to get supper ready," she said.

"Um," Abby said, as if she were having trouble believing the excuse.

"You could have called and asked Grandma to start it," Abby said.

"There was no need for that."

"You were visiting with an old friend, someone you haven't seen in a long time. That should qualify as a need."

"Abby—"

"You never put yourself first, Mama." Disapproval laced

Abby's voice, something she had never before aimed at Becca.

"Where is this coming from, Abby?" Becca asked.

"Well, it's true, isn't it?"

"I have no reason to complain."

"Maybe I'm complaining for you." She folded her arms and glanced out the window. "I saw the way he looked at you."

Becca had no idea what to say. Abby had learned the art of waiting, though, and she was silent for so long that Becca finally said, "I think you were seeing something that wasn't there."

"When you knew each other before, he was serious about you, wasn't he?"

Becca sighed. "We were very young, Abby."

"How young?"

She wanted to end this conversation, and yet she knew not answering would only give Abby more fuel for this fire she'd started to stoke. "He was eighteen. I was seventeen."

"So what happened? Who broke it off between you?"

"I did," she said.

"Why?"

"Honey. It was all a long time ago. Matt and I. . .it would never have worked."

Abby stared out the window, her expression distant. Becca glanced at her cherry-stained hands, feeling something in her heart flip. Surely, Abby was comparing what happened with Matt and her to what might happen with her and this boy she had fallen in love with.

"Are you sure?" Abby asked.

She nodded, not trusting her own voice to hold up under such a question.

They drove another mile or so before Abby spoke

again, determination underlining each word. "It's not going to be like that for Beau and me. I won't let it."

Becca could only hope she was right. Because how could she tell her that sometimes people didn't get what they wanted? That maybe they were wrong to ever want it in the first place.

∞

Then

THE DAYS FOLLOWING their encounter at the Dairy Queen were awkward to say the least.

Becca did her best to avoid Matt. But it didn't seem that she could walk three feet on any corner of the farm without running into him. It was almost as if he were seeking her out, then changing his mind when he actually had the chance to speak to her.

It wasn't until one afternoon when they'd finished the last milking, and they found themselves alone in the barn together that he approached her and said, "Could we go for a walk or something?"

Becca blinked once, a trio of excuses at the ready, each of which instantly dispersed beneath the look in his blue eyes like dandelions to a spring wind. "I have a few minutes before I need to help with supper."

"Good, then," he said, stepping aside to let her lead the way through the back door of the barn. Outside, they walked next to one another, the sinking summer sun warm on their shoulders, the smell of fresh cut grass in the air. "I wanted to apologize for the other night."

"You don't need to," she said.

"Yeah, I do. Wilks can get a little carried away sometimes."

"Is that what you call it?" Becca said, startled by her own anger.

Matt looked out across the field, as if considering his next words. "He hasn't had the best example to grow up by. When we were in the second grade, I spent the night at his house. We were outside playing in the yard when his Daddy got home from work. He was yelling and cussing about some guy who 'was too stupid to know piss from a Mountain Dew if it came in a green can.'"

"So just because his daddy sees the rest of the world as falling short of ideal, it's okay for Wilks to do so, too?"

"I didn't say that. But maybe it means that some people can't help what they grow up hearing."

Becca was quiet for a moment and then, "At some point, doesn't it have to become about our own choices? Aren't we ultimately responsible for what we decide to be?"

"He's my friend, Becca."

To this, she said nothing. What was there to say?

They headed across a recently mowed hay field, the land dipping and lifting until they reached the creek, tall oaks and maples throwing dappled shade across its gurgling surface. Becca resolved to put aside what had happened the other night. She didn't want to think about that. Right now, she just wanted to savor being here with Matt.

"I love the sound of the water against the rocks," she said. "It's like music. If you listen, you can hear the individual notes."

"It's peaceful," he said. No one had ever spoken like this to him before. Turning to look at her, he kept his hands deep in the front pockets of his jeans as if he were afraid they might do something he hadn't given them permission to do. "You come out here a lot?" he asked.

"When I can."

"It's good to have a place that's yours. Remember that secret room I told you about when we were kids?"

She leaned back. "You remember that?"

"Yeah. Your mama wouldn't let you look."

"I really wanted to," she said. "Is that where you go? To be alone."

He nodded. "Sometimes. When I need to think about things."

Becca found a grassy spot at the edge of the creek and sat down, folding her legs beneath her. Matt hesitated and then sat down next to her. "You have a lot to think about?" she said, aiming for a light note.

"More and more."

She turned to look at him, a half-smile lightening her words. "From the surface, it seems like you've got it all together."

"Glad to know I've got somebody convinced," he said.

Becca leaned forward, dug her fingers into a sandy spot and then let it sift back through. "Could I ask you something?"

"Sure," he said.

"What happened to your mama and daddy?"

Matt picked up a small rock, skipped it across the creek's surface. He didn't answer for a good while, and when he did, his voice wasn't that of the overly-confident baseball player who had come to work on the farm just a few weeks before. "They died when I was six."

"Oh," she said, wishing suddenly that she hadn't asked. "I'm sorry."

He shrugged, as if it had all been too long ago to matter.

"Do you remember them?"

"Sometimes," he said. "Not a whole picture or anything. Just pieces. Like my mom's smile when she would wake me up in the morning. Or my dad's laugh when he thought something I did was funny."

Becca swallowed hard and put her hand on his, not knowing what to say.

He was quiet for a few moments, and then, "I was with them that day. In the back seat when we hit the ice. I remember the car starting to slide and the way it felt like it would never stop."

"Oh, Matt," she said.

"Right before it happened, they were laughing at something on the radio. Then all of a sudden, it stopped, like someone had pushed a button. And everything just got really quiet. All I could hear was the sleet against the car, and then we hit a bank on the side of the road and flipped over."

Becca reached out and put her other hand under his, squeezing hard because she couldn't find any words of comfort.

"No one could explain why I wasn't hurt. I wasn't even wearing a seat belt. They were." He pulled his hand away, as if he didn't deserve the comfort. "And you know the really funny thing?"

"What?" she said, her voice soft.

"There was a circus in Roanoke, and they'd been promising to take me all week. My dad had to work late every night, and so this was the last day. Mama said she didn't think we should go because of the weather. But I pitched a fit until they gave in. And then they died."

"Matt." Becca reached for his hand again, ignoring his stiff resistance, feeling somehow that he needed her to push through it. "You can't blame yourself for what happened to them. You were a child. You didn't make the decision to go. They did."

He looked at her then, and she saw the regret in his eyes, wondered how this wounded boy had hidden himself so well that she had not caught even a glimpse of him until now.

But then maybe he'd been there all along. Maybe she just hadn't been paying attention, looking only at the surface details. Whatever the explanation, she was wholly drawn to him, a well of tenderness forming somewhere deep inside her so that she only had to think his name to feel its pulse.

She reached out then and put her hand to the side of his face. Her touch startled him, as if it were the last thing he had expected. And yet, instantly, she saw his relief in it, mirrored acknowledgement of her own yearnings.

She had no idea where her courage came from. She'd only been kissed one other time in her life, and she had not been the initiator of that seriously disappointing encounter. But she leaned in now and placed her lips to the line of his jaw, light as a butterfly's landing, then the corner of his mouth, imbuing each kiss with her own unyielding need to heal him. To somehow bring closure to the Matt of here and now, the Matt who had let himself be defined by the unwitting actions of a six-year old boy.

It was Matt who kissed her then, really kissed her, laying her back against the sandy bank, as if this weren't the first time, as if they already knew how to please one another. Becca had no idea how this could be so, but she loved the heavy feel of him, the way she felt small and protected beneath him, as if she had finally found the place where she belonged.

Around them, the heat of the summer afternoon began to give way to dusk, the air cooling and thinning beneath the lightening humidity. Becca heard the sounds of the farm in the distance, cows lowing, the start of a tractor engine. Entwined with it, the rasp of their own breathing.

Matt kissed her neck and then her ear, propping up on one elbow to look down at her with questions in his eyes.

She heard them clearly, as if he had voiced them out loud. "I don't know," she said.

"I do," he countered.

"Matt-"

"I know what you're going to say," he said, winding his hand through her hair. "That your parents won't approve. That we're too different. That this will never work."

"I wasn't going to say it. But that doesn't mean it's not true."

"It's only true if we let it be."

"You really believe that?"

"Yeah. I do."

And in that moment, as the summer dusk began to descend into evening, she thought he really did. In truth, so did she.

32

Connection

In nature we never see anything isolated, but everything in connection with something else which is before it, beside it, under it and over it.
– Johann Wolfgang von Goethe

Now

After supper, Abby took her aunt a plate of cherry pie, putting it on a tray, along with a glass of milk and a yellow paper napkin.

Upstairs, she knocked at the door, then opened it to find the lamp beside Emmy's bed on. Emmy stared at the shadows on the wall, and Abby wondered, as she always did, what she was thinking. She wondered if she had real thoughts or if there was just emptiness where hopes and memories used to live.

She set the tray on Emmy's nightstand and sat down on the corner of the bed. "Mama made this pie," she said. "I know you like it, so I brought you some."

Emmy continued to stare at the wall, and Abby wasn't sure she even knew she was there. "Here, I'll help you," she said, picking up the plate.

Emmy looked at her then, a jerk of her head, as if she had just realized she was in the room. Abby offered her a bite of the pie, and she took it, a little flash of pleasure lighting her face as her taste buds absorbed the flavor. The sight of it made Abby happy. She rarely saw anything but blankness in her aunt's eyes.

She fed her the rest of the bowl, and Emmy drank half of the milk. Abby put everything back on the tray with a sudden sense that her aunt was glad she'd been the one to bring it to her. It had been this way between them for as long as she could remember. Emmy had never spoken a single word to her, but Abby had always sensed a connection between them, waves of understanding that felt almost like a kind of telepathy. She'd even gone to the library one time and checked out a couple of books on the subject, trying to figure out if what she felt was real. She still didn't know whether it was or not. But at some point, she'd decided to just accept that whatever it was, it didn't need an explanation.

"Would you like for me to take your hair down?" she asked, leaning over to remove Emmy's bonnet. She'd seen her mama do this a thousand times, and she kept her hands gentle in the same way she did. She lay the bonnet on the bed, opened the nightstand drawer and removed a brush. She pulled the pins from the bun at the nape of her aunt's neck, her long, thick hair tumbling down her back.

It was still beautiful, dark and shiny, although the gray streaks were becoming more noticeable. Abby slid the brush through it, and Emmy leaned her head back as if the attention felt good. She kept going long after the tangles were gone, just because it seemed like a small thing to do if it gave Emmy any kind of pleasure at all.

The lamp threw a shadow across the room, and through the cracked window on the other side of the bed,

Abby heard the frogs start up. "There they are," she said. "Just like clockwork."

Emmy turned toward the sound and tipped her head back, as if it reminded her of something good from long ago.

Abby wondered what it would be like to live as her aunt lived. Here, but not really. She'd been like this Abby's entire life. Abby didn't remember her any other way. She wondered what Emmy had wanted when she was young, before this happened to her. If she'd had dreams of being something, doing something. It seemed like the cruelest of fates, hanging suspended between a world she couldn't really be a part of and the one waiting for her in the distance.

No one really knew how much Emmy took in of the world around her, whether she understood what was said to her. Abby liked to think she did. It was too awful to imagine otherwise.

The door opened. Her mama stepped into the room, a soft smile on her face. "Hi," she said. "Everything all right?"

"Yeah. I was just brushing Aunt Emmy's hair."

"Want me to finish?" she asked.

"I'm okay."

Becca walked over to the bed and sat down. She picked up her hand and smoothed her fingers back and forth across Emmy's wrist. "Are you tired tonight?" she said.

No answer came, but Abby liked that her mama talked to her aunt this way. As if there were every chance that one day, she would answer the way she once had. Grandma talked to her in a completely different way, like Aunt Emmy was a three-year-old with no ability to understand anything at all. Abby knew she meant well, but she thought her mother's way showed that she still had hope for Aunt Emmy.

"Why don't we go ahead and get your nightgown on?" Becca said now, getting up to open a dresser drawer and pulling out a freshly laundered one.

They both removed Emmy's shoes, then her dress and cape, before helping her into the nightgown. They settled her into bed against the pillows then, tucking the covers around her waist.

"I can read to her for a little while," Abby offered.

"I will tonight," Becca said.

"Okay. I've got some homework, anyway."

"Good-night, honey."

"Good-night." Abby kissed her mother on the cheek and then reached over and kissed Aunt Emmy as well. Her hand fell across Abby's, and for a moment Abby thought she felt the briefest squeeze.

In that moment, she remembered something that had happened at church one Sunday when she was a little girl, maybe four or five years old. It had been one of the big meetings of the year where visitors from Ohio and California attended, and people literally spilled out the doors of their small white church. Mostly her memory of that day was fuzzy except for one part. She'd been sitting at a picnic table with her family when Mr. Bowman, one of the church elders, came over and said something to Aunt Emmy. Abby couldn't hear what it was, but he looked at her next with something on his face she'd never seen before. A kind of rejection she did not understand.

Abby had started to cry, although she had no idea why now. She remembered her mama jumping up from the picnic bench and gathering her in her arms, pressing her face to her neck and putting an arm around Aunt Emmy's shoulders at the same time. She knew Mr. Bowman had said something else, had the feeling that she heard it, even though she couldn't remember now what it was. It felt as though there was a hole in the memory, a blank spot that nagged at her like a sore tooth.

Several times, she'd started to ask her mother about that day, what Mr. Bowman had said. But something always stopped her. Along with the fragments of that memory, she'd had the sense that her mama had tried to protect her from something. And maybe Aunt Emmy as well.

Abby let go of her aunt's hand then and headed for the door. But just before she closed it, she watched as her mama sat down on the bed next to Emmy and opened the book. A wave of love washed over her, and she thought how lucky Aunt Emmy was to have such a sister. And how lucky she was to have them both. It hurt to think of leaving them, of choosing a life that would take her away from here. Part of her didn't ever want to leave, and yet another part of her wanted to know what else lay beyond here for her. It was her fervent prayer that having one wouldn't mean giving up the other.

33

Real Love

The only gift is a portion of thyself.
– *Ralph Waldo Emerson*

Now

Once when Abby was five years old, she brought a tiny kitten up from the barn to let me hold, sneaking it past Mama who would have immediately sent her back outside with it. I held it in the palm of my hand, a little gray fluff of life, its soft mewling for its mother bringing tears to my eyes.

"I'm sorry, Aunt Emmy," Abby said, the happiness lighting her face fading to dismay. "I didn't mean to make you sad. I shouldn't have brought him up."

I stared at her, unable to turn off my tears, and equally unable to explain that she had done nothing wrong.

Long after she'd taken the kitten back to the barn, I sat on my bed, a part of me yearning to open the window and call her back. I have thought many times to reject her efforts at kindness, to sever whatever sense of obligation she feels toward me. But it is something I haven't been able to bring myself to do, the reasons entirely selfish. Her visits are like being bathed in warm light, and she has a way of appearing when the world around me seems at its blackest.

I look for myself in her, but there is little to be found beyond a certain set of her mouth when she's giving something her full attention. Without doubt, she has Becca's questioning mind. I have no idea whether this is genetic or simply something she's learned from my sister.

I think of the ways in which Becca tries to share Abby with me, how when we're alone, she refers to her as our daughter. And each time I hear this, it's like I've been handed a gift. One I know doesn't come from pity, but from a mutual understanding of how special Abby is and a recognition of the part we've both played in her existence.

And, too, maybe Becca's generosity stems from a lesson we both learned somewhere along the way. That real love doesn't set boundaries or guard with jealousy those at which it is directed. Real love, whatever its origin, is to be shared. Welcomed. Valued.

34

A Clean Heart

In the long run, we shape our lives, and we shape ourselves. The process never ends until we die. And the choices we make are ultimately our own responsibility.
– Eleanor Roosevelt

Now

At just after two a.m., Martha gave up on sleep and got out of bed, reaching for the soft cotton robe Daniel had given her more than a dozen years ago. She slipped it over her shoulders, wincing once when a pain shot through her left elbow, arthritis a nagging reminder of time's passing.

She left her room and took the stairs to the kitchen, keeping her steps soft in an effort not to wake anyone else. She filled the stove-top percolator, which had belonged to her mother, with water and then retrieved the coffee can from the pantry, spooning in an extra tablespoon to chase away the fatigue weighing on her like a wet blanket.

But even caffeine seemed to have little effect these

days. It made no sense that a person could stay so tired and yet not be able to sleep.

Martha waited for the pot's last upward sputter and then poured herself a cup, adding a bit of cream from the glass pitcher in the refrigerator. She retrieved her Bible from the top drawer of the walnut Hutch that sat against one wall of the room, then lowered herself into a chair at the table. She heard a sound in the hallway and looked up to find Becca standing in the kitchen doorway.

"You couldn't sleep either?" Becca asked.

Martha shook her head. "Coffee's ready if you want some."

Becca walked to the pot and filled a cup, thick silence hanging over the kitchen. She sat down at the table, cupping the mug with both hands.

Martha noticed the circles beneath her eyes. "I'm worried about you, Becca."

Becca took a sip of her coffee. "You don't need to be, Mama."

"I'm worried about the choices you're making."

"To accept a gift from someone I cared about?" Becca replied, the words sharp in a way that was not characteristic of her. And then, evenly, "What could be so wrong with that?"

"We both know it's more."

"Do we?"

"Have you thought about how this will make Aaron feel?"

Becca looked away then and sighed, as if the fire behind her last words had suddenly been doused with water, losing their flame. "I'm not doing this to hurt Aaron, Mama."

"But you know that it will."

"Mama, I—"

"I know what you believe you gave up, Becca. I knew

when you married him that you didn't love him the way he loved you. But I really thought you would come to. Aaron is a good man. He's been there for you, for all of us."

"I know he has."

"Isn't that worthy then of at least your loyalty?"

"He has that."

"Does he?" Martha heard the judgment in her own voice and felt the sharp sting of guilt. She was quiet for several moments, rubbing the rim of her cup with one thumb. "I saw Jacob's wife in Wal-mart the other night."

Becca looked up then. "You talked to her?"

Martha nodded. "She had the boy with her."

"Michael, you mean," Becca said.

"Yes. Michael," she said, realizing she had never said it out loud before.

"Was Jacob with her?"

Martha shook her head, feeling her daughter's questioning stare and yet unable to bring herself to meet it.

"May I ask you something?" Becca said.

Martha looked up then. "Go ahead."

"How could you go all these years without seeing him?"

Martha glanced down at the pages of her Bible, trying to focus on the words, but finding their edges blurred and barely readable. "I never wanted things to be the way they've been."

"Jacob loved us, Mama. But he loved her, too."

"And he made his choice." Martha could hear the waver in her declaration, and it startled her, made her wonder where her conviction had gone.

"That's the part I don't understand," Becca said. "Why it had to be a choice."

Martha started to say something, then pressed her lips together, her thoughts a sudden mass of confusion. For so long she had carried the strength of her beliefs inside her like a staff of righteousness, solid as the old oaks that sheltered the farm. Whenever she yearned to see Jacob, when the ache seized her so that it seemed possible she might actually die from it, that staff of truth was all that kept her going.

Now, she felt hollow at her very core.

Becca pushed back her chair, leaving her steaming coffee on the table and walking out the back door.

"Becca," Martha called out. But the door closed, and the kitchen was silent again except for the steady click of the clock on the stove. She started to get up and go after her, but what was there to say?

Her eldest daughter could see no right in anything she had done. And Martha felt suddenly exhausted by the thought of defending herself.

A wrenching sense of loss swept over her, and she got up from the table and walked to the living room. A pine table with a wide drawer sat in front of the upholstered sofa. Martha sat down on the edge of the couch and raised the lid.

Inside were the scrapbooks in which she'd saved the childrens' school art and other things she hadn't been able to bear parting with. She lifted out the top one, opening the cover to see Jacob's childish scribbling across the front page. He'd begun drawing early, around four or five, his eye for reproducing the likeness of the chickens scratching out lunch by the barn or a cow grazing in the field, amazingly good.

She wondered if he'd ever done anything with the talent or if he'd simply put it away and never used it.

She turned the pages of the book, smiling at a watercolor he'd done of their family in a familiar pose of getting ready for church on a Sunday morning. There was Daniel, his easy nature reflected in the smile on his face. And she herself beside him, stern-faced in a way that contradicted her husband's take-life-as-it-comes stance. Becca and Emmy were next to her, pretty and happy in their Sunday dresses, the two of them standing straight as sticks and holding hands, the remains of a giggle on their faces.

Martha turned the page. Glued to the orange construction paper was a letter Jacob had written her in the second grade. The occasion had been Mother's Day, and even now, so many years beyond the first time she'd read the words, her heart lifted with the memory of their sweet sincerity.

Dear Mama,

You are a good mama. I like yur cooking and the close you make for us. When I grow up, I want to mary a woman just like you. I love you.

Your son,

Jacob

Martha ran her hand across the words. She supposed no son could give their mama a greater compliment than this.

She thought about the polite young woman who had introduced her to her own grandson and admitted to herself that she had never given Linda a chance. She had failed to trust her son's judgment, relying on her own, instead, and as a result, alienating the son she loved dearly.

She put the scrapbook away and went back into the kitchen where her Bible lay open on the table. She sat back down in the chair and glanced at the open book, the words on the page now clear and focused, as if someone had turned a lens and allowed her to see them again.

For the whole of her life, Martha had read from this book each and every morning. As a child, her mother had taught her to start the day this way, and she had never veered from it, her intent to show the Lord what she put first in her life. For years, she had read from beginning to end, starting over again each time she finished the book in its entirety. But lately, she'd begun reading as her own mother had in her later years. Opening the book at random and reading whatever lay before her. Her mother had once told her that if she would leave the choice to Him, God would show her the words that would apply to that day's struggles.

This morning, Martha had opened to the book of Psalms, immediately focusing on a single verse. *Create in me a clean heart, O God; and renew a right spirit within me.*

Martha read the verse a second time, then sat back in her chair and closed her eyes. Just minutes ago, she'd been ready to defend her choices, to remind her daughter that it had been Jacob who had rejected his family, not the other way around. But Martha's thoughts turned to Michael, the grandchild she did not know. Michael. And with his name, the flatness of her own argument. All these years, she'd told herself she was standing up for what was right, for all that she had been taught to believe.

Her eyes were drawn to the verse again. A clean heart. A right spirit. She leaned forward then, propped her elbows on the table, and bowing her head, began to pray.

35

Even When

"Yesterday is gone. Tomorrow has not yet come. We have only today. Let us begin."
— Mother Teresa

Now

Becca spent the remaining early hours of the morning in her potting shed where she anchored several dozen seedling plants into fertile, receptive soil. She put her hands to the task of outrunning her thoughts, but without success. She couldn't quit thinking about what her mother had said about Aaron. She wanted to deny the accuracy of it, but in truth, she couldn't.

Aaron was all the things her mother had declared him to be, and this was the part that made her grieve inside. The fact that Aaron had done nothing more wrong than love her. And she had tried to return that love in the same way it had been given, had convinced herself for a very long time that her feelings for him had grown into something resembling what they should be.

Until Matt came back. All the old wounds inside her were as fresh as yesterday, and now she wasn't sure of anything anymore.

When the sun began to peep over the crest of Tinker's Knob, Becca left the shed and climbed into the truck.

She drove the twenty minutes to Jacob's house with the window rolled down, the fresh morning air cool on her face. Like her own, Jacob's body clock was set for farmer's hours, and sleeping past the sunrise rarely happened for either of them. She found him in the barn, feeding a half-dozen of the goats he and Linda raised. Linda was a vegetarian, and their agreement had been that none of the animals they raised would be used for meat. At first, Jacob had been clearly skeptical about the prospects of Linda's ideas, but they had gone on to make a nice living from the sale of organic chicken eggs, goat's milk and cheese. Becca loved visiting their farm because the animals here felt like an extended part of the family. She also loved that despite being raised to understand that cows went to slaughter on a regular basis, Jacob respected Linda's beliefs and had fine-tuned his own to complement them.

A quiet bleat from one of the goats announced Becca's arrival. Jacob turned and spotted her in the doorway of the barn, a smile cracking his handsome face wide. "Hey, stranger," he said.

"Hey, yourself," she said, walking over to give him a hug and then pulling back to let herself take him in. He had changed amazingly little over the years, a few lines in his face, very little grey in his dark hair. She wondered, not for the first time, if happiness was its own fountain of youth. At least for her brother, it appeared to be true.

Jacob touched the back of his hand to her face, and said, "You haven't been over in a while. What are you doing out with the chickens this morning?"

Becca shrugged. "I just wanted to see you."

"Hm," he said, skeptical, and then with real interest behind the question, "And how are you?"

"Okay," she said.

He gave her a long look. "Translation, not okay."

"So who made you an expert on female tone?" she said with a half-smile.

"Actually, I believe you yourself were a primary contributor to my gender-bias education."

She bent over to rub the neck of one of the female goats, loving its silky texture and its short bleat of greeting. "Mama said she ran into Linda in Wal-mart the other night."

Jacob went still, silent for a moment before nodding, "Yeah. Linda said she was nice."

Becca straightened, unable to keep the bitter edge from her voice when she said, "High praise for a grandmother who'd never met her own grandson."

Jacob reached out and squeezed her shoulder with one hand. "Hey, sis. Water under the bridge."

She looked him in the eyes, shaking her head. "How do you do it, Jacob?"

"What?"

"Accept what she's done?"

"Ah, Becca," he said, taking her hand and leading her over to a long wooden bench. They sat down, and he clasped her right hand between his own two, squeezing hard. "There's living. And there's living in the past. I just really want to live. What good would it do for me to spend my time dwelling on something I can't change?"

"Even when she can't see—"

"Even when," he interrupted softly.

She tipped her head and looked at him. "How'd you get so levelheaded?"

"The aid of a good woman," he said.

"Apparently." And then, "Linda's lucky to have you."

"And I'm lucky to have her."

They sat for a while, the silence easy in the way of two people genuinely fond of each other. Becca visited her brother and his family as often as she could, insistent on maintaining her own relationship with them.

When Jacob finally spoke, his voice held an edge of concern. "I saw in the paper where Mrs. Griffith died. Matt came back for the funeral, I guess?"

Becca nodded, not adding anything further.

"Have you seen him?"

"Yes," she said, the word barely audible.

"And?"

"And nothing."

"And you're driving out to see me at the crack of dawn. Must be something."

She shrugged. "Water under the bridge."

"Somehow, I don't think so. Y'all left a lot of stuff unfinished, Becca," he said.

Just hearing it now made her eyes fill with unexpected tears. With anyone else, she managed to keep her composure, but with Jacob, it was different. He'd somehow always managed to know what she was feeling. "He's married. I'm married. End of story." The words were flat, leeched of emotion.

"You're not happy. Is he?"

Becca glanced up. "I'm not unhappy, Jacob."

"Becca. You might have the rest of the world fooled. But you haven't fooled me."

She sighed, leaned her head against the wall. "Jacob, I really didn't come here to talk about me."

Jacob took her hand, rubbed the back of it with his thumb. "You did an honorable thing all those years ago, Becca. But honorable things aren't that easy to pull off. I know what it's cost you."

"I have a good life."

"You married a man you don't love. And lost the one you did. I suppose it could be argued that you've made good of it. But don't tell me you're happy."

A knot of emotion rose in Becca's throat, the tears in her eyes spilling over and slipping down her cheeks. She tried to speak, but couldn't get the words out.

Jacob hooked an arm around her shoulders, tucked her against his chest. She started to cry in earnest then, as if someone had turned on a faucet inside her, and she had no way of shutting it off. He pressed a kiss to her forehead. "You're debating whether to see him, aren't you?"

She nodded once, unable to answer out loud.

"It might look bad from here, sis. But maybe life has to force us into a corner sometimes before we can take an honest look at where we are."

"Where I am is where I'll stay," she affirmed, even as she heard the weakness in her own voice.

"Maybe so. But if you do, make sure this time that it's because of what's right for you. Right for you, Becca. And not anyone else."

∞

Then

THEY STARTED TO date.

The two of them meeting at the county library in town where they would make out behind the Nancy Drew shelves. The recreation park off 919 where they would linger for hours, talking and kissing, sometimes not seeing another person the whole time they were there.

They did all this in secret. Not so much by any open declaration on their part, but instead with an unspoken understanding that once others knew, it would no longer be about just the two of them.

And on some level, Becca didn't want to share it. She felt the fragility of it, and she wanted to protect it. Nurture it. Give it a chance to grow like the Heirloom seeds her grandmother had taught her to start in tiny black pots each spring.

Becca had been working in the garden for a couple of hours, sweat making the back of her dress stick to her shoulder blades. Her hair was damp beneath the straw hat she wore to protect her face from the sun.

She was considering going to the house for a drink of water when she looked up from the row of beans she'd been weeding to find Matt walking toward her, his face set and serious.

He didn't say anything when he reached the spot where she'd been working. He took her hand, pulled her up, not letting go as he walked faster, and then began to run, jumping the rows of vegetables and following the edge of the field at the back of the garden to where the apple trees started.

"Is something wrong?" she called out, worried now.

He didn't answer, but led her deep into the orchard before he finally stopped and gathered her up in his arms, leaning in to kiss her deep and hard, as if he had been thinking about nothing else the entire day.

Becca tipped her head and returned the kiss, her hands clasped at the back of his neck, her hat falling to the ground.

They sank to their knees, and he kissed her again, before easing her down against the shady grass beneath the apple tree. There, they curled into one another, pressing as close as they could manage with a barrier of clothes between them. His hands locked at the base of her spine, and he kissed her forehead, each eye, the tip of her chin, then finally her mouth again.

"Becca," he said.

"What?" she said, smiling and running the back of her hand across his jawline.

"You're killing me. Your dad thinks I'm addle-brained.

Half the time when he tells me something to do I have no idea what he said because I'm wondering where you are and exactly how long it will be before I can see you again."

She laughed softly. "I'll tell him you're really smart. That you're just trying to figure out ways to get me alone. And that you're actually pretty good at it."

"Oh, you'll tell him that, will you?" He began to tickle her then, finding the spots that most tormented her until she was breathless with laughter.

"Stop!" she pleaded, trying to wriggle free.

He did finally, and she lay there, breathing hard and staring up at his beautiful face. She did find him beautiful, like some near perfect specimen of youth and strength.

Her dress was halfway to her waist, and Matt's eyes took in the length of her bare legs. "I love looking at you," he said, reaching out to touch the inside of her knee with one finger.

"I love looking at you," she repeated with utter sincerity.

They stared at one another. When Matt spoke, his voice was low and serious. "Is this going somewhere, Becca?"

She could have made light of the question, but she didn't. She felt his confusion, knew the chaos of it in her own heart. In the beginning, she'd assumed she would be the vulnerable one. Matt was the star baseball player, the guy who dated the school's most popular girls, a guy who ran with a crowd she barely knew how to talk to. She had grown up in a family that shunned the world and its excesses.

But lying here with him, she realized they were both vulnerable. And in that moment, the bond that had begun to form between them deepened to a new level. "I don't know," she said, tracing a finger across the hollow at the base of his throat. "Sometimes, I think we'll both end up getting hurt."

"I don't want to hurt you," he said.

"I don't think you would mean to." She sat up, hugged her knees to her chest and stared out across the rows of apple trees with their nearly-grown fruit. "But I don't think we should kid ourselves, either."

"About what?"

She considered her words, not wanting to say the wrong thing, not wanting him to think she was trying to make him feel guilty. "About where this can go."

He was quiet for a bit and then said, "Can't it go where we want it to?"

She looked at him, a needle of sadness piercing her chest. "I know we haven't been acting this way, but it's more than just the two of us. You have plans. College. Playing baseball. And that's good."

"Yeah," he said. "Do those things mean I can't see you?"

"How could that ever work? You there. And me, here."

He wound a finger through her hair, lifted up to kiss her once. "It could work."

She shook her head. "You make it sound so simple."

"Maybe it is. Maybe it's people who complicate things."

Behind them, an apple dropped to the ground. They both turned at the sound. A crow swooped down and immediately began to peck at the red-green skin.

"Becca!"

At the sound of her mother's voice calling from the house, Becca straightened her dress and brushed the grass from its skirt. "I have to go," she said.

"Meet me at the lake tomorrow afternoon. It's Sunday. I don't have to work."

"Matt—"

Her mother called out again, her voice closer this time. Becca backed up, torn between wanting to say yes and knowing she shouldn't. "I'll try," she said and ran for the house.

36

Searching

The sharp thorn often produces delicate roses.
- Ovid

Now
Matt loved the drive from Ballard out to the lake. Had always admired the way the land along the way dipped and rose, then leveled out to straight, flat stretches of green hay and cornfields. Loved, too, the blue-hued mountains that loomed in the distance, rising up to meet the skyline. As a boy, he'd always thought of them as a wall of sorts that protected the county from the rest of the world the way moats had once protected castles and other places of worth.

Certainly, there were cities and towns in the world far prettier than Ballard County, and he'd seen a lot of them. Florence, Italy. Cannes, France. The Caribbean's Anguilla. But he'd never felt at home in any of those places. He'd been a visitor there, and being a visitor to a place wasn't the same as belonging by birthright.

It wasn't something he'd ever let himself think about to any extent until now. Now when homesickness swirled through him, the intensity of which he could not explain. But it was as if it had built up inside him during all the years of being away, and he could not deny, even to himself, that some part of him belonged here.

He made the turn off 122 onto the smaller road that led to his grandmother's house. Becca's house now. Half-way down the gravel drive, he stopped the Land Rover and draped both arms across the steering wheel, stalling. Was he making a mistake in coming here?

He'd lain awake half the night debating the wisdom of it, aware that he'd crossed a threshold yesterday in asking Becca to meet him. He considered turning around and heading back to town, his gut telling him it would be the best thing for them both. But logic lost its footing beneath the lure of eighteen years of wondering.

He put the vehicle in gear and rolled forward, gravel crunching beneath his tires. A quarter mile more, and he spotted the white truck parked near the back door of the house. Matt pulled up beside it and got out, ran a hand through his hair, nervous in a way that was not characteristic of him.

He walked through the overgrown yard and stuck his head inside the back door, calling her name. No answer. He circled around to the front of the house and found her pulling weeds from the base of the old rose bushes he remembered his grandmother planting along the porch when he'd been a small boy.

"Champlain roses," he said, leaning one shoulder against the corner of the porch railing and sticking his hands in the pockets of his jeans.

Becca straightened and turned toward him. "Is that what they're called?"

"Gran planted them from some bushes my great-grandmother had grown."

"So they come with history?"

He held her gaze and said, "Yeah. I guess they do."

Becca brushed the dirt from her palms. "Then that makes them even more special."

They were silent then, the words echoing between them. A crow cawed in the distance, another answering back.

"Looks like the weeds are going to give you a run for your money," Matt said.

"It's not too bad once you get past the stuff with real roots. Those are the ones that aren't so easy to persuade into leaving." Becca began pulling again, making a neat pile just out from the bush.

Matt knelt beside her and followed her lead.

"You don't have to help," she said, quiet surprise in her voice.

"I want to," he said.

They worked for the better part of two hours, much of the time quiet, the only sounds the tug and release of the weeds letting go of the soil. When the pile got bigger, Matt loaded it into a wheelbarrow and dumped it at the edge of the yard, making the trip back and forth a couple of times.

It was almost twelve-thirty when Becca sat back, wiped the sleeve of her cotton dress across her forehead and said, "Thank you. Four hands are definitely better than two."

Matt stood, surveying their work, pleased to see that the bushes were no longer choked with undergrowth. "They look just like they did when Gran took care of them," he said.

Becca's face softened with the praise. "That's good."

"It is."

She folded her arms, hesitating and then saying, "I brought lunch. Are you hungry?"

"Starving."

She nodded once and went inside the house. Matt used the faucet out back to rinse his hands, finding an old t-shirt in the back of the Land Rover to wipe the sweat from his face. When he returned to the front yard, Becca had spread a blanket on the grass close to the water. At the sight of her waiting for him, he walked the short distance from the house under an onslaught of feelings too tangled to sort out.

An old pear tree grew near the spot she'd chosen. He remembered planting it with Gran when he'd been seven or eight years old. Every August, they would pick up buckets of the small green pears, and Gran would make preserves on the stove in a big copper kettle, filling small glass jars with them and giving them as Christmas presents.

Now, the tree threw dapples of shade across the containers of food Becca removed from a brown wicker basket. Matt stood by the edge of the blanket, not sure what to do.

She scooted over and made room for him, opening a bowl of green beans with boiled white potatoes, yellow corn on the cob, biscuits that looked as though they'd been made that morning and bright pink slices of watermelon.

"It's a lot of food, I know," she said. "Abby only had a half day of school today. I thought she might come out at some point."

"I don't want to eat her share."

"She'd be here by now if she were coming." She passed him a thick white paper plate along with a plastic fork and knife. "There's iced tea in the cooler."

"Great." He reached inside for the pitcher and filled a plastic cup for them both, handing her one.

"Thank you."

They loaded their plates and in silence, began eating

with the kind of appetite fostered by working outdoors. The summer day was warm but not unpleasant, and a breeze drifted in off the lake. A grasshopper found its way onto the blanket and then made a perfect landing atop one of Matt's potatoes.

Becca gently picked it up and put it back in the grass.

Matt smiled. "I thought ants were the picnic invaders."

"Apparently, they have competition."

"Keeps things healthy, I guess."

With amusement in her eyes, Becca took a sip of her tea, then set it down at the edge of the blanket. "So tell me about you and what you do, Matt."

"You first."

"There's not much to tell. I've turned my gardening into something of a small business."

"Your grandmother's Heirloom seeds." Matt could see that she was pleased he had remembered.

"People seem to like things grown with a little extra care."

"As I remember it, you have a special touch with making things grow."

"It's not complicated," she said. "It's just paying attention to what they need."

"That's something most of us have trouble with when it comes to anything other than ourselves."

She considered the words, but didn't deny them. "So tell me about what you do."

"I work for a pretty big law firm. Litigation. Contracts. Refereeing disputes between battling corporations."

"Sounds complicated."

"It can be. And boring. It can be that, too."

She hesitated. "And your wife?"

"She's an attorney, too."

Becca nodded, looking at her plate. She didn't say

anything for several moments, and then, "Pretending not to care. It's hard, isn't it?"

He put down his plate, his appetite suddenly gone. "Yes."

She glanced away, her eyes suddenly turbulent with uncertainty. When she finally looked at him again, she studied his face for several long moments before saying, "We shouldn't be doing this."

"Eating?" he said, trying for a light note.

"It's more than that, and we both know it."

"Becca."

She held up one hand, looking off at the lake. "Matt, don't. Please."

"We need to talk," he said.

"It's too late for that."

"Why is it too late?" he said, anger igniting inside him like kerosene beneath the flick of a match.

She made a sound that was half laugh, half sob. "Because we both have other lives."

"And that means we can't talk to each other?"

She glanced back then, resignation in her voice. "And where would it go?"

"Is it so wrong for me to want to understand what happened to us?" he said then, the words harsher than he'd intended.

"There's nothing to understand."

"There's everything," he said.

She looked down, rubbed a thumb across the back of her hand. "I wrote you that one letter, and I never heard from you again."

"That one letter changed my life."

She glanced up then, her voice soft when she repeated, "And I never heard from you again."

He looked at the lake, not answering for a minute or more. "You remember how I told you once what happened to my parents. That they died when they did because I pressured them into doing something they didn't want to do."

She nodded. "I remember."

"After you wrote to me and said that you couldn't be with me, that things would never work between us, I actually got in the car and started driving home. About halfway here, I had this awful feeling that if I talked you into doing something you didn't want to do, something bad might happen, and I would have to live with that the way I've lived with my parents' death."

"Matt," she said.

He held up a hand, as if he needed to finish. "A week or so later, I'd finally convinced myself that I had to at least talk to you. I came home and drove out to your house. Your mother told me you'd gone away for a while. She said that you didn't want me to know where you were. And then, later, I heard that you'd married Aaron."

Matt's words hung in the air, moments ticking by, and then Becca stood suddenly and started putting the bowls back in the picnic basket, her hands clumsy and shaking. "It's pointless to dredge all this up. To create regret for something that can't be changed."

"Becca." Matt got to his feet, reaching out to stop her with a hand on each of her shoulders. "Wait."

"I can't do this," she said, her voice breaking.

He tipped her chin up, forcing her to look at him. "We're not doing anything wrong."

"Oh, Matt." She was silent for a few seconds, and then with a hand to her chest, "I know you're sad now. That you're grieving, and I think not just for your grandmother." She stopped, started to say something, then hesitated, as if struggling for words. "You're obviously going through a lot of changes in your life. Coming back here must not have been an easy thing.

But what happened between us was. . .we were just kids. And looking back isn't going to help fix anything for you now."

Matt blinked once, considered his response and then, "Is that how you see this?"

"I think you're searching," she said, her voice soft, not unkind. "But there's nothing here, Matt. Don't look to the past to fix the life you have now."

She gathered up the rest of her things and straightened. "I shouldn't have let this happen today."

"Nothing happened."

"We opened a door. And now we have to close it again."

She was halfway back to the house when he called her name again. She faltered, as if she might change her mind and turn back. But she didn't. She kept walking, disappearing around the corner of the house, the still afternoon interrupted only briefly by the sound of her truck heading down the gravel road.

∞

Then

THE SIGHT OF her made him nearly dizzy with longing.

Matt had been waiting for an hour or more at the back of the house, watching for her car to appear in the curve of the gravel drive. His palms were sweaty, and he kept checking his watch to make sure she wasn't yet late.

At just after one o'clock on Sunday afternoon, he heard a car turn in off the main road. A minute later, she pulled into the driveway and cut the engine. Matt walked out to meet her, leaning down to kiss her through the lowered window. "Hey," he said.

She smiled. "Hey."

"This might have been the longest day of my life."

"Why?" she said, her voice teasing as if she already knew the answer.

He opened the door and pulled her out, backing her into the side of the black Impala and anchoring his hands in her thick blonde hair. "Because of this," he said, kissing the side of her neck. "And this." Another kiss at the back of her ear. The tip of her nose. And finally her mouth. Long, deep, lingering. "And that."

"And that," she repeated, her eyes soft in the way he lay awake at night thinking about when they weren't together. When all he could think about was wanting her, needing her as he had never before needed another human being.

They leaned back to stare at one another, taking their time. Matt was glad to be able to look at her fully, to not think about who might see them, her mother, her father, Wilks. This wasn't something he'd ever had to think about with any of the girls he'd dated. For the most part, parents liked him. And while he told himself that the Millers didn't have anything against him personally, their disapproval made him uncomfortable.

"You up for a canoe ride?" he said.

"Only if you're doing all the rowing."

He took her hand and pulled her toward the house, "Deal. Come on."

"Wait," she said, running back to the car and grabbing a canvas bag from inside.

"Bathing suit?" he said.

Her cheeks brightened with color. "I went into town last night and bought one. I felt like I was buying something illegal."

Matt reached out to touch her face. "You don't have to wear it if you don't want to."

"I want to," she said.

They went into the house, and Matt showed Becca a

room where she could change. "I'll be outside getting the canoe ready," he said.

She nodded and closed the door, while he thought about the bed in that room and all the things they could do there. He forced himself to walk outside and down to the dock where he'd tied the canoe earlier.

He got everything ready to go and then sat down, letting his feet dangle in the water. Ten minutes passed. Another five. And then another. Just as he was heading back to the house to check on her, Becca let herself out the back door and walked toward the water in a light blue one-piece that while modest by some comparisons, made his heartbeat kick up several notches.

He met her half-way. "Wow," he said. "You're beautiful."

She glanced down, looking awkward. "I feel like I'm trying to be someone I'm not."

"Funny, you look just like this girl I'm crazy about."

She smiled then, clearly pleased. "So you're rowing?"

"I'm rowing."

Matt untied the canoe, held it steady while she slipped into the front seat. He handed her an oar and then slid in the back with his own. He pushed them off, and the canoe glided across the surface, light and quick.

The July air was thick and hot. The sun sat high in a blue sky, the lake water reflecting back the same hue. The pinks and purples of thistle and blueweed colored the fields along the shoreline. "We might have to take a swim before long to cool off," Matt said.

She looked over her shoulder, shot him a grin. "You just want to see me in this bathing suit again."

He dipped his head. "Not denying that."

Becca laughed and trailed her hand in the water, letting her fingers make little wakes while Matt moved them through the cove with long, steady strokes.

He had a destination in mind, a spot around the bend

where the land formed a u, natural sand blanketing the shoreline, a poplar tree lending shade to part of the beach.

It only took five minutes to get there, but Matt was sweating by the time he brought the canoe to a stop.

"It's beautiful here," Becca said.

Matt climbed out first, then helped Becca from the front. The canoe tipped side to side, and she lost her balance at the last second, falling forward against his chest. He caught her with one arm around her waist, and they stood there in the shallow water, looking into each other's eyes.

Matt was suddenly conscious of their breathing, the sound of it drowning out everything else around them.

Becca drew his head down to hers and kissed him, her lips soft and searching. In that single moment, Matt felt as happy as he had ever felt in his life. Still holding her in the air with one arm, he carried her to the beach. She was giggling now and telling him to put her down. He ignored her until he reached the grassy area just beyond the sandy beach.

He dropped to his knees then, both arms around her. They studied each other, the laughter fading away, leaving behind a stillness, a sudden understanding of his own feelings. The moment hit Matt like an axe to the back.

"Becca," he said.

"I know," she said, pressing a hand to his face. "Me, too."

"I want to say it, though."

"Maybe you shouldn't," she said.

"Why not?"

"It might—"

"What?"

"Change things."

"It won't."

"How do you know?"

He tipped her chin back with one finger, looked into her eyes. "I know."

"But—" She shook her head a little, her protest weak now.

"I love you. Becca Miller. I love you."

Tears welled in her eyes. She blinked them away, pulling his face to hers and kissing him with her own deep and thorough answer. She didn't have to say anything. He knew she felt the same way, knew it with a kind of certainty he had never known about anything else in his life. She filled spaces inside him, sealed seams where the edges had come undone.

"Matt," she said a few moments later, pulling back to look up at him. "I don't know where this can go. If there's anywhere for it to go, but I love you, too."

"There's everywhere for it to go," he said. "There's the whole world." He kissed her then, pressing her back against the grass beneath them and stretching alongside her, half his body covering hers.

Matt had been with his share of girls, but none of it had ever meant what he now realized it should have. Before now, it had always been about the end game. Guys in a locker room bragging about whose pants they'd gotten into over the weekend.

He laced his hand through Becca's long, soft hair, aware, too, for the first time in his life of what a different thing it was to care more about pleasing than being pleased. As far as sex was concerned, for him it turned the whole thing inside out, so that every smooth move he'd cultivated with other girls felt exactly like what it had been. A meaningless act with nothing remotely selfless at its core. And none of it, none of it, applied to what he felt for Becca.

"Matt." Becca put a hand to his face, looked into his eyes.

He pulled back, shifting his weight. "Am I hurting you? Do you want me to stop?"

"No," she said, shaking her head and cupping the side of his face with one hand. "No. Don't worry so much, okay? I just want you. The real you."

All his uncertainty fell away then, and he turned onto his back, pulling her along with him so that she sat up, her legs straddling either side of him. He anchored a hand on the back of her thigh, and she leaned down to kiss him with all the sweet innocence he was so drawn to in her.

Eventually, she stretched out on top of him, his hands sliding to her waist and up to her shoulder blades, sealing her to him with an undeniable knowledge that she was what he wanted for the rest of his life.

A boat roared down the channel, bringing the world back to them, its engine wound out, loud voices making themselves heard above the sound. Matt sat up, recognizing the group as Wilks and some of the other players from the team. There were a few girls with them, Angie's dark hair visible at the front where she stood next to Wilks.

Becca sat up. "They're looking for you."

"Yeah, I guess."

They listened as the boat disappeared around the bend and into the cove. They heard the boat slow at Matt's dock, idling for a minute or more while voices called Matt's name. When they got no answer, the boat revved up again and came flying back out of the cove, then jerking to a near stop as Wilks glanced over and spotted Matt and Becca in the inlet.

"Hey, there they are!" he called out, whipping the steering wheel toward them and then dropping the engine back and beaching the boat on the sand next to the canoe.

They were all drunk. That much was obvious from

twenty feet away in their unsteady balancing act with the boat. Joey Mathers and Dale Brooks stood in the back, beers in their hands. Angie looked uncomfortable, and for a moment, Matt was sorry about it. It hadn't been his intention to hurt her.

"Hey, man," Wilks said, catapulting off the boat and splashing his way to the shore. "You didn't invite us to the picnic."

Matt reached for Becca's hand and pulled her close to him. "This one was private."

"I can see that," Wilks said, looking at Becca in a way that made heat rise in Matt's chest. "I don't blame you for making this one a solo gig." He glanced over his shoulder. "'Course Angie's wondering why she didn't get an invitation. Maybe that would have been awkward though since she's supposed to be your girlfriend and all."

"Shut up, Wilks," Matt said, steel in his voice.

"Matt, let's go," Becca said, taking his arm.

"Wilks, stop," Angie called out from the boat.

He turned and threw an arm her way. "What? You're okay with getting dumped like yesterday's trash? Isn't that what he's done with all of us? Got himself a new girlfriend, and now we're not on the call list anymore."

"Wilks, get on the damn boat," Dale said.

"You guys are a bunch of wimps. You're willing to cut him behind his back, but in front of him, it's 'no problem, Matt. We'll be here when you're done with your farm girl."

Matt let go of Becca's hand then and bolted through the water to where Wilks stood. He shoved him once with everything he had. Wilks tumbled backwards, splashing heavily into the shallow water, then leaping back up with Virginia red clay painting the legs of his white swimming trunks.

"You two used to be like brothers," Joey said, hanging

over the edge of the boat. "What the hell's wrong with you?"

Anger edged out any remorse Matt might have felt. He'd made so many excuses for Wilks, and the truth was he refused to do it anymore.

"Matt, stop, please," Becca said from behind him.

Wilks stumbled to his feet, running a hand across his face and hair to clear the water. "You've gone over the edge, you know it?"

"You don't know when to quit, man," Matt said. "Get out of here."

Wilks climbed over the side of the boat, throwing a last glance at Becca and then Matt. He put an arm around Angie and pulled her against him. She looked once at Matt and then glanced away.

"You don't mind then, if I pick up where you left off?" Wilks yelled out. He slammed the gearshift into reverse and wheeled the boat around, flooring it out of the cove.

Matt stayed in the same spot until the sound of the engine disappeared altogether. He turned then and found Becca standing on the grass, her arms folded across her chest, the joy he'd seen in her face moments ago completely gone now.

"We should go, Matt," she said.

"Becca—"

"Who are we kidding?" Her voice was soft and reasoning. He would have preferred her anger, anything over the quiet acceptance with which she posed the question.

"I don't care what they think," he said.

"Maybe not now. But you will."

Matt ran a hand through his hair, frustration in his voice when he said, "If they can't accept you, Becca, then they're not my friends."

She shook her head. "You've known them for a long time. I don't want to change your life, Matt."

He walked toward her, not stopping until he stood directly in front of her. He tipped her chin up with a single finger and kissed her mouth. "You already have," he said. "You've changed everything."

37

Drowning

> *"Give sorrow words; the grief that does not speak knits up the o-er wrought heart and bids it break."*
> — ***William Shakespeare***

Now

After leaving the lake house, Becca nearly made it to the end of the driveway before she had to pull over, leaning forward with her arms wrapped around the steering wheel, grief rising up from deep inside her.

Here, alone, with no one to hear her, she gave in to it, the force flattening her the way a summer thunderstorm flattens an otherwise perfectly stout field of corn.

Granny Miller had once told her that pain was like that, quiet inside a person until roused, a sleeping monster intent on devouring everything in its path. She hated now the sound of her own weeping, hated herself for giving in to it, for her inability to stop it.

She'd never known that Matt had come to see her. All those years, and her mother had never told her. Both sadness and anger tore at her, while above, thunder clapped and lightning streaked across the darkening sky.

Raindrops splattered the windshield, only a few at first, and then increasing in number until they hit the truck in unrelenting, unforgiving sheets. Becca opened the door and got out, standing in the middle of the gravel road.

She cried until she was spent, the sound drowned beneath the downpour, the sorrow folding in upon itself as the storm above steadied to a gentle rain and then subsided altogether. She leaned against the truck, her dress plastered to her skin, while the old sense of loss settled within her, every bit as familiar as it was unwelcome. For so many years, she had kept it locked away, refusing to let its power sway her. But in meeting Matt here today, she had given it entrance, and she didn't know if she had the strength to turn it back again. For all these years, she'd managed her wants and needs with an unyielding resolve, the way some people managed chronic illness, keeping it just at bay. And maybe she'd seen them that way, her regrets, as a disease with the potential not only to ruin her own life, but so many others as well.

AARON WAS HALF-WAY between the house and the barn when Becca pulled into the driveway some twenty minutes later. She sat for a moment, willing normalcy into her face. Aaron didn't deserve any of this. This was the part that sat like a rock on her chest.

She got out of the truck, going around to the passenger door to gather up the gardening tools she'd taken with her out to the lake.

She heard the crunch of Aaron's boots on the gravel drive and turned to face him. "Hi," she said, hearing guilt in her own voice and yet unable to wipe it away.

Aaron was a tall man and carried himself with a kind of straight-backed dignity. But she noticed now that his shoulders seemed to tip forward, as if there were a strong wind at his back, the resistance of which he could no longer maintain.

His gaze dropped the length of her wet dress, questioning. "Where have you been, Becca?"

"I went out to Mrs. Griffith's house."

"Becca." Aaron's voice held a note of something she'd never heard before, and it actually struck a chord of fear inside her. Not of him, or of anything he might do, but of foreboding. As if they had both arrived at a point from which there was no turning back. "You saw him today."

The words were without question or accusation, but imbued with a regretful sadness that turned her heart. "Aaron."

"Why would you do that to yourself, Becca? Why would you do it to us?"

There was pain beneath the words, an entire ocean of it, and it was this that collapsed the wall of self-pity inside Becca. She could see now with clear eyes the wrenching result of her absorption, how easy it would be to break a man as strong as Aaron. A man who had done nothing to justify the hand fate had dealt him.

He walked forward, reached out to grasp her shoulder, reminding her suddenly of the little boy she'd once saved from drowning at a baptism service in the creek behind their church. It had been a cool April morning when the water was really too cold to use for the service, the candidates three teen-age boys certain enough of their hardiness that they were unwilling to consider other options.

The toddler had wandered too close to the creek's edge and lost his footing, toppling into the water, the splash so quiet that even with dozens of people milling about, Becca had been the only one to turn at the sound. She'd jumped in after him, instantly sinking beneath the weight of her own shoes and coat. She'd struggled her way back to the surface, frantically reaching for the child. For as long as she lived, she would never forget the feel of his small hand clutching her sleeve, the only connection between him and certain death.

Standing here now, Aaron's large hand anchored to her shoulder, she knew that same feeling of responsibility, as if his very life depended on her. On whatever action she took. Whatever choice she made.

She stared into his quietly pleading eyes, pity infusing her heart. She reached up then and placed her hand over his, felt his relief in the quiet release of his breath, as if he had been holding it all along, uncertain whether she would choose to save him or let him drown.

38

Clear Signs

"Sister – if all this is true, what could I do or undo?"
— ***Sophocles***

Now

Martha heard the truck pull into the driveway. She left the sheet on Emmy's bed unfinished and joined her at the window where they both watched Becca get out and Aaron walk up from the barn to meet her. The exchange between them was short, but the tension between them impossible to miss.

For a moment, an old sense of duty rallied inside her, and she considered going downstairs and talking to Becca about where she'd been today. But she knew, simply from the look on her daughter's face, that wherever it was, it had involved Matt Griffith.

On the heels of obligation, though, came a wave of weariness so intense that she had to sit on the chair beside the window, her limbs suffused with a heavy tiredness whose origin she thought more mental than physical.

All these years, and they thought she did not

understand. That she was simply set in her ways, and had no idea what it was to want something she could not have.

But they were wrong.

She knew. Too well, she knew. Far better than either Becca or Jacob would ever believe.

She quickly finished Emmy's bed and guided her back to it, propping her pillows up against the headboard and then leaving her with a book by her side, knowing she would never read it.

Martha left the room and went to her own, closing the door and staring hard at the cedar chest at the foot of her four-poster bed. She couldn't remember the last time she'd actually let herself look back, convincing herself there was nothing to be gained from it. Some pains never dulled, though, no matter how many years passed.

She got up from the chair and knelt down in front of the chest, her right knee cracking with the effort. She turned the latch and opened the lid, running a hand across the carefully folded quilts on top. Her mother had made these, using scraps from the dresses she'd sewn for Martha and her sisters. She lifted one and pressed her face to it, imagining that they still held the wonderful smell of the family kitchen where her mother had gone back and forth between cooking daily meals and working on the quilts she had loved.

She lifted two more rows from the chest and then saw the small box at the very bottom. It, too, was made of cedar, a gift she supposed she should have given away a long time ago. Something she had never been able to bring herself to do.

To her knowledge, Daniel had never seen the box. But what reason would he have had to rifle through her quilt chest? Daniel had trusted her without question. With this admission came a pang of guilt for the fact that her secret had outlived her marriage. Somehow, it seemed doubly wrong that Daniel had died without ever knowing she had loved another man.

She opened the lid to the box, the letters and photos exactly as she had left them. She touched the edge of the black and white picture on top, a too familiar ache setting up in her heart the way bursitis found the same weaknesses in her joints each winter.

Taken nearly fifty years ago, the photo had faded, softly blurring her face and that of the young man standing next to her, his arm around her waist. Martha had been eighteen, her hair dark and shiny, her skin glowing with youth, the girl here barely recognizable to her now.

She touched a finger to his face while something she had felt long ago sliced through her, as real to her now as it had been when she had been too young to appreciate its rarity. Mitch. Dark-haired, smile-at-the-ready Mitch.

There were only two photos, ironically, a beginning and an ending. This first taken at an outlook on the Blue Ridge Parkway during a picnic they'd gone on with two other couples, Mitch the only non-German Baptist boy among them. She remembered how much they'd laughed that day, how then it had seemed as if laughter would always be a part of their lives.

They'd actually met at church one summer Sunday when Mitch had come to visit with Esau Austin. From the moment they'd been introduced, Martha hadn't been able to take her eyes off him, and so, he later told her, it had been for him as well. For three months, they'd dated in secrecy, Martha afraid to tell her parents she had fallen in love with someone outside their faith.

But on the day Mitch had asked her to marry him, he'd done so with the declaration of converting, to live with her as she had grown up living. He didn't care, he said, as long as they were together.

Martha touched a hand to her face now, feeling the deep grooves in her skin and finding it hard to believe that a boy as young and handsome as Mitch had ever said such things to her. She wondered, as she had many times, what would have happened if he had not been drafted, if they would actually have made that life together.

The last photo had been taken on the day he'd left for Korea. Esau had driven them to Newport News where the ship that would take him across the world had been docked. He'd taken this picture of them, their arms locked tight about one another in a good-bye kiss.

She remembered, clearly, the fear she'd felt in those moments,

"Please come back," she'd whispered against his cheek.

"I will," he'd said.

He'd only been away for six months when his parents received a visit from officials with news of his death. Esau had been the one to bring the news to Martha, and to this day, the cut of it lay raw in the deepest recesses of her heart.

With his death had come a sort of confirmation for her. Proof that she had been wrong to veer from a path she had always believed to be right. She had gone on, eventually, marrying Daniel and having a family with him. She had loved Daniel. He'd been a good man, but she understood the difference between the kind of love a woman was simply taken over by and the kind she chose in a rational decision.

Becca had no way of knowing any of this, and in her daughter's eyes, Martha knew it must seem as if she'd never had the ability to think with her heart. But she had. And she knew the price of it. Had learned from her experience that sometimes people were given clear signs that they had made the wrong choice.

For Martha, Mitch had been just such a sign.

Like Becca, she had allowed her heart to sway her from logic. And like Becca, she had lived to regret it.

39

Sacrifice

We don't see things as they are, we see them as we are.
– Anaïs Nin

Now

It is easy to feel sorry for Aaron. In all that has happened, he's been as much a victim as anyone, his only crime in this life that of loving my sister.

By any definition, his offer to marry Becca and give Abby a name was a selfless one. But in truth, the only way he could ever have had her. I think he must have known this when he drove to Ohio that winter where Becca and I had gone to stay with Mama's sister for the duration of my pregnancy.

In most eyes, Aaron's offer to marry her and give Abby a name could be considered an act of chivalry. It certainly made our coming back to Virginia an easier thing for Mama and Daddy to bear. I wonder though if he knew when he made that offer how great the cost would be. That the sacrifice would be his own heart.

The truth is that she was never really his to have. I think he had to know this on some level, that there are things we are intuitively aware of, although we can't let ourselves admit them out loud. Sometimes we want something so desperately that we never consider the possible outcome. Maybe it's out of desperation that we force the pieces together, even when the joints don't quite fit, so that in the end there is really no chance for permanence.

40

Too Far Gone

Relationships are like glass. Sometimes it's better to leave them broken than try to hurt yourself putting it back together.
– Author Unknown

Now

The clock on the end table by the sofa read nine-thirty. Matt had spent the past two hours sitting in front of his laptop under a pretense of losing himself in work. So far, the effort had been a wasted one. He couldn't get his thoughts off the afternoon at the lake with Becca.

He heard the car turn into the driveway, saw the lights flick off outside the front window of the house. Hope surged up inside him.

He opened the front door of his grandmother's house to find his wife poised in mid-knock, a look of uncertainty marring her normally confident features.

"Hey," she said, hands shoved inside the pockets of a light jacket.

She normally wore her dark hair pulled back in a clip of some sort, but she'd left it down tonight. It hung against her shoulders, thick and glossy in the way he'd once liked for her to wear it. "Phoebe, what are you doing here?"

She glanced away, as if gathering reserve strength for what she was about to say. "I came because I think you need someone, Matt."

He ran a hand down the back of his neck and tried to keep his irritation in check. "If I did, what would possibly make you think it would be you?" His voice reverberated with a low anger, and he instantly saw the imprint of it on her face, as if he had physically slapped her. He couldn't deny wanting to hurt her, even as he hated himself for succumbing to the base instinct.

"May I come in? I don't have to stay, but can we at least talk?"

Matt didn't want to talk. He didn't want to look at her, much less listen to her. They'd attempted the irrelevant effort of explanation a number of times in past weeks, and for him, it had led nowhere that offered anything resembling enlightenment.

Down the street a dog barked, and a door opened, then closed. His own sense of decency prevented him from immediately sending her on her way. "Five minutes," he said, stepping back and waving her in.

"Thank you, Matt," she said, pressing a hand to his arm.

Matt recoiled as if she had touched a hot iron to his skin. He saw the rejection register in her eyes, but he couldn't bring himself to care.

He led her to the kitchen since it was the most neutral place in the house. He'd brought her home only once when they'd first started dating. Gran had already moved to the nursing home, and they'd spent a single night here. Phoebe complained about the aging appliances and the fact that there wasn't even a microwave to heat up the cold pizza they'd picked up on the way. "How could anyone live without a microwave?" she'd asked.

Matt had read enough about the radiating of food not to care if he ever subjected his own to it again. But Phoebe argued the path of convenience, and they agreed to disagree that night. As they had done so many other times.

Ironically enough, this was the conversation that surfaced the day he'd stood in his office and finally put together the pieces of her affair. That evening after work, he'd walked straight into their kitchen and yanked the power cord to the oversize microwave out of the wall, then carried the thing out to the curb where it would later be rescued by two teenage boys on bicycles before it ever made it to the trash truck. Phoebe had only stared after him and never said a word about it. He wondered now if they'd done virtually that same thing for the duration of their marriage, dodged their differences with alternating concessions, trying too hard to be what the other wanted instead of what they really were.

He leaned against the sink counter and folded his arms across his chest. "Why are you really here?"

She hung her purse on the back of a chair and swallowed once, a hand to her throat. "May I have some water?"

He opened a cabinet door, handed her a glass, which she filled from the faucet. She took a long sip and then set it on the counter and turned to face him. "I don't expect you to ever forgive me for what I did, Matt. But people make mistakes. *I* made a mistake. My God, we've been married for ten years. Can't you at least let me try to make up for it?"

He looked at her for a long time before he said anything, a half-dozen answers that were nothing resembling kind springing to his tongue. But he bit them back, reaching for something that wouldn't leave the taste of bitterness in his mouth once he'd said it.

The refrigerator clicked on, humming an off-key note of advanced age. "I've tried to figure out the why," he said finally. "Gone over and over the possibilities. There has to be a why. People don't do things without motivation. But for the life of me, I haven't been able to figure out yours."

"Matt—"

"Subterfuge isn't you, Phoebe," he interrupted. "We both know it. If something is bothering you, you print it on a big flag and run it up the pole until it gets noticed."

"I waved that flag in front of your face for a very long time," she said, her voice breaking at the edges. "You just didn't see it."

Denial instantly sprang up and then wavered beneath a memory. A Saturday morning when Phoebe had gotten up earlier than usual and driven to Starbucks for coffee and chocolate cream cheese muffins. She'd brought them back upstairs to their bed on a large silver tray, but he'd already been up, planning to go in to work. When she'd offered to join him in the shower, he'd said he didn't have time.

Looking at her now, he felt a rush of guilt for the fact that there had been nothing urgent waiting for him at the office that morning. Memories of other mornings, other nights when she'd made similar efforts scattered through his consciousness like marbles on a wood floor. And under the onslaught, his own indignation suddenly wilted.

She stared at him and then shook her head. "We were both to blame, Matt," she said. "That's all I'm saying."

"It's too far gone, Phoebe."

She stared at him, not letting her eyes leave his. "Is it?"

The refrigerator kicked off, the room going suddenly silent. He didn't answer. Couldn't have said in that moment why he didn't.

She moved close and splayed her hand in the center

of his chest, staring at the back of it as if she could see through it to his beating heart. She looked up then. "Matt," she said. She leaned in and kissed him, the touch more question than promise.

When he didn't pull away, she deepened the kiss. He let her, all the anger draining out of him, and in its place a deep-rooted weariness. He let his wife kiss him while thoughts of that afternoon with Becca taunted him. He'd never really left her.

He knew the futility of the path they'd started down by meeting at the lake house, had seen it written clearly in her regretful eyes when she'd told him she had to go. It wasn't that he thought she was wrong. After all, what kind of idiot saw the land-mines-ahead sign posted clearly in front of him and just kept walking as if there were no possibility of one exploding beneath his feet?

He slid his arms around Phoebe's waist and pulled her to him, replacing her initiative with an unyielding resolve to put himself back in a place he understood. Even if it wasn't a perfect place, his heart had taken this hit and survived. He understood this place.

With Becca, he'd taken a hit of an altogether different magnitude, and that, he had thought he wouldn't survive. That was a place he couldn't go again.

He bent and slipped an arm around the back of Phoebe's legs, lifting her without letting his mouth leave hers. He carried her to the stairs and then up, until they reached the door to his room. He'd left a lamp on earlier, and the circle of light touched her face and the tears in her eyes.

He placed her on the bed, and she sat up, her legs over the side. She reached out and began to unbutton his shirt, her fingers clumsy at first, and then finding a steady rhythm. When the last one was undone, she pushed the shirt from his shoulders and unbuckled his belt. Becca's face flashed across his vision. Becca, laughing. Becca, leaving. He squeezed his eyes shut and leaned down, one hand on either side of Phoebe. He kissed her again, while she unbuttoned her blouse and shrugged out of it.

On the bed, he stretched out alongside her and slid his palm into the curve of her stomach. She made a soft moaning sound and changed the pace of the kiss to something far more urgent. He followed her, removing the rest of her clothes and then his own. And it was only after they were both lying naked side by side that it hit him in a sudden swoop of realization that they were both trying to fight their way back to a place of understanding.

He pulled away and looked down at her, pushing the hair from her face with a sudden tenderness marked by acceptance and regret.

She began to cry then, tears sliding down her cheeks and onto the white sheets beneath them.

He reached out a thumb and rubbed one away. "Shh."

"He asked me to marry him," she said.

Matt dropped back against the pillow, one arm across his forehead. "And we've both just figured out your answer."

"Oh, Matt. If this could work—"

"But it can't," he said.

"It can't."

They lay there for a while longer, quiet. Finally, Phoebe got up and slid her clothes on. She stood at the side of the bed, buttoning her blouse without looking at him. She slipped her shoes on and then sat down on the edge of the mattress, running the back of her hand across the center of his chest.

"For you, the only why that really matters, Matt, is yours. And I suspect the answer is here in this place. That's where your heart is. I think it always has been."

She leaned in and kissed the side of his face. "I hope you figure out what it is. I really do."

She got up then, and without looking back, walked out of the room and down the stairs, the front door clicking open and then closed in a sound as defining as it was final.

41

Promises

> *Choices are the hinges of destiny.*
> *– **Pythagoras***

Now

On the morning following her afternoon with Matt at the lake, Becca carried Emmy's breakfast tray upstairs to her room. She opened the door to find her sister curled up in a tight ball at the center of her bed, quietly sobbing.

"Emmy?" Becca set the tray down on the nightstand and slid across the mattress to put a hand on her shoulder. "What is it? Are you all right?"

Emmy stiffened at her touch, but did not answer. Becca lifted Emmy's chin and looked into her eyes, red-rimmed and swollen, as if she hadn't slept at all.

Becca went to the closet, pulled out a dress and shoes, went back to the bed, and helped her sister sit up. "Come on, Emmy. I think we need to go see the doctor today."

Emmy followed each of Becca's gentle instructions, putting her arms into the sleeves of her dress, her head hanging as Becca helped her with her shoes. All the while, she cried as if someone had opened a valve inside her, as if she simply could not stem the flow.

The door to the room opened, and Martha stepped inside, assessing the two of them and then closing it quickly behind her. "What is it, Becca?"

"Emmy needs to see Dr. Hayes," she said, resolve in her voice.

"Becca. I think you're overreacting. This will pass."

"You don't know that."

"And you don't know that it won't."

Becca turned then, unable to keep her voice even when she said, "How many days should we wait? A week? A month? She's suffering, Mama. She needs help."

"And have the doctors really helped her the other times? This medication you insist she needs. Has it done any good at all? Has it helped her have a normal life?"

"There is no shame in needing help, Mama." Becca reached for calm, opening a dresser drawer and retrieving Emmy's brush before looking at her mother again. "Sometimes, the medications need to be changed," she said, repeating what Dr. Hayes had told her the other times when this had happened. "Sometimes, they stop working."

Martha started to say something, then pressed her lips together, a look of utter weariness coming over her.

For a moment, Becca's determination softened, and she questioned herself, not for the first time. "Will you help me get her downstairs?"

But Martha didn't answer, instead turning and leaving the room.

"I'll be right back," Becca said to Emmy, going down the hall to Abby's room. She knocked once, then stepped inside. Abby was already dressed and brushing her teeth.

"It's Emmy," Becca said. "She's not doing so well this morning. I think her medicine may need to be changed."

"You're taking her to the doctor?"

"Yes."

"I'll go with you," Abby said.

"You have school today, honey."

"I can miss it. It's no big deal."

Becca reached for Abby's hand, squeezed it once. "We'll be fine, okay? I just need some help getting her downstairs."

With each of them on either side of Emmy, they eased their way out of the house and into the truck. Emmy sat where they put her, the seat belt secured at her waist, tears still streaming freely down her face.

Becca turned to Abby. "Want me to drop you at school?"

Abby glanced away and then back again, something close to apology in her voice. "Beau's picking me up this morning."

"Ah," Becca said. "Abby, your father still doesn't know about this."

"No," Abby said.

Becca sighed once, leaning in to kiss Abby's forehead. "You know this won't be easy."

"I know."

A look of understanding passed between them.

"He's really important to you," Becca said.

"He is."

"Sometimes we don't get the chance to remake our choices. Be sure, okay?"

Abby leaned in and pressed her cheek to Becca's chest, the same as she had as a little girl. Becca put a hand to the back of her head, wishing for the capacity to offer her the guarantees and reassurance for which she was silently asking.

Becca glanced inside the truck at her sister and then back at Abby. In her eyes, she saw the same question she'd asked at Abby's age.

"Sometimes, it isn't enough, sweetheart," Becca said. "It just isn't enough."

∞

Then

THE REMAINING WEEKS of the summer flew by.

Becca grew to dread going to bed at night, knowing the next morning would bring them one day closer to Matt's leaving for school.

At first, they just didn't talk about it, letting it loom like some enormous genie hovering above them, ready to zap the happiness they'd found with one another into the starkest kind of loneliness.

But one Saturday night when they'd driven into Roanoke to eat at a restaurant downtown, Becca talked less than normal, leaving most of her sandwich and chips on her plate. Matt had tried several different threads of conversation, but she heard the heaviness in his voice and realized he was feeling the same things she was feeling.

He reached across the table and took her hand, squeezing once. "Hey," he said, "the summer's not over yet."

"I know," she said, trying to smile.

He signaled a waitress and paid their bill, then led her outside to his grandmother's station wagon, holding her door and waiting until she slid inside before closing it.

He drove down Jefferson Street, taking a left and crossing the bridge that led to Mill Mountain. They took the winding road to the top and pulled into the parking lot behind the city's well-known landmark star.

"I've never seen it this close," Becca said. "It's so tall."

"Close to ninety feet if I remember right," Matt said.

She leaned forward to look out the windshield at the view of the Roanoke valley below. "It's beautiful from here."

Matt turned in his seat, touched her face with his hand. "Hey."

She looked at him then, biting her lip to keep from losing the composure she'd worked so hard to maintain all night.

"Everything's going to be all right," he said.

"Oh, Matt," she said, shaking her head.

He reached for her then, folding her into his arms and pressing his face against her neck. "It really is. It's up to us, you know."

She let herself take comfort in his embrace, tried to believe it was that simple. But doubt had crept its way into her every thought these past weeks, and she could no more shake it now than she could turn herself into something other than what she was. She pulled back to look at him. "Are we kidding ourselves about this?"

"What do you mean?"

"You're going to college. I'm not. You're going to be in a whole new world. I'll be here."

"I'll come home on the weekends. It's only a two hour drive."

"That doesn't seem fair to you."

He touched her cheek with the back of his hand. "How about letting me decide what's fair to me?"

She was quiet for a moment. "I just don't want you to miss out on all the college stuff."

"I may not be too experienced in the ways of the world, but I do know that it isn't possible to have everything. And I want you. I want you, Becca."

Part of her felt as if she should argue further. To not do so seemed selfish. But the truth was that she wanted him, too. Already, she couldn't imagine life without him. Couldn't imagine going back to the days before he had come to work on the farm. That life now seemed impossibly bland. And if she were to admit it, lonely.

"You have to promise me something," she said.

"Okay. What?"

"That if you get there and change your mind—"

"Becca," he interrupted.

"No," she said, holding up a hand. "Please. Let me finish. If you start to feel that this isn't what you want, that you just want to go to college and not have a girlfriend back home, you'll tell me. And I'll understand."

He looked at her for a few moments, then leaned in and kissed her on the mouth. When he pulled back, he kept his eyes on hers. "I think you're underestimating one thing."

"What's that?" she said, her voice soft.

"The fact that I'm crazy about you. That I can't go to sleep at night because I can't quit thinking about you. That you're the first thing I think about when I wake up in the morning. And that I have no idea how I'm going to get through the days between when we see each other."

Becca looked down at her lap, swallowing hard. "Matt."

He ducked in then and kissed her again. She slid her arms around his neck and sought to get as close to him as she could.

They kissed until they were both breathing hard and impatient with the console separating their seats. The radio played a slow song, and the light from the star made stripes across them through the windshield.

A vehicle pulled into the lot, turning into a space twenty or thirty yards away. Becca pulled back and smoothed her hands over her hair. "There's something I need to say, Matt. So, please, let me say it."

He looked at her for a moment, his voice soft when he said, "Go ahead."

"I don't want to be the wedge between you and everything else in your life. You have a lot ahead of you.

And already, so many things have changed. Your friendship with Wilks—"

"Hey," he said, interrupting her there. "That's not your deal, okay? Neither one of us is going to make him a different person. He's the only one who can do that."

"But the two of you were friends for so long."

"Yeah, maybe I didn't really know what a friend was." He leaned against his door, his eyes on her. "Will you promise me something?"

"What?" she said.

"That you'll consider going to college."

She shook her head. "Matt, I didn't finish high school."

"But you could if you wanted to."

She started to say how crazy that sounded, but stopped herself, recognizing the little leap in her pulse as excitement for the possibility. "I don't see how I could—"

"I see how you could. I've heard you were an excellent student."

"I liked school."

"Why did you quit?"

She hesitated, trying to find words that would make him understand how different their lives had been to this point. "It was what my family expected of me."

"Did you agree?"

She turned her head and looked out the window into the dark night. "Not completely," she said.

"Then just think about it. That's all I ask."

"It sounds impossible."

"I think we both know that we have some roadblocks in our path. It seems to me that the key is making sure we figure out how to go around them and not let them trip us up for good."

"You make it sound so easy."

"If we do what's right for us, I think it is."

She glanced at the clock on the dashboard. 11:30 p.m. "I need to get home," she said.

"You'll think about it?"

She smiled. Nodded once. "I'll think about it."

"Excellent," he said, grinning. He started the car and pulled out of the lot, passing the truck that had joined them at the overlook a few minutes ago. The shape of a boy and girl shone through the back window, the girl's head resting on the boy's shoulder. Becca reached for Matt's hand, entwining her fingers with his. They didn't let go of one another until they were back in Ballard County, and he dropped her at the front door of her house.

42

Questions

Life is simple, it's just not easy. – ***Author Unknown***

Now

Matt didn't feel like running this morning, but he made himself anyway. He needed to clear his head, and short of a stiff bourbon at eight a.m., it was the only way he knew to do so.

He left the house at a pace faster than he normally started out, finishing the first mile of his loop through town in just over six minutes. He slowed down for the second mile, the end of which he ran past Ballard Family Medicine, a practice now housed in what had once been the home of one of the town's early founders.

He topped the knoll, winded and sweating, spotting Becca's white truck just as she pulled up in front of the doctor's office. He slowed and then stopped short of the driver's side door.

Becca glanced up and saw him, surprise widening her eyes, and then something else he couldn't readily identify. She rolled down the window with obvious reluctance.

"Hi," he said.

"Hi."

He ducked his head to speak to her passenger, recognizing her then as Becca's sister, Emmy. She did not respond to his greeting or glance his way at all. He looked at Becca again. "Are you okay?" he asked, feeling that something wasn't right.

She glanced down at her lap and then back at him with a forced smile. "Yes. Fine."

"Do you need some help?"

"No," she said quickly. "Thank you."

He stared at her for a moment, not sure what to say, but certain that she wanted him to go. "Okay," he said, backing up a step. And then, against his better judgment, "Becca. Will you call me?"

"It's better if I don't," she said.

Emmy still had not looked at him. "Becca-" he said.

"Matt. Go, please. Just go."

With reluctance, he turned then and ran on, glancing back once to see that she hadn't yet gotten out of the truck. There was something undeniably odd in what had just happened. As if she were hiding something, although what he couldn't imagine.

Half-way down the next hill, he stopped, pulled back to the top by his own curiosity. He watched as Becca crossed the street with her arm around Emmy's waist, all but carrying her.

She glanced his way then and stumbled a step, righting herself with a look of pain.

"Becca, let me help," he called out.

"No." She raised one hand to stop him, anger in her voice now. "I don't need your help, Matt. We're fine. Really. We're fine."

She didn't look his way again, but crossed the street to the sidewalk and then helped Emmy through the front door of the clinic. Matt stood, transfixed. *We're fine.* Why then was he left with the sense that they were anything but?

BECCA'S WORDS ECHOED in Matt's head the remainder of the morning, a thicket of questions forming in their wake. What had happened to Emmy? And why was Becca so protective of her?

He hung out in the house until noon and then got in the Land Rover, needing a change of scenery. He drove through town, deciding to stop at the cafe on North Main for lunch. The place was a landmark in the county and had been around for as long as Matt could remember. He went inside and took a booth out front, lifting a hand to a few familiar faces. He gave his order for the daily special of grilled chicken and mashed potatoes to a friendly waitress who took it back to the kitchen and then returned with his iced tea.

"You're Matt Griffith, aren't you?"

He found nothing familiar in her face, but wondered if he should know her. "Yeah, I am."

She smiled, white teeth flashing against caramel-colored skin. "You used to date Becca Brubaker, didn't you?"

"You know her?"

"Sort of. Her brother married my cousin. Linda."

"He did?" Matt said.

"He did."

"Good for him."

She glanced over her shoulder at the kitchen, then said, "It's kind of disgusting how in love those two are."

"Still?" he said.

"Still."

"They're lucky."

"Either that, or they knew a good thing when they saw it."

"Jacob never struck me as a dumb guy."

"No," she said. "Well, I better get back to the kitchen and check on your order."

"Thanks," he said.

"You bet."

She'd turned to go when he stopped her with, "Excuse me."

"Something else you need?"

He hesitated, and then, "Do you know their sister? Emmy?"

"I knew her in school. We were the same age. Shame what happened to her. They said she was never the same after John died."

"John?"

"Rutrough. The boy she dated. They were supposed to get married, apparently."

"When did he die?"

She thought for a moment. "It was the same year Jacob and Linda got married in September. It happened right before that. Must have been August, I guess."

August. The same month he'd left for college. The same month Becca had cut him out of her life.

43

Understanding

The price of anything is the amount of life you exchange for it.
– Henry David Thoreau

Now

Throughout the morning Martha tried to stay busy, cleaning rooms that didn't need cleaning, baking two pies when she'd just made two others the afternoon before. She tried to tell herself she hadn't been too harsh with Becca earlier. And yet she knew she had. Knew, too, that Becca was doing what she thought best for Emmy.

It was almost noon when Martha walked outside and stood staring at the crest of Tinker's Knob, one hand to the small of her lower back where a permanent ache seemed to have lodged.

She glanced at the fence that ran alongside the left edge of the yard and the line of marigolds she and Becca had planted earlier in the spring. Their bold yellow beckoned her forward, and she crossed the grass, bending to pick a dozen or so.

With the bouquet in one hand she let herself through a metal pasture gate and walked through the field where in between tugs of green grass, black and white cows grazed, each noting her progress with big, curious eyes.

The walk from the house to the family cemetery took her a good fifteen minutes. On a younger person's legs, it could be accomplished in five at the most. At the far end of the pasture, Martha let herself through another gate and climbed the short hill where a single enormous pine tree lent shade to the fenced graveyard.

She stood for a moment, staring at the rows of tombstones, many of the oldest ones a single rock that marked the burial spot. Generations of her own family had been laid to rest in this place, and although she had attended the burials of many of her relatives here, she had always found it to be a spot of great peacefulness.

She opened the single latch gate and walked through, closing it behind her. A worn path encompassed the perimeter of the cemetery. Martha followed it to the right hand corner where a single large headstone and a smaller one sat side by side. She dropped to her knees in between the two, a hand resting on each. The larger one was Daniel's, the chiseled text across the top reading, GONE TO BE WITH THE LORD, DANIEL MILLER. The smaller one read WILLIAM MILLER, PRECIOUS INFANT, RESTING IN GOD'S ARMS.

William had been born to Martha and Daniel in between Becca and Emmy. He'd arrived two months early and lived only a few hours after his birth, his lungs not strong enough to sustain him. He'd been born in their home, and when his last breath left his little body, Martha sat for hours just holding him, unable to let him go, rocking him in the chair she had rocked both Jacob and Becca in. Daniel had finally taken him from her, wrapping him in a soft blue blanket, pulling one corner over the baby's sweet face.

Even now, so many decades later, she could still feel the

pain of that moment, a pain that never again left her but stayed dormant in one of her heart's chambers, able to flare to life with a single memory, a single reminder.

She ran her fingers over the words on the tombstone and imagined Lydia Rutrough sitting in front of her nearly grown son's tombstone, ragged pain consuming her fresh with each visit. Empathy flooded through Martha, and she didn't know which would be worse, having a child for so short a time, or having him for sixteen years and then to lose him.

But if there was anything Martha had come to understand about life, it was that people didn't get to choose their tragedy. Tragedy chose its people.

Martha divided the marigolds she'd brought with her, placing half on William's grave and half on Daniel's. She pulled stray weeds from the sides of the headstones until they were neat again.

When she was done, she knelt in front of Daniel's and tried to bring to memory his face as it had been when they'd first met, young and handsome, his eyes full with love for her.

Now, when she looked in the mirror each morning and saw the lines so clearly etched in her face, it was hard to believe anyone could have loved her as both Mitch and Daniel had loved her. But the certainty of this had never left her, and for this, she was grateful. Especially when she thought of herself as Becca must surely see her. A bitter old woman who had forgotten how to smile or laugh.

She was worried about Becca and Emmy. She'd considered, even, driving into town and waiting for them outside the doctor's office. She couldn't say for sure what had prevented her, respect for Becca's decision-making ability or worry for what news the doctor might have given her about Emmy.

She wasn't naïve. She could see Emmy's downward progression. She knew, too, that Becca was right to be concerned. How did she explain then her own behavior this morning? Her reluctance to admit that Becca was right?

She stared at her husband's tombstone and wondered if she had come here today thinking she would somehow find answers. Looking to Daniel for guidance when he was no longer here to guide her.

A breeze lifted the boughs of the pine standing guard over the small cemetery. For Martha, the sound of the wind sifting through the pine needles was a lonely sound. It echoed inside her, and brought with it the resounding realization that she was alone in this. She could no longer rely on Daniel to steer her in the direction of right. Since his death, she had limped along on the assumption that everything they had done was for the best. And now, she no longer knew.

Sitting here in this place where she had lain both husband and son to rest, it was suddenly, painfully clear to her that from this point on, she would have to choose her direction for herself. Choose it and then live with it.

44

There Comes a Day

Are we not like two volumes of one book?
– Marceline Desbordes-Valmore

Now

The appointment with Dr. Hayes did not go as Becca had expected. There was a concern in his expression today that she had not seen before, or perhaps had not let herself see. This morning, she felt the weight of it like a leaden blanket across her shoulders.

Once he'd finished examining Emmy, Dr. Hayes asked his nurse to wait with her while he spoke privately with Becca.

They walked down a short hall to his office. "Have a seat, Becca," he said, closing the door behind him and walking around the desk to sit across from her. She had known Dr. Hayes for twenty-five years or more. He had been involved in Emmy's treatment from the beginning, recommending early on the hospital in North Carolina where she had stayed for a few months with little to no change in her condition.

"Becca," he said, sitting back in his chair and giving her

a long look. "I'm not happy with the changes in Emmy. I think you should consider hospitalizing her."

Becca leaned back, caught off guard by the abrupt admission. "Based on what?"

"Her weight is down significantly. Clearly, the medication isn't controlling her depression."

"Can't we try something else?"

"We would be switching back to something she's already taken. I don't have to tell you that she's eventually declined on every medication we've tried."

"Why are they not working?" Becca asked, hearing the note of helplessness in her own question.

"There is no magic button, Becca," he said, not unkindly. "As I've explained before, Emmy's depression isn't like a broken arm where we can locate the exact spot of the fracture and reset it. Recovery depends on finding the most effective treatment. And to be honest, on the patient's willingness to want to be helped. I'm getting off the medical facts track here, but I hope we know each other well enough for me to speak from the gut. I think it might just be easier for Emmy to stay in retreat mode than to come out and face the things she's not able to face."

In eighteen years, Dr. Hayes had never been this blunt with her. And it scared her. "We can't know what she's thinking," Becca said. "What she feels."

"No. Not for sure. But we do know that Emmy's trauma was severe, and that she has never been the same since. More and more is being learned about the effects of post-traumatic stress disorder. I know I've said most of this to you before, but scientists believe a traumatic event can actually change the biology of the brain. No one knows for sure if it's reversible. Emmy's depression has obviously complicated all of this."

Becca absorbed this before saying, "What could they do for her that we're not already doing?"

"Maybe nothing. Maybe something."

She laughed a hollow laugh. "That's certainly a glowing recommendation."

"I'm not sure you're going to have a choice, Becca," he said, his face drawn with regret.

"I can't send her away, Dr. Hayes."

"Becca," he said, his tone losing the distance of doctor-patient, infused now with compassion. "There are very few families who would do what you've done. But this kind of dedication doesn't come without a price. How long can you keep carrying your sister?"

Becca looked at him and said the only thing she knew to say. "For as long as it takes."

Dr. Hayes reached for his prescription pad, writing for a few moments and then tearing off the single paper. "At some point, you need to start thinking about yourself, Becca. That's okay, you know."

Without answering, she took the prescription from him and left the office.

IT WAS THE kind of early summer day they used to love as kids. The sun so bright against the blue sky that it was nearly painful to look at it. The air smelled like fresh cut grass and fully bloomed flowers.

With Emmy in the seat next to her, Becca waited in the CVS drive-through while the new medicine was filled. She paid the cashier and pulled back out to the main road. She started to make the right hand turn that would take them back home and then on impulse, turned left instead. "I think maybe you need a change of scenery," she said to Emmy, grinding the old truck's gears to fourth and rolling down her window to let in the warm air.

She stopped again at the McDonald's drive-through,

ordering them each a Big Mac, fries, and a Coke, foods they rarely ate. Today, Becca felt the need to step outside normalcy. Today, she felt as if the boundaries were choking her. And it was only as they sped down Route 40 toward the lake and the house she had begun to think of as hers that she felt them begin to loosen.

45

The Light

Our roots say we're sisters, our hearts say we're friends.
– Author Unknown

Now

Please don't worry, Becca. Everything is going to be all right.

Of course I don't say the words out loud. My lips are no longer capable of making their sound even as they run through my head, perfectly formed.

Becca's hands grip the wheel with the kind of determination that gets a person places in this life. This is Becca. Always looking ahead to the next roadblock, trying to foresee the inevitable, plan a way around it.

I want to tell her that I know bad things happen to everyone in this world. That sometimes people get past them. And sometimes those bad things break them. That some things just happen no matter how much we fight against them. She wouldn't believe me though. It's simply not in her nature to give up. And given the choice, she will never let me, either.

I look at my sister, at the worry drawing her mouth into a tight line where smiles used to form so readily. I wonder which of us has suffered the most. I think it could be easily argued that Becca has, that as long as I am here, she will continue to do so.

Here in this admission is the answer for us both.

There is only one way out. The understanding came to me some time ago, my mind glimpsing the solution in pieces at first. It was a relief, really. To finally see that I have an exit, one I can step through at any time.

Riding along in our old truck, warm spring air swirling through the lowered windows, I know without question that time has come. The certainty of this lifts some of the heaviness from my chest, and I can actually breathe better. I can only pray that in the end, all will be forgiven.

46

Embers

Our hearts are lamps for ever burning...
– Henry Wadsworth Longfellow

Now

Matt was at the hardware on Franklin Street when he saw Becca drive by. He'd been buying a couple gallons of white paint for the front porch railing on his grandmother's house. Searching, in truth, for a physical distraction from the incessant round of questions looping through his head.

He paid a talkative cashier, and then without giving himself time to consider the wisdom of it, got in the Land Rover and drove after Becca. From the stoplight on Tanyard, he spotted her white truck a half-mile or so in front of him. He followed her out of town and took the left turn onto 122, hanging back a bit, certain she would stop if she saw him.

Twenty minutes later, she took the right to the lake house. He followed still, close enough now for her to easily see him in the rear view mirror. But she didn't slow down until she pulled in at the back of the house. She got out of the truck and walked over to his window.

Becca looked at Matt for several moments, her face revealing an inner struggle, a pain he didn't recognize. "Matt," she said. "You shouldn't be here."

"No," he agreed. "I probably shouldn't."

She considered this, then glanced over her shoulder at the truck where her sister sat on the passenger side. "I thought Emmy might like a picnic out here."

"Good day for it," he said. "Would it be all right if I join you?"

She hesitated. She knew she should send him away. This, of all things, was none of his business. But she simply did not have the stamina for another battle today. "Two Big Macs should be enough for the three of us."

He got out of the Land Rover and walked across the grass with her to the truck. She opened the door and took Emmy's arm, helping her out. Matt went to Emmy's other side and put a hand to her elbow, glancing at Becca for permission. In her eyes, he saw relief, as if it were the last thing she'd expected him to do, the last and most welcome.

They chose a spot close to the lake's edge where they could hear the gentle lap of the water against the red clay shoreline. They spread out the quilt Becca had brought along, and Matt set the food at one corner, before helping Emmy to sit on the opposite end.

She looked up at him once, and he was hit with the feeling that she recognized him. She didn't speak though and looked off at the tranquil surface of the lake.

Becca divvied up the food, putting a portion in front of each of them.

"I'm really not hungry," Matt said, feeling guilty now for horning in on their lunch.

"There's plenty," she said.

They ate without talking, neither Becca nor Matt doing

their food justice. Emmy picked at hers, eating almost nothing.

Matt brought up a variety of subjects, uncomfortable with the silence. They talked in generalities about the growth at the lake, how people were selling their homes up north and moving to Tinker's Knob for their retirement years. How the population increase would change things. Some, for the good. Some, not so much.

Once they'd finished eating, Becca stood and said, "I think I'll get Emmy a chair from the porch."

"I'll give you a hand," Matt said, following her to the house. They each took one side of the old rocker and carried it back. Becca helped Emmy to stand and then sit in the chair, facing the water.

"There," she said. "That's better."

Emmy folded her hands in her lap and tipped the chair back and forth, something in her face lightening with the motion.

Becca looked at Matt. "Would you like to walk along the shore?" she said.

Matt nodded. "Sure."

"I'll be within sight, Emmy," Becca said, placing a hand on her sister's shoulder and then walking toward the water.

Matt followed, glancing back once to make sure Emmy was okay. He caught up with Becca, and they walked side by side, silent, until they reached the shade of a large oak that grew close to the water.

"Is she like this because of what happened with John?"

Becca glanced up, her eyes wide, the question clearly startling her.

"This morning over at the cafe," he explained, "someone was telling me about how he died. One of the waitresses there."

"What did she say?"

"That it was a horrible accident. And Emmy never got over it."

She stared off at the lake. "I guess she never did," she finally said, her voice wavering with emotion. "You think that it will get better. That with time, a person can heal. But some wounds aren't like that. Some wounds are . . . forever."

Matt absorbed the words, felt their hollow echo. "I'm sorry, Becca."

She nodded, and then, "A few times, we thought a medication might be making a difference, but eventually, they all seem to stop helping. Doctor Hayes says she has to want to get better, that there must be a balance between medication, our love for her, and her own will to live. I guess I've thought we could keep pulling her along until one day, she would reach out, and that she would want to come back."

"This all happened just after I left for college," he said. "Why didn't you tell me, Becca? Why didn't you let me know?"

"You had another life to go on to."

"And I thought you were going to be a part of that life. Is this why you ended things between us? So that you could take care of her?"

She glanced away, shaking her head. "Oh, Matt, that was so long ago."

"And I've never forgotten any of it." He made no attempt to hide the emotion in his voice.

She looked at him then, her eyes brimming with tears. "We both knew it would never have worked."

"Did we?"

"We should have."

Several beats of silence passed, and then Matt reached for her hand, the action automatic. He wasn't thinking of vows or lines that shouldn't be crossed. Of the different lives they had led. Or what such a gesture meant. He saw the pain in her face and felt it reverberate through him like the whiplash that follows a sudden stop in motion. He didn't know what to say, so he said nothing, just held her hand, comfort his intent. But with the connection came awareness of other things. Of the delicacy of her hands, as surprising to him now as it had been eighteen years ago, hands capable of making things grow, hands capable of making him feel things he had never before felt.

Something bowed within him, and for a moment, he didn't let himself look up, certain she would pull away. When he finally looked at her, her eyes were liquid with sadness and regret, for her sister, he knew. But he sensed there was more. That here, in this moment, she had let down her guard. That she felt the same grief he felt for the loss of what they had once been to each other. And for the walls separating them from ever finding their way back to it.

"Becca," he said.

"Don't," she said, her voice little more than a whisper. "It will only make it worse."

"How could it?"

"Matt, please."

He glanced at the spot where Emmy still sat, rocking in a barely discernible motion. He stood in pained silence, certain that nothing could feel worse than the forced release of something you never wanted to let go of in the first place.

∞

Then

NEVER IN HIS life had Matt both dreaded and looked forward to something so much. On the one hand, the thought of leaving for college and being separated from

Becca filled him with the kind of anxiety that kept him awake at night wondering if he could stand being apart from her. And on the other hand, he told himself it was just a matter of time before they could be together again in the same place.

Becca had already made some calls about completing her GED. And although at first she had been hesitant, as if she was considering doing something wrong, she had told him just the day before that she was excited about the classes she would be taking and getting back into studying again. She had yet to tell her parents about her plans, saying she would do so when she felt the time was right.

Matt had finished his last day at the farm two days before, using the time since then to pack and tie up loose ends before driving to Charlottesville on the eighteenth. For their last night together before he left, he had planned something special, telling Becca only that she would need a bathing suit and an appetite.

He picked her up at four o'clock, getting out to open the station wagon door for her, then glancing up to see her mother standing at the living room window, watching them go. At the look on her face, he faltered for a moment, lifting his hand and offering a respectful nod as he walked back to his side of the car.

From the beginning, he had been aware of Mrs. Miller's disapproval of his interest in Becca. She had made little attempt to hide it. Today, though, it wasn't disapproval he saw in her lined features, but something more like concern. Fear, even.

He had no idea what to make of that, telling himself that eventually she would come to see that he would never hurt her daughter.

Matt pulled out of the driveway and headed for the main road, silently reaching for Becca's hand and clasping it in his. He felt her sadness, saw, too, how she tried to hide it beneath a cheerful expression.

"Hey," he said.

She looked at him then, her blue eyes going liquid.

"We're going to be okay. I promise."

She nodded, biting her lip.

"Did your mom give you a hard time about going out with me tonight?"

"You could say that," she said.

"It'll take time, I know," he said. "But I'll prove to her that I'm good for you, that I would never hurt you."

She leaned over then and put her head on his shoulder, linking her arm with his. They drove the rest of the way out to the lake house in near silence, the imminence of their parting hanging heavy on them both.

Matt pulled up at the back of the house, turning in the seat to look at her. "I came out earlier today and did some things. I want this night to be special, Becca."

She leaned in and kissed him. "Thank you. And it will be."

They got out then and walked to the house, Matt stopping her at the back door. "Wait here a minute, okay?"

"Okay," she said, smiling.

He went inside and hustled through the few things he had left to complete, opening the door finally and waving her in. "Close your eyes and take my hand," he said.

She did as he asked and followed him down the short hallway and into the small dining room, which he'd transformed with white candles and yellow roses. In the increasing dimness of dusk, the candles flickered shadows across the floor and ceiling.

"Okay," he said. "You can open your eyes."

She did so, staring for a moment at the room and the

table set with white plates and crystal glasses. “Oh, Matt,” she said. “It’s beautiful.”

“Gran gave me a few tips. Plus she did the cooking.”

“I think I’m actually glad about that,” she said, smiling.

They went into the kitchen, warming up the food on the stove and doing their best to avoid talking about what was ahead, even as it loomed over them like a huge black cloud.

They took their time with dinner, the roast and potatoes tender and delicious. For dessert, there was chocolate cake with chocolate icing, but by this point, they both picked at it, their appetites decreasing as the few hours they had left together slid by.

Becca pushed her plate away after a few bites, saying, “Everything was wonderful.”

“Why don’t we go for a swim?” he said.

“Okay.”

They cleared the table and put the dishes in the dishwasher, working side by side, mostly silent. They changed into bathing suits then, meeting outside on the porch that faced the lake.

By now, dark had settled, the moon a circle of light on the water in front of the dock. They walked across the yard hand in hand, not saying anything until they reached the end of the pier.

“Are you up for a swim?” Matt said, running his hands through her long hair.

“Only if you promise not to let go of me.”

“That’s easy,” he said, lowering himself into the water and then turning to look back at her. She unbuttoned the cotton cover up she wore over a pink bathing suit, letting it drop to the floor. Matt swallowed once, his body responding the way it always did at the sight of her.

She put her arms by her sides and dropped into the water straight as an arrow, only to resurface sputtering and laughing. She reached out an arm and slipped it around his neck.

They swam out a bit and then back, teasing and splashing water, grabbing onto the dock's edge and kissing until they were both breathing hard.

Matt slipped his free arm around her waist and pulled her up close. They stared into each other's eyes, Matt letting everything he felt for her show there. And then he spoke the words he'd been holding inside for weeks. "What would you say if I said I want to marry you someday?"

Her eyes widened, as if it was the last thing she'd expected him to say. She glanced off, and then looked back at him, shaking her head. "Don't say things you'll wish you could take back at some point."

"Why would I take it back?"

"For all the reasons we've talked about before."

"Becca," he said, brushing the back of his hand across her cheek. "I'm not going to go to Charlottesville and decide I want another girl. You're just going to have to trust me on that."

She didn't say anything for a few moments. "I guess I will," she said.

He smiled. "You guess you'll marry me? Or guess you'll trust me?"

"Both," she said, reaching up to kiss him again.

Her mouth was soft and seeking against his, and there with the water making gentle slapping noises against the sides of the dock and the buzz of a boat in the distance. Matt had no idea how he was going to bring himself to leave her the next day.

She tipped her head back and looked up at him. "I want to be with you tonight," she said.

Matt said nothing for a few moments, his heart

thrumming hard. He leaned in, kissed her, and then said, "Are you sure?"

"Yes. I'm sure."

She let go of him then, climbing the ladder to the dock, and turning to wait for him. They walked back to the house in their wet bathing suits, bare feet noiseless on the dew-damp grass. Inside, Matt led her to the bedroom just off the living room and closed the door behind them. The moonlight found its way in through the cracked wooden blinds. He put his arms around her and drew her close, kissing her with all the feeling inside him.

She pressed herself to him and kissed him back. They undressed each other, Becca unable to look at him at first, and then finally doing so with eyes full of love and appreciation.

He led her to the bed, and they lay down together, fully exploring one another for the first time, as if they needed this memory to carry with them over what they knew would be difficult months ahead.

They took their time. Matt wanted to be able to think back on this night as a vow to one another, a commitment from the heart. In that single moment when they were as close as it is possible for two human beings to be, he looked into her face and said, "I love you, Becca Miller."

She looked back at him, eyes wide open. "I love you, Matt Griffith."

And with those words, whispered with utter sincerity, Matt had every reason to believe they would spend the rest of their lives together. That they would get through the next year and figure out a way to be together for good.

Little did he know that when this night ended, eighteen years would pass before he ever saw her again.

47

Middle Ground

"Neither should a ship rely on one small anchor, nor should life rest on a single hope."
– Epictetus

Now

From the kitchen, Martha heard Becca pull up at the front of the house, the engine of the old truck groaning a sigh of relief as it reluctantly settled into silence. She'd been listening for them for hours now, worry beginning its deep dance, until she could think of nothing beyond an image of the two of them stranded along a road somewhere.

She'd called the cell phone Becca carried with her a number of times but had only gotten the message system.

And so by the time she heard the truck's familiar rattles on the gravel drive, she felt weak with gratitude. She walked to the front door as fast as her arthritic limbs would allow and then down the steps to the walkway where Becca helped Emmy slide out.

Martha stopped just short of them and said, "I was worried."

"I'm sorry, Mama," Becca said. "I thought Emmy could use a change of scenery. We drove out to the lake."

"Oh," Martha said, in the next breath starting to chastise Becca for not calling and then stopping herself. "Did she enjoy it?"

Becca glanced up then, clearly surprised by the question. "I think so," she said.

"Good," Martha said, hearing the effort in her own voice. She took Emmy's other arm, and together they led her into the house and up the stairs. In Emmy's bedroom, they settled her in her favorite chair by the window, the two of them working in a quiet harmony that Martha could not remember feeling between them for many years.

It was only after they'd gotten her settled and walked back downstairs to the kitchen that Martha said, "What did Dr. Hayes say?"

Becca ran a hand around the back of her neck, fatigue etched in her face when she said, "He changed her medication again."

Martha could tell by the look in her daughter's eyes that there was more. "And what else?"

Becca didn't answer for several moments, her voice cracking at the edges when she finally spoke. "He thinks we should consider another hospital program."

Martha leaned against the counter behind her, one hand anchoring her against the sudden unsteadiness in her legs. "And what do you think?"

Becca shook her head. "I don't know what to think. I just know she's getting worse."

Martha crossed the floor and sat down at the table, every inch of her body suddenly weighted with a tiredness that went to her very bones. She didn't speak for several moments and when she did, weariness laced each word. "Do you think we should send her to another of those places?"

"I can't bear the thought of it," Becca said.

"Neither can I."

Martha looked up then and met Becca's gaze. There was a softness there, an empathy, that she had not seen directed at her in longer than she could remember. It made something in her heart simultaneously dip and soar. "So what do we do?" she asked, honestly hoping Becca had the answer.

"Trust that the new medicine will help her."

"And if it doesn't?"

Becca stepped forward and put her hand on Martha's shoulder. "Let's not try to figure that out until we have to."

Tears welled in Martha's eyes. She wiped them away with the back of one hand, nodding in silence. They didn't say anything else. It was nice, though, the way Becca didn't move off right away, but remained where she was, her hand an anchor between them, steady, soothing.

48

Enough

"Love is never lost. If not reciprocated, it will flow back and soften and purify the heart."
*– **Washington Irving***

Now
Becca sat at the table long after her mother went upstairs. Lethargy had attached itself to her limbs, and it seemed far easier to stay where she was than to try and figure out a direction from here.

Aaron walked up from the barn, wiping his forehead and the back of his neck with a blue bandana handkerchief before folding it and putting it away. He stopped when he saw Becca. "Where were you this afternoon?" he asked, reluctance in his voice, as if he didn't really want to know and thought he had no choice but to ask.

"I took Emmy out to the lake," she said.

He glanced off, then looked back at her again. "Just the two of you?"

Becca would not lie to him, painful as the admission was. "No," she said.

He made a sound of disbelief. "What are you doing, Becca?"

"Aaron—"

"No," he said, his voice rough with emotion. "I deserve an answer to this. Have you spent our entire marriage waiting for Matt Griffith to come back?"

She drew in a quick breath, feeling the sharp stab of the accusation. "That's not fair—"

"Fair?" he said, the question marked with a short laugh. "You want to talk fair. How is it fair to marry someone you love, certain that if you just wait long enough, they will one day love you back, only to end up realizing you've been a fool? That there was never any possibility of that. Where's the fairness in that?"

Becca tried to answer, but no words would come. Anything she said would sound trivial, unworthy of the questions he'd just thrown at her. Said out loud, the accusations made it sound as if her every action had been premeditated, Aaron's hurt an inevitable thing. And yet, it hadn't been that way. She'd never wanted to hurt him. She had thought when she married him that she could love him in a way that would be enough for them both.

"Well," he said. "I guess that pretty much says it all."

"Aaron—"

He backed away, raising a hand to stop her. "Don't, Becca. Just don't." He stood there for several moments, and then without saying anything else, turned and walked away.

49

A Place to Hide

"Judge a man by his questions rather than by his answers."
— Voltaire

Now

Matt was sitting in the old green glider on his grandmother's front porch when the white truck turned into the driveway.

It was after eleven, and he hadn't yet considered the possibility of going to bed, his head too full with everything that had happened that afternoon to even consider sleep. He instantly recognized the truck as Becca's, even as he blinked hard to make sure it wasn't his imagination. All evening, he'd been restless, pacing the kitchen and then the living room, with no interest whatsoever in sitting down at his laptop or picking up the novel he'd tried to start a half dozen times.

He wondered now if this was why. If he'd known on some level that she was coming. If what they'd started that afternoon couldn't possibly be finished as they'd left it.

The headlights flashed across the porch and then

eclipsed altogether. Matt stood and walked down the steps and along the brick path until he reached the door of the truck.

Her window was rolled down. She said nothing, just looked at him with something like defeat in her eyes. He could feel it in the air between them, too, a thick cord of submission, as if they'd both lost the will to fight any longer.

He opened the truck door and stuck out his hand. She took it and slipped down from the seat. He led her back up the walkway and onto the porch where he motioned for her to sit on the glider and then took the spot beside her, feeling a simple relief in the fact that she was here.

"Could I get you something to drink?" he said, conscious of the few inches that separated them, shoulder to hip.

She shook her head. "I'm fine, thanks."

"What is it, Becca? What's wrong?"

She started to speak, then pressed her lips together. Tears leaked from the corners of her eyes and slipped down her cheeks. She began to cry then, her shoulders shaking beneath the onslaught.

"Becca," Matt said. "Don't. Please." He put his arm around her, tucked her into the curve of his shoulder and pressed his lips to her forehead, tenderness welling up and spilling over.

She cried as if it had been a very long time since she'd allowed herself the indulgence, grief lowering over her like a curtain of rain.

He wrapped his other arm around her, helpless to do anything other than hold her in silent consolation.

He didn't know how long they sat this way, but when her sobs softened and then finally subsided altogether, he felt her wilt against him, her energy spent.

Around them, the night had come alive with the sounds

of encroaching summer. Crickets chirped in harmony. A dog barked somewhere nearby. From the tennis courts, one street over came the whump of ball against racket.

"Do you want to tell me what's wrong?" he said.

"It would take far less time to tell you what's not."

"We could start there," he said.

She straightened then, slowly, one hand against his chest, her eyes locked with his. They drank each other in, as if this quenching of thirst had been too long denied.

"I'm sorry, Matt," she said finally, sitting back to put distance between them. "I shouldn't have come here like this."

He brushed her face with the back of his knuckles. "If not here, then where?"

The truth of the question struck him with its stark clarity, as if the eighteen years they had lost were nothing more than a bridge between then and now. It seemed only right that he should be the one here for her. In fact, it seemed unimaginable that he could be anywhere else.

"Hey," he said, "you remember that room I told you about when we were kids?"

"Your secret room," she said.

"Wanna see it?"

She smiled then, a watery smile that brightened her eyes and collapsed something heavy inside him. He stood, took her hand and led her inside the house. He flipped on lights as they went, leading her to the back of the main staircase. He released her hand to slide aside a heavy walnut bookshelf.

A short door stood in the center of the wall. Matt opened it, then flipped a light switch just inside. He took Becca's hand again and led her through a short hallway and then down a set of steps into an underground area. He also turned on lights here and pulled a few drop cloths off the backs of upholstered chairs.

"Incredible," Becca said. "No one would ever know it was here."

"It's like its own little world. It must have come in handy during the Civil War days."

Becca walked around the room, touching the furniture, brushing her fingers across the paintings on the walls, as if to confirm they were real. "The day you told me about this room, all I could think about was how amazing it would be to have a place where you could slip away and hide whenever you wanted."

"I used it a lot," he admitted.

"I love it," she said.

He walked over to her, stopped just short of touching her. She looked up at him, the longing he felt inside himself reflected clearly in her eyes.

"Matt," she said, her voice breaking.

"I know," he said.

She moved closer while he refused to take his gaze from her, certain that if he blinked, he would wake up, and none of this would be real. He would be alone again, without her.

With a tentative hand, he slipped the white cap from her head, needing suddenly to see her hair as he remembered it, to know the feel of it against his fingers. He found the pins at the back of her neck, hesitated. "Is it okay?" he asked.

She nodded.

He pulled one pin loose and then another until her long, still-blonde hair fell in a curtain to the middle of her back. He leaned in and pressed his face to the top of her head, breathing in the scent of her, remembering.

She slipped her arms around his neck, and they stood that way, holding each other as they had when they were young. Matt barely breathed, afraid to move for fear that if he did, she would pull away. In this moment, he could not bear the thought of it.

He wasn't sure how much time had passed when she finally leaned back and looked up at his face. She touched a hand to his jaw, curving her fingers against his cheek. "I don't want this to be happening, Matt. But I don't know how to stop it."

He knew that she meant more than this moment, more than this night. For him, it was more as well. Since the day he'd returned to Ballard County, the present had begun a slow winding back to the past, until now it seemed that the two had merged, and all that he had once felt for Becca, he felt for her again. "All this time," he said, his voice raspy. "And I remember this . . . I remember."

He leaned in then and kissed her. A soft, gentle kiss, a reintroduction of souls. It was as if a match had been lit to something inside him long thought dead. He felt the instant flare of it and recognized it as hope.

They kissed until thought of anything else was lost.

Becca pulled back first with a sound that was half-gasp, half-sob. "Oh, Matt. I never thought it could still hurt this much."

"I never stopped loving you," he said.

"Don't," she said, stepping away from him. "We shouldn't say these things."

"I'm sorry, Becca," he said. And he was. "But I can't change what's true."

She moved behind one of the upholstered chairs, her hands anchored to the back of it, as if she needed both the barrier between them and the upright support. "Everything is so messed up. I don't know if it's because you came back, or if it was already that way, and I just hadn't let myself see it." She hesitated and said, "For my entire adult life, I've been able to be content with the way things are. I've had a good life. I have nothing to complain about."

"I loved you, Becca," he said. "And I thought you loved me."

"I did," she said, the words sounding as if they had been torn from her. She glanced away, clearly regretting them.

"Then why?"

"There is no single answer."

"I'll take one, if it will help me to understand."

She shook her head, tears streaming down her face. "I can't," she said. "Not now."

"Okay," he said, going to her, putting his hand to the back of her neck and pulling her to him. "Okay."

"Would you just hold me?" she said. "Please. Just hold me."

He took her hand and led her to the sofa where they both sat. He pulled her close, and she rested her head on the center of his chest, one arm around his waist.

"What are we going to do?" she said.

"We'll figure it out, Becca," he said.

"There are so many people to hurt. I don't want to hurt anyone."

He bent his head and kissed her hair, wishing he could tell her they didn't have to. Wishing it could be true.

Minutes passed, one hour, then two while they stayed where they were, tucked away in the secret room, absorbing comfort from each other, as if this exchanged energy would fortify them for what lay ahead. As if they, in fact, could hold at bay a river that had long ago begun its flow.

50

Free

"Peace is always beautiful."
— Walt Whitman

Now

I let myself out the screen door at the back of the house, allowing it to click quietly closed behind me.

The moon is high in the sky, fat and full, a summer moon that cuts a wide swath of light along my path to the barn. It is a night much like that last one with John, a night when I'd honestly thought we were at the very beginning of our lives. At fifteen years old, I guess there was really nothing else I could think. It's true that when you're that young, you don't really believe your life can end. That it can be snuffed out before you've even thought to appreciate it.

I open the big sliding doors and step inside, my head instantly filled with the events of that hot August evening when everything changed forever. It all comes back to me, fresh in my memory as if it just happened.

I don't expect that anyone will understand what I am about to do, but I feel lighter with the knowledge that I will finally be free of this body in which I have become little more than a prisoner. And with this freedom, I have something I have not had in all these years. Hope. For me. And also for those I love. Maybe that is the one thing I still have left to give.

51

A Dream

All the art of living lies in a fine mingling of letting go and holding on.
– Havelock Ellis

Now

Becca stood at the end of a long white tunnel. She could see Emmy at the far side and heard herself calling her sister's name over and over again. But Emmy could not hear her. She kept walking, never turning to look back, just walking, moving farther and farther away until Becca could barely make out her silhouette. And then she disappeared altogether, as if she'd stepped out into nothingness and was simply gone.

"Emmy!" Becca called out, starting to run after her. "Wait! Emmy! Come back!"

Becca woke with a start, her dress damp with sweat, her chest tight with its own inability to pull in enough air.

Matt's arm dropped from her shoulders. He made a sound and then sat up, opening his eyes and saying, "What is it, Becca? What's wrong?"

"I—a dream. It was a dream."

Matt reached for her hand and said, "Are you all right?"

"I don't know," she said, overcome by the sudden feeling that something was wrong, that she had to get home. "I have to go."

"It's late. Let me drive you."

"No," she said. "I'm fine."

"I'll walk you out then."

Becca grabbed her purse and the white bonnet and hairpins where they lay on the small table at the edge of the couch. Matt took her hand and led her from the room back to the main part of the house and then to the front door where they took the steps to her truck.

"I don't feel right letting you leave like this. Are you sure you're okay?"

"Yes," she said.

"When will I see you again?"

She shook her head, feeling in that moment a too familiar wrenching in the center of her heart. "I don't know."

He pulled her to him, kissed the top of her head. Becca squeezed her eyes shut against the tears that instantly welled up. She got in the truck and backed away, not letting herself look at him as she drove off.

The few stoplights she encountered seemed to take forever, and she pushed the speed limit along the Route 40 stretch leading away from town.

The farther she drove, the more real her dream seemed, the more real the sense of foreboding hanging over her. Something was wrong. She couldn't describe it other than as a bone-deep awareness that something monumental had changed, shifted like the very particles in the air, so that she had to consciously think about how to breathe against the panic inexplicably escalating inside her.

She brought the truck to a quick stop in the driveway, jumping out and leaving the door open. She let herself in the house and then took the stairs two at a time, her shoes loud on the wood steps. She went straight to Emmy's room, turned the knob quietly and stepped inside. The bed was neatly made, the lamp on the nightstand throwing a circle of light on the rag rug in the center of the floor.

"Emmy?" she said.

No answer.

She looked in the bathroom down the hall, her heart racing now. She flew down the stairs to the kitchen but found no sign of her sister.

And then she noticed that the back door had been left ajar.

She stepped outside, the dark penetrating beneath the cloud that had settled over the moon. She called her sister's name again and again. She looked at the barn, and her heart started to race. She walked across the dew-damp grass and then began to run, frantically calling as she went.

She opened one of the sliding doors, stepping in and blinking as her eyes adjusted to the dimness. From a stall at the back, a cow mooed, her calf echoing the complaint.

"Emmy?" Becca said again.

Still no answer. Becca walked to the center of the barn, glancing into the alcove where a wooden staircase led to the hayloft.

And then she saw her. Suspended from the rafter at the end of the aisle like a broken doll, her neck and head bent at an odd angle. A ladder lay on the floor beneath her.

Becca screamed then, a high, piercing wail that she did not recognize as coming from herself. "Oh, Emmy, no. No. Emmy. No!"

Sobbing, she ran to the storage room a few yards away and grabbed a knife from the toolbox sitting on the floor. She struggled with the ladder, righting it beneath her sister and then climbing up to try to cut the rope from which she hung suspended. Great, heaving cries of rage and anguish engulfed her, echoing within the otherwise silent barn. Her hands couldn't go fast enough, and in her hurry, she sliced a finger on her left hand, the pain failing to register even as blood spurted out and dripped onto her dress.

When the rope gave, Emmy's body fell into Becca, knocking her to the ground. She lay for a moment under her sister's weight, her lungs refusing to take in air. She forced herself up, rolling Emmy gently onto her back.

Her blue eyes stared up at Becca, wide and clear.

Becca pulled her sister's head into her lap and draped herself across her.

She began to cry then, a great ocean of tears, the pain so deep and horrible that all she could do was give in and let the waves take her where they would.

52

A Keening

> *"Death is no more than passing from one room into another. But there's a difference for me, you know. Because in that other room I shall be able to see."*
> ***— Helen Keller***

Now

The rooster woke Martha at just after four o'clock.

She sat up, stretching and then wincing when a pain nipped at the ridge of her shoulder.

She got out of bed, walked stiffly to the bedroom window and saw that the truck was in the driveway, the driver's door open, the interior light shining dimly.

Martha raised the window and called out, "Becca?"

When there was no answer, she left her room and walked down the hall to Emmy's door. It stood ajar, and the lamp was on. A feeling of unease rippled through her, and she turned for Becca's room on the other end of the hall.

The door was closed, so she knocked.

"Come in," Aaron called out.

She stuck her head inside. "Is Becca here?"

He came out of the bathroom, fastening the top button of his shirt. "I haven't seen her," he said, his voice hard.

"Something's wrong," Martha said. "Emmy isn't in the house. I'm going outside to look for them."

Martha took the stairs down as quickly as she dared, slipping through the front door and stopping for a moment on the porch to search the yard in the darkness.

One of the barn cats eased its way from beneath a boxwood and up the short steps to rub at her ankles, purring softly. She bent to smooth a hand across its fur and then straightened abruptly when she heard another sound.

It came from the barn, the kind of keening she'd heard animals make for lost babies. Alarm hit her in the center of her chest, and for a moment she had to grab the porch railing to keep herself from stumbling backwards. She hurried down the steps, running through the yard as fast as she could manage, the hitch in her hip instant.

The barn's big sliding door was open. "Becca! Emmy!" she called out, fear nearly choking her now.

She ran down the aisle, following the sound, which she recognized as coming from her oldest daughter. Halfway down the concrete, she stopped at the alcove to her left.

Becca sat on the floor. Emmy lay across her lap, her head resting against Becca's shoulder. Above them, part of a rope dangled.

It took a few moments for the image to process, for Martha's mind to register as true what her eyes saw. Grief rose in her chest, an awful black curtain. She dropped to her knees and uttered. "Oh, Emmy. Dear, God, no. Emmy."

53

A Letter

> *"Any fool can know. The point is to understand."*
> — ***Albert Einstein***

Now

Becca had lived through difficult things. Or at least, she thought she had. But nothing had ever compared with standing in the front yard of her house and watching the black funeral home hearse pull away with the body of her sister inside.

There in the middle of the green grass, she sank to her knees and wrapped her arms around herself, feeling as if her very insides were being ripped out. She dropped her head, while great, heaving sobs overtook her, draining her of every last ounce of energy.

"Becca."

She glanced up to find Aaron standing next to her. He put a hand on her shoulder and said with compassion, "Come on. Let's get you inside."

"How could this have happened?" she said. "How could she be gone?"

"Your sister was sick, Becca," he said, his voice gentle. "That wasn't your fault."

"Why didn't I see? How could I not have known she was going to do this?"

"We don't know what Emmy felt all these years. God tells us to care for our brothers and sisters. That's what you did, Becca. What else could you have done?"

"What about Abby? What am I going to tell Abby?"

Aaron didn't say anything for several long moments. "I suspect it's time you told her the truth," he said, and then squeezing her shoulder once, walked inside the house.

Becca knew Aaron was right. She wanted to throw back the curtains and let every last beam of truth find its way into the crevices of their lives. And yet another part of her was simply terrified of the thought.

When she could force herself to do so, she got to her feet, so weak it was all she could manage to place one foot in front of the other and make her way up the steps of the front porch.

Once inside, she climbed the stairs to her sister's room, standing in the doorway and staring at the empty bed. She forced herself to walk over and sit on the mattress. She lay down and pressed her face into Emmy's pillow, breathing in the scent of her shampoo.

She cried quietly, soaking the white case with her tears until there were no more left to cry.

She sat up, finally, pulling the pillow with her and pressing it to her stomach. On the sheet-covered mattress where the pillow had been, lay an envelope addressed to her. She stared at it, not sure she wanted to know what was inside.

Finally, she reached for it, rubbing her thumb across the familiar handwriting. She turned it over and slipped the flap free from the back. She pulled out a single sheet of paper, along with a smaller envelope that had been sealed.

She unfolded the paper and began to read.

Dearest Becca,

Thank you. I don't know any other words to say for what you've done for me. Please know that I'm not doing this for you. I know that's the first thing you'll think. That I wanted to set you free from the obligation you feel for me. But it's not that. I'm really doing this for myself. I just don't want to be here in this world anymore. I can't be here anymore. And if you are the one to find me, I am sorry for that.

Please read the letter in the other envelope here to Abby. It gives me comfort to think that your voice would be attached to my words. Sweet Becca, please find a way to be happy, and know that I love you.

Emmy

Becca folded the letter and stared at the grass field visible through her sister's window. How many days had Emmy stood before this very window and looked out at the view beyond, the colors and textures altering with each passing season while the pain inside her stayed the same, unchanging?

Becca began to shake as if the temperature in the room had dropped thirty degrees, while outside the day went on, beautiful and warm.

54

Awake

"A child said What is the grass?
fetching it to me with full hands;
How could I answer the child? I do not know
what it is any more
than he."
— Walt Whitman

Now

Abby woke to a knock at her door. She propped herself up on one elbow to squint at the alarm clock. It was just after six, the rising sun slipping through the slats of her window blinds.

"Come in," she said, her voice still groggy with sleep.

The door opened, and Becca stepped into the room, hesitating for a moment and then walking over to the bed. She said nothing, but sat on the corner of the mattress, one hand smoothing across Abby's hair.

Abby looked up into her mother's face. "You've been crying. What is it? What's wrong?"

"Oh, Abby," she said, her voice breaking, "I don't know how to tell you this, except to just say it."

"Mama, you're scaring me," Abby said, sudden fear sitting tight and hard in her chest. "What is it?"

In a painful stretch of silence, her mother glanced away, and then looked back at Abby before saying, "It's Emmy, honey. She died this morning."

As if she had been struck, Abby sat up on the bed, shock draining all feeling from her face and hands. "What?"

Becca put her arm around Abby's shoulders and pulled her close. "There's more," she said, the words breaking in half. "She took her own life."

"No," Abby said, placing a hand over her mouth to keep the scream from coming out. "No!"

"I'm sorry. I'm so sorry."

"Oh, Mama," Abby said, starting to cry. "Oh, no."

Becca put her arms around her again while Abby sobbed against her chest, her shoulders shaking with grief. They sat this way for a very long time, until Abby could finally speak again. "How? How did she do it?"

"In the barn," Becca said so softly Abby could barely hear her.

Abby started to ask how, but stopped herself. Somehow, she already knew. "Oh, Mama," she said, starting to cry again. "Mama."

55

Son

"Proud people breed sad sorrows for themselves."
— Emily Brontë

Now
Martha stood in the center of the kitchen floor, listening to the sound of her granddaughter's heartbroken sobs.

Becca had said she would go to see Jacob once she had told Abby, but Martha wanted to tell him herself, needed to tell him herself. She forced movement into her arms and legs, the effort taking every ounce of her mental, as well as physical, strength. She climbed the stairs and changed her clothes, a heaviness in the center of her chest that she knew would be with her for the rest of her life.

She drove the old black Impala along the winding roads that connected to Route 40 and led to Jacob's home in Ferrum. The drive was only twenty minutes or so, but felt as if it took days.

While she'd never paid an official visit to her son's house, she knew exactly where it was, having driven by many times over the years. But she'd never once been able to loosen the iron apron of righteousness behind which she justified her estrangement from Jacob and his family long enough to stop.

Today, though, it had been removed for her.

A white mailbox stood at the entrance to the farm, a neat gravel road leading to the plain, two-story house, similar in appearance to her own and the one where Jacob had grown up.

Martha stopped the car just short of the maple tree in the front yard. The boy, Michael, came out of the house, waved once and then ran back inside.

She got out of the car, her hand clutching the door for support. Jacob came out onto the porch, staring without words, as if certain he must be imagining the sight of her.

"Mama?" he said. "What's wrong?"

Linda walked out of the house to stand beside Jacob.

Martha started to answer her son's question, tried to force the words from her mouth. But they wouldn't come. She pressed a hand to her throat and shook her head.

Jacob ran down the steps and took her hands. "What is it?" he said, alarm in his face now.

"It's Emmy," she said, the words breaking under a wash of sorrow. "Oh, Jacob. She's gone."

With that, she let herself step into her son's open arms. And for the first time that morning, she allowed herself to cry.

56

Sorrowful News

Every wall is a door.
– Ralph Waldo Emerson

Now

At just after eight a.m., Matt walked into the cafe and sat down at a table near the cash register. He'd gone for an early run and then decided to come here for breakfast because the house was now infused with Becca's presence, and he couldn't stand being there without her.

"What can I get you?"

Matt looked up to find the same waitress he'd talked with the last time he'd been in standing next to the table. Her face was drawn this morning, her eyes troubled.

"Some coffee, please," Matt said.

"I'll be right back with it."

She turned to go, but he reached for her arm and stopped her. "Are you all right?"

"No, actually," she said. "I guess I'm not. You haven't heard the news then?"

He shook his head. "What news?"

"A volunteer for the rescue squad was in a little bit ago. They'd just finished a call out to the Miller farm." She hesitated, her face a sudden cloud of sadness, then said, "Emmy hung herself sometime last night."

Matt blinked, the words registering but not penetrating. "What?"

"Yeah, I know," she said, shaking her head and exhaling a weary sigh. "We were just talking about her the other day. You wonder how a person can get to such a place. How things can get so bad that trying is just impossible."

"Yeah," he said, his voice barely audible.

"I'll go get your coffee."

"No," he said, sliding his chair back and standing. "Thanks. I don't think I want anything now."

"I'm sorry," she said. "Come back again, okay."

Matt pushed through the glass door and walked to the Land Rover, his mind numb with what he'd just heard. Dear God. Emmy. Becca.

He stuck the key in the ignition and turned it quickly. He had to see her. He had to make sure she was all right. But no sooner had he started to back out of the parking place than another thought hit him, forcing him to stand on the brake.

The truth was that he couldn't go out to the Miller place this morning. The truth was that he had no right to do so.

Plain and simple. He had no right.

57

Threads

"Be the change that you wish to see in the world."
— Mahatma Gandhi

Now
In the two days following her sister's death, Becca felt as if she were walking around in a fog of disbelief. Her rational mind accepted that Emmy was gone, but her heart knocked with hope each time she climbed the stairs and walked past her room.

She busied herself with the details of the funeral and burial, picking out the clothes Emmy would wear, writing the obituary for the newspaper. Each of these things she approached as a task to be completed along with a line of duties that would somehow lead her out of the dark and into the light again.

Jacob came by the house a couple of times to help however he could. At first, Becca could not believe he was actually there, stunned to hear that her mother had told him the news of Emmy's death in person. As grateful as she was to hear of it, she could not help but wonder what had prompted her mother to yield now when not even their father's death had led her to do so.

Martha thought it best that they not have a visitation night, but the single service and burial only. At first, Becca had disagreed, but she couldn't deny that it would be difficult enough to get through the single day of services.

Having heard the news, Matt had left numerous messages for her on her cell phone, but she could not bring herself to return any of them. She was holding herself together by pure strength of will, and if she spoke to him now, she feared she might simply shatter into a thousand pieces. Everywhere she turned, there was a reminder of Emmy, each room holding some memory that tore at her heart.

The eleven a.m. service was to be held at Billings Funeral Home. The morning dawned with a full sun and blue sky, and Becca was grateful that the day would not reflect the grayness she felt inside. She spent the early hours in her potting shed and garden, feeling that at least there, she had some control over life and death.

At nine-thirty, she went inside to change, meeting her mother, Aaron, and Abby downstairs just after ten o'clock. The four of them made the drive to town in complete silence. Becca stared out the window, not really seeing the familiar landscape. She felt numb, as if all her senses had ceased to function.

At the funeral home, they went inside and took a seat on the front pew. In a few minutes, Jacob, Linda, and Michael, along with Jacob's youngest son, Thomas, joined them. Jacob sat next to Martha.

People filed through in singles, couples and families, until the rows were full halfway back.

Becca did not allow herself to look around. She kept her gaze focused straight ahead, sitting with her back straight and her arms folded in her lap. She held herself together by blanking her mind and refusing to think ahead to what life would be like without her sister.

Becca's mother had requested a closed casket, the wooden coffin draped in a cascade of white daisies, Emmy's favorite. The service was simple and brief. Becca thought it must be difficult for a pastor to know what to say in circumstances such as these. Throughout her life, she'd heard many people say taking one's own life was an unforgivable sin. But for her, a single verse from the book of Matthew stood out in the pastor's remarks. *Come to me, all you who are weary and burdened and I will give you rest.* It was her fervent belief that Emmy had been welcomed with open arms, that she was at last at rest. How could God blame her for being too tired to keep fighting? She had given it her best for so long.

Next to Becca, Abby sobbed quietly. Becca took her hand and clasped it between her own while the small crowd sang a single hymn, *Just As I Am.* A group of six pallbearers, Jacob included, went forward to carry the casket outside. A man in a black suit indicated that the family should follow. Becca walked down the aisle with her gaze down. At the last row, she glanced up and found herself staring into Matt's eyes. It was the empathy there that nearly undid her. She stopped, drawn to the comfort she knew his arms would offer. Aaron took her elbow just then, and she forced her feet to keep moving with the same will she had dredged up within herself all these years, going where now she did not know.

THEY BURIED EMMY in the family cemetery at the back of the farm. An enormous pine tree stood sentry over the enclosed area, headstones made of oval rock marking the resting places of generations of their family, including their father and baby brother. Emmy had always loved the spot, and it seemed right to Becca that she be here instead of some public cemetery far from the people who had loved her.

They stood at the side of the grave, Abby crying softly, Becca with an arm around her shoulders. The pastor made his remarks, words that were supposed to comfort, but somehow failed to do so. When he finished, Abby broke a daisy from the arrangement sitting nearby and dropped it onto the top of the casket.

Martha swayed forward, and Jacob caught her, pulling her into the circle of his arms. The pastor said a final prayer, bringing the burial to a close. In silence, they turned from the grave and began to walk away, Abby clinging to Becca's hand.

Again, Matt stood at the back of the crowd, as if unsure that he was welcome here. This time, instead of walking by, Aaron stopped and leveled a look at him. "What are you doing here?" he demanded in a low voice.

"Paying my respects," Matt said, equally quiet.

Aaron stared at him for several long seconds, and then said, "Perhaps you should consider that if it wasn't for you and your friends, we wouldn't have a reason to be here today."

Matt blinked once, as if the accusation had come at him like an unexpected punch. "What are you talking about?"

Aaron shook his head and walked away.

Matt looked at Becca, his eyes full of questions.

"Please, Matt," she said. "Just go."

"Becca," he said. "What did he mean by that?"

She didn't answer. She couldn't. She felt Abby's questions boring into her, and all she could think right now was that she had to hold onto her composure just a few minutes longer. If she could just make it to the house. Be by herself for a little while.

She walked quickly, Abby trying hard to keep up with her. "Are you all right, Mama?" she said.

Those words alone undid her, grief unraveling like a ball of yarn tossed to the wind. She let go of Abby's hand and began to run, not stopping until she reached the house and the safety of her sister's room.

There, she threw herself onto Emmy's bed and cried until she thought her bones would break beneath the force of her grief.

She lay there, aware on some level of the sound of cars leaving, voices downstairs, and footsteps along the hallway. There was a soft tap at the door, and then, "Mama? May I come in?"

Becca sat up, straightening her dress and rubbing the back of her hand across her face. "Yes," she said.

Abby stepped into the room, her face shadowed with uncertainty. "Are you okay?"

"I will be," she said, patting the edge of the bed.

Abby walked over and sat down. "What was Daddy talking about when he said those things to Matt?"

Becca reached for Abby's hand, holding it tight for a few moments before she said, "Oh, Abby. I suppose this is all long overdue."

"Mama, you're scaring me."

Becca drew in a deep breath and closed her eyes for a moment, forcing herself to go on. "There was something Emmy left for you. She asked me to read it to you after the funeral."

Abby's eyes grew wide, and she leaned back from Becca. "What is it?"

Becca opened the nightstand drawer and pulled out the envelope Emmy had left, along with the note she'd written to her. She lifted the flap in the back and removed a single piece of paper. The words blurred in front of her, and she wiped her eyes and then began to read.

Dear Abby,

You're a young woman now, and in reading this, I hope you will understand that things don't always work out in life as we plan. Sometimes, we make a decision that leads us to a place we never imagined finding ourselves, the road that got us there full of blind curves.

I know that once I'm gone, the truth won't matter anymore. My family has tried to protect me, most especially, Becca. While I know I should be grateful for this, a great deal of pain has been suffered as a consequence.

I did give birth to you, Abby. But in every way that counts, Becca is, and has been, your mother. I beg your forgiveness for my failures where you're concerned, most especially this last one.

It is my hope that none of this will change who you are.

You have my love always,

Emmy

Becca folded the letter and sat for a moment, the lump in her throat impossible to speak around.

Abby turned on the bed and stared at her. "You're not my real mother? She was my mother?"

"Abby—"

Abby jumped up, raising a hand to stop Becca's words. "Is this true?"

Becca glanced down and then met Abby's searching stare. "Yes," she said. "It is."

Sudden tears welled in Abby's eyes and streamed down her face. "Why would you do this? Why would you not tell me?"

Becca stood and reached out for her, but Abby jerked away. "Don't," she said. "What about Daddy? Is he my—"

"No," Becca said, feeling as if her heart were breaking in half.

Abby said nothing for a few moments, her eyes wide with disbelief. "Who is then?"

"His name was John. John Rutrough."

"Was?"

"He died while Emmy was pregnant with you."

Abby wrapped her arms around her waist, as if trying to physically hold herself together. "Everything is a lie. My whole life has been a lie. How could you? How could you?"

With this, she fled from the room, her footsteps pounding down the stairs, the front door opening and then slamming shut behind her.

Becca glanced at the letter on the bed, and leaving it where it lay, went after her.

58

Questions

"Talk sense to a fool and he calls you foolish."
*— **Euripides***

Now
Matt didn't know what to think.

He drove home from the funeral with Aaron's accusation ringing in his head, along with the nagging feeling that there was something he didn't know, something he wasn't sure he wanted to know.

Back in town, he found himself making a turn into the Exxon station where Wilks was out front pumping gas. He looked up and spotted Matt turning in. Maybe it was his imagination, but Matt thought he saw a flicker of something like caution in Wilks's expression before he covered it up with a friendly wave and a smile.

Matt pulled up to the side of the building and cut the engine, getting out and walking over to where Wilks was waiting for his customer to sign a credit card receipt. Matt waited until Wilks stepped away and told the man to come back again before saying, "Is there somewhere private we can talk?"

"Sure. What's up?" Wilks said, his tone light.

"Lead the way."

Wilks shrugged and walked inside the station. He pushed a button on the cash register, opened the drawer and stuck the credit card slip inside.

"There's something I need an explanation for," Matt said.

"Shoot."

"It was something Aaron Brubaker said today."

"Really?"

Matt heard the change in Wilks's voice, a sudden note of caution. "You heard about Becca's sister Emmy?"

"Yeah." He shook his head. "Shame, wasn't it?"

Matt was quiet for a moment, and then, "Aaron said none of it would have happened if it hadn't been for my friends."

"What friends?"

"You tell me."

Wilks held up a hand and uttered a sound of disbelief. "Man, I have no idea what you're talking about."

"Is that right?"

"That's right."

"You know anything about what happened to John Rutrough?"

Some of Wilks's composure slipped, and his voice was sharp when he said, "Where you going with this, man?"

"Just trying to put some things together."

"I hate to tell you, but you're barking up the wrong tree."

Matt turned to the window and looked outside for a few moments. When he swung back around, he pinned Wilks with a deliberate look. "Any chance you came out to the farm the night before I left for school?"

Wilks laughed and threw up his hands. "I don't know what the hell you're talking about."

"I'm asking you a straight question. Give me a straight answer. Did you come looking for Becca and me that night?"

"Shit, Matt," he said, spitting a stream of tobacco juice across the parking lot. "If you've been pining for that little piece of Dunkard tail all these years, don't go looking for somebody else to blame when you're the one who lost it."

Matt's response was automatic. He slammed his fist straight into Wilks's face, hammer hard. He heard the bone in his nose crack, followed by a roar of outrage.

Wilks came at him then, ramming a shoulder into Matt's chest and sending them both catapulting out the glass door of the station. They went down in a body tackle, rolling across the black asphalt, the punches fast and furious. A few men from the grain mill next door walked over and shouted for them to break it up. Neither Matt nor Wilks listened.

In his gut, Matt knew Wilks was hiding something, that he knew more than he was saying. In his fury, he was ready to beat it out of him if he had to.

A car pulled into the station's parking lot, a siren whirring for a moment, then shutting off. "Hey, y'all break it up now!"

Two deputy sheriffs in brown uniforms got in between them, backing them off each other. Sweat poured down Matt's face, and he wiped it off with the sleeve of his shirt, the rage inside him still at boiling level.

"Son of a bitch!" Wilks yelled, holding a hand to his nose.

Matt grabbed for him again, and one of the deputies slapped a pair of handcuffs on him. "All right, girls, we've got a nice little cell over at the county jail where you two can cool off."

The other deputy cuffed Wilks who glared at Matt and said, "This isn't over."

"You're right about that," Matt said. "It's not."

59

Truth

People only see what they are prepared to see.
– Ralph Waldo Emerson

Now
Abby ran until her side screamed, and her heart felt as if it would beat a hole through her chest.

She cut through one of the cow pastures and then a stretch of tall pines that led to the main road. Low-growing briars grabbed at her bare legs beneath her dress and left angry red scratches on her skin. She barely felt them.

Once she got through the woods, she walked alongside the road that led to town. Her mind buzzed with questions, one right after the other so that she couldn't separate them long enough to make sense of anything she had been told.

All she could think was that her mother had lied to her. Becca had lied to her. A sob rose up inside her and spilled out. She no longer even knew what to call her.

A mile or so from her house, she flagged down a

logging truck. The driver was an older man with thick gray hair and yellow teeth.

She climbed into the cab and shut the door behind her. He looked at her with concerned eyes and said, "You all right, young lady?"

"Yes, sir. I just need to get to a phone."

The man reached in his pocket and pulled out a cell phone. "Here you go, miss."

"Thank you." With shaking hands, she dialed Beau's number and winced as voice mail picked up. She left a message and asked him to meet her at the convenience store off Route 40. She handed the phone back to the man and thanked him again.

"Glad to give you a ride. I'm going that way."

"I really appreciate it."

For the rest of the drive, he talked about his grandchildren and how he wanted something better for them than a life spent driving a logging truck.

Abby wondered about that when he dropped her off in the store parking lot a few minutes later — what it was that made parents and grandparents think they had to pave the way for their children, remove all the stumbling blocks. She would rather be given a chance to deal with the truth than wake up one day to realize that nothing was as she'd thought.

He pulled into the parking lot of the convenience store and said, "You want me to wait with you until he gets here?"

"No. Thanks," she said. She opened the door and hopped out of the cab. "I'll be fine."

"All right then," he said, and with a wave, drove off.

She waited almost thirty minutes before Beau pulled up in his parents' old station wagon. They'd made fun of the old car so many times, Beau assuring her that one day he'd have something he'd be proud to drive her around in, but she'd never been so glad to hear its familiar rattle.

She got in the passenger side and said, "Can we go some place where we can be alone?"

"Sure," he said, looking worried. "Are you all right?"

She nodded, not trusting herself to speak.

They drove for a few minutes to a spot just outside of town where they'd often gone to be together. It was quiet here, no houses in sight, and Abby got out of the car quickly. Beau came around to meet her, putting his arms around her and pulling her to him. At his touch, Abby felt instant relief, the world no longer shifting beneath her feet.

She looked up into his handsome face with its chiseled lines. "Thank you for coming to get me."

"What is it, Abby?" he said, the palm of his hand curved against her cheek.

She buried her face in his chest then while painful sobs shook her shoulders. When she could bring herself to speak, she told him everything. That Emmy had been her real mother. That Becca was actually her aunt. That her father had been a boy named John, who died in a horrible accident in their barn.

Once it had all spilled out, Beau wrapped both arms around her and held her tight. "And you're you," he said. "It doesn't matter how you came to be. What matters is you're wonderful."

"How can you say that?" she said, her voice breaking. "I don't even know who I am now."

"I know who you are," he said, tipping her chin up and forcing her to look at him. "And I love you."

"Beau—"

"Let's get married, Abby," he said, his voice soft, determined.

She pulled back and looked at him. "What did you just say?"

"I want to spend my life with you," he said, touching her cheek. "I think we've gotten a pretty clear picture these past few days that there are no guarantees out there. I don't want to define what we have by someone else's definition of how, why, or when we can be together. I love you, Abby. You love me. That's all we need to know."

She leaned in and kissed him then, fresh tears running down her face. This time, though, they sprang not from sorrow, but from joy.

60

To Go Along

Impelled by a state of mind which is destined not to last, we make our irrevocable decisions.
*– **Marcel Proust***

Now

The sun had started to set, light draining from the sky when Martha let herself out the front door of the house and sat down next to Becca on the porch steps.

"You told her then," Martha said, resignation in her words.

Becca looked down at her hands, rubbed a thumb across a callous on her palm. "Emmy left a letter for her. I think she needed to know that Abby would learn the truth from her."

"And who will it help?" Martha said, failing to hide her weariness now.

Becca looked into her mother's face and said, "Isn't it time the truth came out? All of it?"

Martha glanced at the field beyond the house. "Sometimes I wonder if we even know what the truth is anymore." She paused, the silence between them weighted before she said, "There's something I never told you, Becca."

"What?" she asked, hesitant, as if unsure she wanted to know the answer.

Martha looked off into the distance. "Your father and I had a terrible argument the night John died. I didn't agree that our silence would be the best thing for Emmy. I didn't agree that we should keep what we suspected about the accident from John's parents."

Becca stared at her for a few moments, then said, "But I thought you both felt it was the best thing."

"The one thing my mother told me before I got married was that in times of serious disagreement, I must let Daniel's decision be the final one. I don't know if what we did was right or wrong, but I couldn't stand to see Emmy suffer more than she already had. I guess I chose to believe that Daniel was right and that our silence would be the best thing for her." Her voice broke under the admission.

They were quiet for a while, a cricket making its lazy summer chirp in the hedge at one end of the yard. Becca reached over and put her hand on the back of Martha's. "I know Daddy was trying to protect Emmy. But I do believe that the truth somehow always finds its way to the light."

Martha turned her hand into Becca's, squeezed once, then got up and went inside the house. She climbed the stairs to her room, retrieved the brown bag from her bottom dresser drawer and made her way slowly back to the porch.

A mockingbird trilled from the gutter of the house. Martha again sat down next to Becca, turning the bag upside down and letting the red and white baseball cap fall onto the apron of her dress. She held it up, looked inside. The initials W.P. were written there with a black laundry marker, the ink as legible now as it had been eighteen years ago on the night Becca had found it lying a few feet from John Rutrough's body.

Becca stared at it for a long time before saying, "You kept it."

"Yes."

"Did Daddy know?"

Martha shook her head, picking the cap up and handing it to her. "No."

Becca blinked hard, running her fingers across the embroidered *Ballard County Eagles* just above the bill.

"These past few days," Martha said, her voice heavy with regret, "I've thought about what you told me that night when you gave me this hat. That the boy was probably looking for you and Matt, that he didn't like that you two were seeing each other. I guess that must have been because you were different, and he couldn't get comfortable with that. I'd like to condemn him for it, but I've done the same thing with my own son. I never gave Linda a chance because she was different from us."

"Mama—"

"Let me finish," she said. "I'm thankful that I have another chance. And that I can try to fix the damage I've done with Jacob. I wish the same could be true for the wrong done to John and Emmy."

Becca reached over and put her hand on top of Martha's, squeezing once. Martha felt a renewed link of love and understanding between them, and on its heels a surge of overwhelming gratitude.

"The truth is in your hands now, Becca," she said, the burden of deceit lifting from her shoulders, as if she had finally done what she should have done eighteen years ago. There was no way to know how things might have turned out had she made this choice then. And that was the part from which there was no escape, a single question she would have to live with for the rest of her days.

61

Evidence

> *"Things that are done, it is needless to speak about; things that are past it is needless to blame."*
> – ***Confucius***

Now

Sheriff Lynch let Matt and Wilks cool their heels in the county's finest holding cells until nearly five o'clock. Matt resisted the urge to dig a deeper hole for himself and sat out the waiting period without saying a word. When a deputy came to open his cell door and told him he was free to go, he forced himself to walk out of the jail without waiting to see if Wilks was being let go at the same time.

He walked the half-mile back to the Exxon station where his Land Rover was parked. He drove to his grandmother's house and went straight upstairs to take a shower, glimpsing in the bathroom mirror afterward the bruise blooming on his left cheek.

Dressed in fresh jeans and a cotton shirt, which he left untucked, he went downstairs and picked up the phone, dialing the number still seared in his memory.

His heart pounded with the knowledge that he was stepping over lines, but he could no more stop himself than he could erase the circle of questions looping through his head. He had to see her.

Mrs. Miller answered the phone. He recognized her voice instantly. "This is Matt Griffith, ma'am. May I please speak to Becca?"

She didn't answer for a few moments, hesitating long enough for Matt to think she might have hung up on him. When she finally spoke, the words were edged with resignation. "She left a little while ago. I suspect she went out to the lake house."

"Thank you, ma'am," Matt said and hung up.

He drove the stretch of road between Ballard and the lake at the upper end of the speed limit, hoping Becca's mother was right about where she had gone. Pulling into the driveway twenty minutes later, he exhaled a sigh of relief at the sight of the white truck.

He got out and knocked at the back door. When there was no answer, he let himself inside, walking through the kitchen and calling her name. He found her outside on the porch facing the lake.

He stood for a moment, letting himself drink in the sight of her. "Becca," he said.

She looked up at him then, her blue eyes clouded with conflict. "You shouldn't have come, Matt."

He sat down next to her on the high-backed wooden bench, leaning forward with his elbows on his knees, looking out at the lake beyond. "Are you all right?" he said.

"I don't know what I am," she answered softly. "I'm not sure of anything anymore."

He turned to her and said, "I want to know what Aaron meant, Becca. I think you owe me that."

She didn't say anything for a good bit, but then stood

and walked inside the house, returning a couple of minutes later with a brown bag in her hand. She handed it to him. He looked up at her, then reached in and pulled out the contents.

He stared at it for a moment, recognizing it instantly, even though it had been nearly two decades since he'd seen it. He picked it up, knowing who it belonged to, even before he saw the initials written in the rim.

"I gave this to him," he said. "I drew that baseball bat on the side. I don't understand. Why do you have it?"

"I found it beside John's body in the barn the night he died."

Matt stared at her, shaking his head. "Wilks was there?"

"Yes."

"And what?" he said, shaking his head. "You think he killed John?"

"I don't know exactly what happened. I just know John and Emmy weren't alone there that night. After you left, I went upstairs to get ready for bed. Emmy wasn't in her room or anywhere else in the house, so I went outside to look for her. I found her at the barn, sitting next to John's body. She wasn't able to tell me what happened. She never did."

"Becca." He reached for her then, pulling her against him and wrapping his arms tight around her. "Why didn't you come forward with the evidence then?" he asked, his voice low.

"My parents believed Emmy would be forced to relive what had happened again and again if someone were charged with John's death and there was a court proceeding. They didn't want to put her through that after we saw how Emmy had been affected."

"And so all this time you kept the hat?"

"I gave it to Mama that night. My father asked her to

throw it away, but she kept it. She gave it back to me today and said it was up to me what to do with it."

Matt didn't know what to say. He couldn't imagine that Wilks would ever have actually done anything to cause another boy's death, and yet he held in his hand evidence of his involvement. He remembered then the times he had defended his friend to Becca. The remarks he'd made, remarks Matt had written off as harmless. "Becca," he said, feeling suddenly sick inside. "I'm sorry."

"It wasn't your fault, Matt."

"I could have talked to him—"

"Maybe it would have made a difference. Maybe not."

He stared at the hat, realizing this was something he would never know. "What are you going to do with it?"

"I've asked myself that question over and over again. Maybe it's better to just leave it all alone."

"Do you really believe that?"

She looked at him then, her eyes brimming suddenly with tears. "No," she said softly.

He reached for her hand, laced his fingers with hers. "I'll go with you," he said.

She stared at their interlocked hands, then looked into his eyes. "Thank you," she said. "Thank you."

62

Good-byes

Only in the agony of parting do we look into the depths of love.
– George Eliot

Now

They drove in their separate vehicles, and there were moments during the trip back to town and the walk through the parking lot to the sheriff's office when Becca wasn't sure she could go through with it.

Matt walked beside her, holding her arm the entire way, standing behind her chair when she placed the hat on the sheriff's desk and told him everything she knew.

When she was done, Sheriff McBride folded his hands across his considerable stomach and said, "You do realize that I could file charges against you for not bringing this forward at the time of the incident?"

"Yes, Sheriff," Becca said.

"Sheriff," Matt began.

The sheriff raised a hand. "Stay out of this, Matt."

"It's all right," Becca said. "I understand."

He picked up the hat, turned it over once, and then

looked up at Becca. "I'll see what I can work out with the D.A.," he said.

"Thank you, Sheriff," Matt said.

"Thank you," Becca repeated softly.

THE TWO OF them walked outside together, stopping next to Becca's parked truck.

It was dark now, the light from a street lamp throwing shadows across the pavement.

"John and Emmy both deserve to have the truth known," Matt said. "You did the right thing."

"Did I?"

"Yes."

Becca looked up at him then, her eyes wet with tears. "There's something else I need to tell you, Matt."

"What?" he said.

"Emmy was pregnant with John's baby. She gave birth to Abby the following March after he died."

Matt blinked wide, as if he'd been completely blindsided. "But I thought—"

"I've raised her as mine," she said. "Aaron and I."

Matt didn't speak for several moments, and then finally said, "Is that why you married him? To give the baby a name? To help your sister?"

She struggled with the answer, compelled to offer one that would inflict as little pain as possible. But then she had no idea what that would be. And so she chose the truth. "Yes," she said. "Yes."

"Becca." He cupped her face in his hand, his eyes dark with emotion. "There are so many things I want to say."

"I know," she said, putting a finger to his lips. "But you can't. We can't."

"Is this how we're to end it then?" He raked a hand through his hair, made a sound of frustration. "Becca, I love you. I've always loved you. It nearly killed me the first time to let you go, but I did because I thought it was what you wanted. Now . . . now I don't think I can let you do it again. This time, it has to be your choice."

"But it's not really," she said, shaking her head. "I have other people to consider. If it were just me—" She stopped, not letting herself finish the sentence.

"If it were just you?"

She leaned in then and lifted her face to his. He lowered his head at the same time, and they kissed with a kind of desperate longing, tempered with the unspoken awareness that this was good-bye.

Becca pulled away first, fully aware that if she did not, she might never bring herself to do so.

"Becca," he said, his hands on her shoulders.

"I have to go," she said. "Good-bye, Matt." She made herself walk away then and get inside the truck.

It was only when she reached the edge of the lot that she let herself glance up at the rear-view mirror. And when she saw that he was still standing there, watching her go, she began to cry, grief for Matt and grief for her sister a single rising tide inside her, the crest so high and wide that she wondered if she would ever manage to find her way above it again.

BECCA SLEPT DOWNSTAIRS that night.

She couldn't bring herself to go up to the room she shared with Aaron, aware that her actions would only be a lie when compared to the turmoil in her heart.

The living room couch did little to entice sleep, and she mostly turned from one side to the other until the grandfather clock struck four. When she opened her eyes again, the clock was striking the hour as five. She sat up to find Aaron sitting in a chair a few feet away, watching her, silent.

"Is this where we are then?" he asked, his voice surprisingly even.

"Aaron. I never wanted to hurt you."

He looked off, his gaze on the window where morning light was beginning to replace the dark. "The sad thing is I know that. But what I don't understand is why you can't close the door on what you feel for him. Your life is here, Becca."

"I'm not leaving," she said.

He stared at her for several long moments, and then said, "You already have."

"No, I haven't."

"I guess I always believed that love could be a choice. I know now that isn't true. Because I know that you've tried to love me in the same way you love him. But you don't. And I would be a fool to let myself believe for a moment longer that you ever will."

Tears welled in Becca's eyes, emotions clogging her throat so that she couldn't speak. When she finally found her voice, she said, "We'll get through this."

"Ah, Becca," he said, shaking his head. "Last night when I lay awake waiting for you to come to bed, I told myself exactly that. That we would get through this. But then I realized that's not enough. Marriage has to be about more than getting through. And then it hit me that I've been ignoring the truth all along. The truth is that when something doesn't begin right, it can never end right. I wanted you so much that I was willing to overlook what I knew to be true. I knew you didn't love me in the same way that I loved you. And maybe you thought I was playing the hero, marrying you to give your sister's child a name. But I wasn't that selfless. I married you because I wanted you for my own. However I could have you."

Tears streamed down Becca's cheeks now. She wanted to deny everything he'd just said, but her heart was heavy with the realization that she could not. She did love Aaron, for his goodness and steadfastness. For the good father he had been to Abby. For his kindness with the animals on the farm. For so many things. But just not in the way he needed her to.

Aaron stood and walked over to the couch, touching the back of his hand to her hair. "It's time for me to let you go, Becca. It's time."

He turned then and left the room, the front door closing quietly behind him a few seconds later.

Becca sat for a while after he'd gone, not moving, just trying to absorb all that had been said. She wanted to go after him, tell him he was wrong, that she could be what he needed her to be. But it wasn't true. She knew it wasn't. And maybe it was time she let him go. He was a man who deserved to be loved with the entirety of a woman's heart, and in this way, she had failed him completely.

BECCA WENT UPSTAIRS and got dressed, hearing her mother up and moving around in her own room. She came back down a half hour later, stopping at the foot of the stairs just as Abby let herself in the front door.

"You're home," Becca said, a wave of relief washing through her. "How did you get here?"

"Beau drove me."

"Oh, honey, I'm so glad you came back."

Abby studied her for several moments and then said, "I'm not angry with you. I don't want to spend my life second-guessing what you and everyone else did. I know you loved Emmy, my mother," she said, breaking off there, flustered. "I know you loved her, and you must have done what you thought was best for her. I also know that you paid a price for that."

Becca reached out and touched Abby's cheek with the back of her hand. "I'm sorry for hurting you. That's the last thing any of us wanted."

"I know."

Becca sat down on the steps, gratitude weakening her knees.

"Do I have other grandparents?" Abby said.

Becca blinked, caught off guard by the question. "Yes," she said.

"Do they know about me?"

"They thought it best if—"

Abby held up a hand. "I don't want to know anymore right now. I had to ask, but I think I'll wait for the explanation."

"Oh, Abby, I wish I could make this easier for you."

"How can it be easy?"

"It can't."

She sat down next to Becca, reached across and took her hand between her two. "I'm going to marry Beau. At five o'clock this afternoon in town at the Methodist church."

For a moment, Becca could not speak. When she finally did, concern underlined each of her words. "Oh, Abby. Please don't do anything hasty. You've been through so much these past few days."

"Yes, I have," Abby said, a new maturity in her face that Becca could easily see. "But what I understand now is that people make all sorts of life-changing decisions for reasons that are sometimes not within their control. That they lose people they love because life takes a turn they never expected."

Becca felt the well of familiar tears at Abby's reference to the words Emmy had left her.

"Beau and I love each other. The way my mother must have loved my father. The way you loved Matt." Abby's voice broke there. "We love each other. Isn't that all that should matter?"

Becca turned then and pulled Abby into her arms. Abby

cried softly while Becca held her, rubbing her back and pressing her lips to the side of her hair.

Eventually, Abby pulled back and looked up at Becca, her lashes moist with tears. "You understand, don't you, Mama?"

Becca's heart constricted with the simple word. Mama. "Abby—"

"We're not promised anything," she said before Becca could finish. "If I've learned anything in the past few days, it's that. Love is a gift. A gift I don't want to turn away from. If Beau and I wait, if we put off what we already know we have, we may not have another chance. The way my mother and father lost their chance. The way you and Matt—"

She didn't finish the rest, as if she knew the words were painful to Becca. In a soft voice, she added, "Neither of us is willing to risk losing each other. You'll be there for us today, won't you?"

"Oh, Abby," Becca said.

"You don't have to answer now. But I hope that you'll come. You're my mother. It will mean everything to me if you do."

She got up then and walked to the front door. "I'll go down to the barn now and tell Daddy."

"Do you want me to go with you?"

"No," Abby said. "I think I should do this myself."

Once she left, Becca went into the kitchen, standing at the sink with both hands grasping its edge. She felt as if her life had dissolved around her, the pieces so scattered and shorn that she had no idea how to begin picking them up again, if it would ever resemble anything of what it once was, even if she did figure out where to start.

Through the kitchen window, she could see the sun coming up behind Tinker's Knob. A bright ray of light unfolded itself through the white cotton curtains, and, for

Becca, with it came the sudden understanding of exactly where she should start. It seemed so simple, really, the realization that sometimes a person had to go back to the beginning if she were to ever figure out what the ending would be.

63

Ascent

"What are men to rocks and mountains?"
—Jane Austen

Now

The climb was steep. Far steeper than she had imagined in all the times she'd dreamed of climbing Tinker's Knob. There really wasn't a path, either, so she made her own, winding her way through dense pines and stretches of hardwoods that served as light-dappled canopies for the forest floor, all the while moving steadily upward, upward.

She'd pulled her hair back in a ponytail, borrowing jeans and a shirt from Abby's closet, clothes she was sure her daughter thought no one knew she had. She'd also put on thick leather boots that hit her mid-calf as protection from the rattlers and copperheads known to live on the mountain.

Along the way, she saw numerous families of deer grazing, squirrels darting from tree to tree, already working on their harvest for the coming winter. There were no wild boars, although she did see two wild goats, a male and a female, who studied her from a distance and then turned their heads back to a patch of grass growing between two old oaks.

The higher she went, the rockier the terrain became, and by the time she reached the top, exactly two-and-a-half hours from the time she left the farm, she was winded and sweating.

She stood for a moment, hands on her knees, drawing in deep breaths. She straightened then, looking behind her at the valley from which she'd come. She could see the white house where she'd grown up, the red barn and the black-and-white cows grazing in nearby green fields.

Heart pounding, she turned then and started the walk across the top to the other side. The peak of the knob couldn't have been more than fifty yards or so, mostly rock with some low-growing green bushes scattered in between. She had to crouch down a time or two and work her way from one craggy jut to another.

As she approached the edge, she stopped and closed her eyes, wanting to see it all in one sudden sweep. She opened her eyes then, looking out at the valley below, taking in its vast expanse.

Under the velvet green spell of spring, startling swatches of color burst forth from black locusts, tulip poplars, and yellow sweet clover. Farms much like her own were scattered across the landscape below, cows and horses grazing along lines of white fencing. Like little moving dots, children played in the back yard of a tall brick house. Nearby, she saw a man and woman hug before the man got in a truck and drove away.

She felt in that moment, a swell of disappointment, realizing she had made this climb with the lingering expectation that something different might be revealed to her here. That she might find firm and final confirmation of her mother's long ago warnings about crossing the boundaries of their own world.

But in reality, she found something else, something altogether different, validation in fact, of what she had once believed deep down to be true. That even when lives were divided by boundaries as high and imposing as this very mountain, boundaries imposed by the beliefs of others, the people on either side weren't so different. And even when people looked different on the outside, whether it was in the way they dressed, the color of their skin, or the way in which they spoke, on the inside they were much the same. That for the most part, people had the same needs, the same wants, the same desires. They wanted the best for their loved ones and grieved when life brought them short of that.

It was rejection of this truth that had led to the tragedy of John and Emmy. Led her mother to close Jacob and Linda out for so many years. And, she could finally admit, to her own unacknowledged fear that the love she and Matt had found in each other would never survive those differences. That she could make herself love Aaron in the same way she'd loved Matt if she just tried hard enough.

She knew now that love didn't work that way. That it was something the heart chose of its own accord. And as much as she had wished that she could change this within herself, that she could have avoided hurting Aaron as she had, she knew that she could not. This was something she would have to live with the rest of her life. The injustice she had committed against him.

Becca sat there on the rock, a low breeze lifting the wisps of hair that had come loose from her ponytail. So much pain. So much loss.

Abby's words played through her thoughts then. *We're promised nothing. Love is a gift.*

The truth of this settled around her, and with it came a deep sense of peace and acceptance. In her heart, she knew Abby was right. In her heart, she supposed she always had.

She stood and let her gaze linger for a few moments on the land below her. She turned then and began the return hike down the mountain. She would have to hurry. She had a wedding to attend.

64

A Sign

"Your will shall decide your destiny."
— Charlotte Brontë

Now

Matt had spent the day packing. And most of the previous night arguing with himself about whether he should try to see Becca again, try to convince her that they belonged together.

He'd gotten out of bed a little after four a.m., made himself a pot of coffee and took a cup of it into the secret room at the center of the house. He turned on a single lamp and sat down on the old sofa, all too aware of the last time he'd sat here with Becca next to him.

He considered driving out to her place and pleading with her to give what they had a chance. He knew that she loved him as he loved her. They couldn't lose that again.

But it was here in this room that he finally let himself hear what she had tried to say to him last night.

Becca had made her choice. And loving her as he did, how could he do anything other than honor it?

At eight a.m., he called a Realtor who happily met him at ten o'clock to list the house. He signed all the papers and then watched from the front porch while the woman posted her sign at the edge of the yard near the driveway. He felt a cutting sense of loss with this final step, turning away to go back inside and get the house ready to be shown.

He finished up around four-thirty, then went upstairs to shower and change into clean clothes. He took his suitcases out to the Land Rover, piling them in the back and then going inside to give the house one last check, sadness blanketing him. He closed the heavy wood door behind him, hesitating for a moment, and then locking it with his key.

He walked quickly to the truck, getting inside and reversing out without letting himself glance back at the house. He drove away with a solid lump of regret in his throat, giving in to the need to make one last loop through town.

He headed down past the cafe, cars filling up every parking space out front for an early dinner. He turned left and drove past the Old Simpson's Grocery, the farmer's market, and the hospital. He took another left at the light and headed past the coffee shop next to the courthouse, waiting out a light and then driving toward the Methodist church. He stopped at the light, glancing over at the front of the tall brick building just as the doors opened. A young woman in a white dress walked out, at her side a young man in a black tuxedo.

Matt realized then that the young woman was Abby, Becca's daughter.

The light turned green, and he let the Land Rover roll forward, barely moving.

More people came out of the church, a man and a woman he didn't recognize, and then two more that he did. Becca. And her mother, Martha Miller, older, but clearly recognizable to him.

Matt told himself he should drive on, but his hands turned the wheel of their own volition, and he pulled over alongside the curb just across the street from the church. She wore a light blue dress, simple but flattering, her long blonde hair pulled back in a ponytail. Matt stared at her, unable to look away.

He felt in that moment as if his very existence hinged on her looking up. And as if she had heard his thoughts, she lifted her head, her eyes finding him immediately.

They looked at each other for several long moments, while the church bells began to ring, their deep gong-gong resonating with joy.

He thought then about the losses in his life, and how deep down, he avoided putting himself out there. Aware that doing so meant he would have to live with the consequences if things went wrong.

Driving away today would be the safe thing to do. Or, he could take a chance.

An older woman took Becca's arm and said something to her. Becca answered without taking her eyes off him.

A car tooted its horn, asking Matt to move forward.

He lifted a hand at Becca, and she raised her own to him.

He eased the Land Rover back into traffic, but instead of heading straight along the road that would take him to the 220 connect and the highway that led to D.C., he hung a left and looped his way back to his grandmother's house on Highland Street.

He turned into the driveway, sat for a moment while the church bells still rang in his ears, and Becca's sweet face hung in his memory. He got out then, walking over to the For Sale sign and staring at the words. He pulled the post free of the ground, shaking the dirt from the bottom. He walked back to the vehicle, opened the hatch and threw the sign inside. He gave the house a last glance, a fresh imprint on his memory, and then, sliding in the driver's seat, he backed out and drove away.

Letter from Abby

115 Old Mill Rd.
Chapel Hill, NC 27514
May 10th

Dear Mama,

Things are going well here for Beau and me. He's doing great with his classes, and I suspect he'll make the Dean's list again this semester. I'm hoping I will, too.

It's a beautiful time of year. The streets are full now with flowering trees in pinks and whites. From our apartment window, we can see a park where little children play on seesaws and jungle gyms. Beau has become a volunteer in the local Big Brother program, and once a week he takes twin seven-year old boys to places like the Science Museum, a putt-putt course, or the zoo.

I talked to Daddy last week. He seems happy in Ohio, and I'm glad. I'm going to go up and visit him when school's out.

Grandma called a few nights ago. She sounded good. She said Jacob and Linda are now running the farm full-time.

Michael is going to spend the night next Saturday so Jacob and Linda can celebrate her birthday. I invited Grandma to come down to see us. She said the next time you come, she might come with you.

Tell Matt I said hello and that the next time Beau and I come home, I fully intend to land a bass and upset his new Tinker's Knob Lake record. By the way, I read the article in the News-Post(thanks for the subscription by the way!) on how well his practice is doing. It's nice that he's being compared to his grandfather. I can't believe he actually accepted that miniature donkey as payment from old Mrs.Turner. Did she really ram the mayor's car for saying the new animal shelter was a waste of money? Yay for Mrs. Turner. Did you know mini-donkeys can be housetrained?

I can't wait to see the garden you've planted this year. Did Matt finish putting in the irrigation system?

I'll quit rambling now and get to the real point of why I'm writing. Beau's mom called last night and said she'd heard that Mr. Perdue had moved away from Ballard County, and I'm glad about that, so there's no chance that you have to run into him. No matter where he goes though, he has to take the knowledge of his actions and beliefs with him. And I think the tribute we can pay to my father and mother is to live as we would hope others might, treating others as we would like to be treated. Maybe that's the best any of us can do.

Well, I better go now. Beau's waiting for me. We're heading over to campus for afternoon classes. I miss you, Mama. And I love you.

Your daughter,

Abby

Reading Group Guide

1. Do you think Becca made the right choice in taking on the role of Abby's mother? Do you think her decision to do so was completely out of love for her sister? Or possibly, too, as a way to confirm her own belief that she and Matt could never have a life together?

2. Do you think we are very often led to choose the paths we choose for our lives based on our sense of duty to our families? Why do you think some people like Wilks take pleasure in belittling those who are different?

3. Do you think Matt should have realized the depth of Wilks's prejudice against Becca and the way she was brought up?

4. Were Martha's prejudices equal to those of Wilks?

5. Do you think Martha was wrong to go along with her husband's belief that the best thing for all would be to let what happened to John, Emmy's fiancé, be perceived as an accident? Do you find Martha's unwillingness to disagree with him objectionable?

6. Is it human nature to dislike those who are different from us? Do you think it is the role of the parent to teach children to see others as individuals with the same potential to make the world a better place?

7. Do you think Becca was wrong to keep Emmy at home instead of having her hospitalized?

8. Do you believe Matt's grandmother left Becca the lake house in the hope that she and Matt end up having a life together?

9. Do you think Becca should have stayed with Aaron after Emmy died?

10. Do you think Aarron married Becca knowing she could never love him in the same way he loved her?

11. What do you think Tinker's Knob represented for Becca?

12. Do you think Becca is right to finally choose her own path instead of the one chosen for her?

Books by Inglath Cooper

My Italian Lover
Fences – Book Three – Smith Mountain Lake Series
Dragonfly Summer – Book Two – Smith Mountain Lake Series
Blue Wide Sky – Book One – Smith Mountain Lake Series
That Month in Tuscany
And Then You Loved Me
Down a Country Road
Good Guys Love Dogs
Truths and Roses
Nashville – Part Ten – Not Without You
Nashville – Book Nine – You, Me and a Palm Tree
Nashville – Book Eight – R U Serious
Nashville – Book Seven – Commit
Nashville – Book Six – Sweet Tea and Me
Nashville – Book Five – Amazed
Nashville – Book Four – Pleasure in the Rain
Nashville – Book Three – What We Feel
Nashville – Book Two – Hammer and a Song
Nashville – Book One – Ready to Reach
On Angel's Wings
A Gift of Grace
RITA® Award Winner John Riley's Girl
A Woman With Secrets
Unfinished Business
A Woman Like Annie
The Lost Daughter of Pigeon Hollow
A Year and a Day

Thank You!

I would like to thank you for reading And Then You Loved Me. Reading choices are plentiful these days, and I'm honored that you took time out of your life to read Matt and Becca's story. I so hope you enjoyed it. I would really appreciate your leaving a comment on Amazon if you don't mind taking a little more time to do that. It is extremely helpful and greatly appreciated.

Wishing you many great escapes,

Inglath

38312040R00231

Made in the USA
Middletown, DE
07 March 2019